Should We Stay or Should We Go

ALSO BY LIONEL SHRIVER

Lionel Shriver

Should We Stay or Should We Go

A Novel

HARPER

An Imprint of HarperCollins*Publishers*

SHOULD WE STAY OR SHOULD WE GO. Copyright © 2021 by Lionel Shriver. All rights reserved. Printed in the United States of America. No part of this book may be used or reproduced in any manner whatsoever without written permission except in the case of brief quotations embodied in critical articles and reviews. For information, address HarperCollins Publishers, 195 Broadway, New York, NY 10007.

HarperCollins books may be purchased for educational, business, or sales promotional use. For information, please email the Special Markets Department at SPsales@harpercollins.com.

FIRST EDITION

Designed by Bonni Leon-Berman

Library of Congress Cataloging-in-Publication Data has been applied for.

ISBN 978-0-06-309424-6

21 22 23 24 25   LSC   10 9 8 7 6 5 4 3 2 1

To Ann—faithful, capable,
irresistibly mischievous,
and bound to go
from strength to strength.
Thanks for reliably
fighting my corner—
and for remembering
wine miniatures and
popcorn for our
bleary train journeys home.

There is a natural tendency of any isolated system to degenerate into a more disordered state.

—*The Second Law of Thermodynamics*

Contents

Should We Stay
or Should We Go

1

The Soap-Dish Box

"Was I supposed to cry?" Kay cast off her heavy, serviceable dark wool coat, for this was one of those interminable Aprils that perpetuated the dull chill of January. The only change that spring had sprung was to have stirred her complacent acceptance of wintertime's bite to active umbrage.

"There aren't any rules." Cyril filled the kettle.

"In respect to certain gritty rites of passage, I rather think there are. And please, I know it's a bit early, but I don't want *tea*." Kay went straight for the dry Amontillado in the fridge. She'd had a nip of wine at the reception and didn't fancy going backwards to English Breakfast. A drink at home was an indulgence at five-thirty p.m., and she was using the technicality of occasion to break the household injunction—unwritten, but no less cast-iron for that—against ever cracking open a bottle before eight p.m. Any impression that she was drowning her sorrows was pure conceit. In truth, the sensation that the afternoon's landmark juncture left in her stomach felt nothing like grief. It was more like that vague, indeterminate squirrelling half-way between hunger and indigestion.

To Kay's surprise, Cyril abandoned the kettle and joined her at the table with a second glass, remembering to slice and twist two wedges of lime. Had one spouse been responsible for establishing the eight p.m.

watershed in the first place, it would have been Cyril, though the couple's intertwined habits went far enough back that no one was keeping track.

"I thought I'd at least feel relieved," she said, clunking her cheap wine tumbler from Barcelona dully against the one sitting on the table in a lacklustre toast. Serviceable, like the coat, the tall, narrow glasses achieved a perfect proportion of which much fine crystal fell short. More betrayal of her inadequacy: that she could consider the geometry of glassware at a time like this.

"You don't feel relieved?"

"To be honest, I've looked forward to this turn of the page for at least ten years. Which may be appalling but won't surprise you. Now that what used to be called 'the inevitable' is upon us—"

"Maybe we should call it 'the optional' now," Cyril said. "Or 'the infinitely delayable.' 'The on-second-thought, maybe-we-can-do-that-next-week, love.'"

"Well, I don't feel any lighter, any sense of release. I only feel leaden and flat. My father sucked so much life from everyone around him by the time he passed. Maybe he used up even the miserable amount of energy we'd need to celebrate the fact that he's dead at last."

"What a waste," Cyril said.

"Yes, but it would have been one thing if the waste were restricted to the one life of Godfrey Poskitt and the discrete misfortune that it ended badly. The waste has been so much more ruinous than that. My poor mother, the carers, even our kids, before they stopped visiting. I'm so glad I gave them permission to give up the pretence of being loving grandchildren. Because what was the point? Most of the time he didn't know who they were, and all they got for going out of their way was abuse. He was physically so unpleasant as well. My mother and I tried, but managing the nappies alone was such a trial, because he fought and kicked a great deal, and sometimes, which was mortifying, got a soft little erection—honestly, *my own father*. So we'd put off changing him, and he often smelt."

"In spite of all that, it was decent of two of his grandchildren to make an appearance today."

"Of course Simon came. He's so duty-bound and hyper-responsible that for pity's sake at twenty-six he's almost middle-aged. And whilst I appreciated that she showed up, if only for my mother, naturally Hayley had to be late—allowing for the usual showy entrance and calling attention to herself. Why, I reckon she planned it, watching a bit of telly beforehand, just to ensure she'd not be boringly on time. Roy's absconding in the end was predictable as well. Being a grandson is simply one more undertaking that he can't follow through on."

"As for the waste," Cyril said, looping back, "you omitted a conspicuous casualty. Yourself."

Best that her husband said it. "I hesitate to calculate how many cumulative years of my life that man's infinite dotage managed to destroy."

"At least you miraculously managed to keep working. It was the leisure time your father hoovered up. The evenings and weekends, the early mornings, the emergency trips to Maida Vale in the middle of the night: all time you might have spent with me."

"So you're the injured party?"

"Merely one more."

Restless, Kay got up to sweep some crumbs from the Corian beside the sink, casting a mournful eye at the half-built would-be conservatory off the kitchen: a work in progress for the last two years and another victim sucked into her father's whirlpool of limitless need. These days the children seemed so envious, but she and Cyril had bought this house in 1972, once they'd found out Kay was pregnant with Hayley and needed more room—and in those days, not only was the whole country a wreck, but so was Lambeth, which was why such a grand structure (if south of the river) had been within the means of an NHS nurse and a GP. These three-storeys-and-loft-to-boot had only looked grand from the outside; good gracious, "fixer-upper" didn't begin to describe it. Now that nineteen years of cost overruns and inconvenience were at last rounding on a habitable property, the kids tended to forget having to step over clatters of raw lumber on the way to the loo or shaking crumbles of plasterboard from their hair before school. They put out of mind, too, the warnings in their childhoods about hurrying home from the Tube, because the neighbourhood in those days was beyond dodgy. No, they didn't see a financial stretch for a young couple on the public payroll, who took on a considerable risk that the whole tumbledown interior would collapse ceiling-to-floor like a portable coffee cup. All the children saw now was the imposing, respectable edifice of Mum and Dad's House, a conventional projection of the establishment that they'd never afford for themselves, what with interest rates at fifteen percent; and Roy, if she didn't miss her guess, already saw a kip he might inherit. Roy was always looking for shortcuts.

Now with Dad gone, presumably she'd the spare time to finish the conservatory, yet her appetite for the project had fled. She was already fifty-one. How much longer would they live here? More starkly, how much longer would they live? Kay had imagined that she'd crossed the signal threshold of fifty with aplomb—*Look at me! I'm sophisticated about the passage of time, and this new decade doesn't bother me in the slightest!*—but such morbid thoughts had never entered her head in her forties.

"I wonder if I should have gone back home with my mother, after the reception," Kay said with misgiving. "Percy said he'd go back to keep her company, but I know my brother. He won't stay long."

"Haven't you had enough of all this sacrifice?" Cyril said. "You women! You complain about how you're always the ones taking care of everybody. Then when you get a single moment to yourselves, you hop up and volunteer to take care of someone else."

"We only, as you put it, 'volunteer' because *no one else will do it*!"

Her anger took them both aback. Kay regrouped. "I'm sorry. You know it's not as if I never asked Percy to help. But he lives that bit further out in Tunbridge Wells, and of course he was terribly busy betraying his wife and children."

"That's not entirely fair."

"I'm not saying that he contrived to be gay purely to escape his filial duties. But he's definitely *used* being gay. 'Oh, I can't mind Dad this weekend because he's obviously uncomfortable with my coming out.' Well, of course he's 'uncomfortable,' you git, the man was born in 1897!"

"The problem is much more institutional than sticking the women with bedpan duty," Cyril said, drawing up and sounding more like his regular authoritative self. "Central government needs to take fuller responsibility for social care. It shouldn't fall on you, your mother, or your extended family—"

"Well, it did, and it does, and it will when you and I fall apart as well. Even the slightest helping hand from your local council—like making up your bed, never mind chasing you down the street when you're raving? Qualification for homecare is means-tested, and my father was a solicitor."

"True, the means-testing is pretty brutal—"

"The savings threshold above which the council won't wipe your bum is a measly twenty grand—which is far more cash than Mum has left after all those carers, but she still wouldn't qualify for any benefits because she has the house. If you've stashed nothing away, or next to nothing? The council picks up the whole tab. How do you like that, Mister Socialist? You slave away your whole life like my father, carrying your own financial weight and supporting your family, and then when you collapse the state says you're on your own. Do nothing, earn nothing, and save nothing—make absolutely no provision for yourself—and the state takes care of you for free, soup to nuts. Talk about moral hazard! Obviously, anyone who does anything, earns anything, and saves anything is a berk."

"You're ranting. And you know I think social care should be a universal benefit, just like the NHS."

"Uh-huh. Make it universal, and then the same responsible people who earn anything at all will still pay for their own social care, as well as everyone else's social care, with such sky-high taxes that they can't afford a pot of jam. You're the one who had to go to that big Trafalgar demonstration against the poll tax—which would have raised money for social care and a great deal else."

"Don't start. The poll tax was regressive and you know it. And thanks to protests like Trafalgar, the 'community charge' is well dead and buried. Besides, I doubt on this of all evenings you're in the best frame of mind to design complex government policy."

"All that grooming—clipping those thick, gnarly toenails, pinching the mucus from his hairy nostrils, going through whole boxes of wet wipes cleaning his bum . . ." Kay had started to range the slate floor, for one of the advantages of having opened up the kitchen and dining area was its improved capacity for pacing. "I can't tell you how awkward it is to brush someone else's teeth, and then he'd bite . . . The chasing and corralling and undressing . . . I was halfway between a daughter and a sheepdog. The eternal surveillance, because we had to watch him like a two-year-old, lest he cut himself, or drink Fairy Liquid, or set the house on fire . . . The spoon-feeding, the wiping the muck from his beard . . . The cajoling, for hours on end, to coax him down from the ladder to the loft, of all places . . ."

"Well, paying for all that care for my father alone would have cost the state a fortune. Collectively, caring for all the other train wrecks like him would cost the state the earth, and that's why it's *not* a universal benefit. Honestly, in order to control him, it took the three of us, me, Mum, *and* the hired helper—that is, to *barely* control him. The real problem isn't how that kind of walking decomposition is financed, but that it's financed at all. My father suffered a good four years of steady deterioration, followed by a solid ten of nothing but degradation. Whoever pays for it, it's a grotesque waste of money, and also a waste of younger people's time—my time, my mother's time— that is, the centre cut out of our lives whilst we're in still good health, still sane, and still capable of joy. Waste, you said? *Nothing* but waste, and for what? He should have died when he was first diagnosed. Then I could have come home from his funeral and cried my eyes out."

Kay plunked back in the kitchen chair, eyes dry. Why, they were so dry they hurt.

Cyril scrutinized his wife. This seeming stoicism of hers was uncharacteristic. Of the two of them, she was the far more impassioned. He was the methodical thinker, which meant that others sometimes mistook him for cold-hearted. Nevertheless, she was not an emotional liar. Eight days ago, when the call from Maida Vale awoke them at four a.m., Kay had also been matter-of-fact. The news hadn't been unexpected. Apparently they'd had difficulty feeding his father-in-law for weeks, because the poor fellow had trouble swallowing. (That's what happened: the brain became so dysfunctional that it forgot how to close the epiglottis. At its most extreme end, the disease delivered its coup de grace: the brain forgot how to breathe.) After Kay finished talking to her mother in the hallway, she lodged the cordless phone in its cradle at their bedside and announced without ceremony, "*Dead.*" She'd slid under the duvet and gone straight to sleep.

"You can't stir up any feeling for him at all, then?" Cyril asked. "Sorrow, a moment of nostalgia?" As of her shockingly unsentimental pragmatism last week, it was a little too easy to picture Kay noticing that he himself had just dropped dead beside her and then harrumphing to her side of the mattress with relief: finally, a certain someone would no longer crank the bedclothes systematically to the left, and she'd have the duvet to herself.

"No, I feel absolutely nothing, and I've tried," she said. "This dying by degrees, it cheats everyone. I feel as if he's been dead for years. I've never been allowed a proper bereavement, either. But I shouldn't feel sorry for myself, because for my mum it's been so much worse. My father continually accused her of stealing his things, or of rummaging through his legal papers. More than once he called the police, and he could have periods of lucidity long enough to persuade an officer at the door that the strange woman in the sitting room really was a con artist or a thief. I can't possibly appreciate how painful it's been for her. I'm sure I must have told you that during the last few years he forgot their entire marriage. Instead he fixated on 'Adelaide,' remember? The sweetheart he married after he came back from the Great War. They hadn't been married two years when Adelaide died; maybe it was influenza. Think how it made my mother feel, her marriage of fifty-five years obliterated by an eighteen-month relationship from 1920. It would be as if in my dotage I eternally pined for David Whatshisname—"

"David Castleveter," Cyril filled in sourly.

"See, you remember my old boyfriends better than I do. So my dad kept calling for Adelaide and accusing my mother of having kidnapped his bride. He thought Mum was some jealous harridan who'd trapped him in this strange house. I've seen the portrait, a black-and-white kept high up on his study bookshelf, and Adelaide was a stunner—more of a knockout than my mother ever was, to be honest, and for Mum I'm sure that didn't help."

"Can't you compartmentalize?" Cyril poured her another half glass. He'd heard about Godfrey's demented obsession with Adelaide before, but this rehearsal seemed to be getting something out of his wife's system. "You seemed to have a real soft spot for your father before his decline. Can't you keep your memory of him in his heyday in a separate place?"

"Nice idea, but memory is too fragile. You can't mangle it like that. My memory of what he once was is like a delicate daddy longlegs that the last ten years have stepped on. I think about my father, and I can't control the pictures that pop in my head. Naked below the waist, purple with rage, and covered in faeces: one of my favourites."

"I still have a fair recollection of Godfrey when he was younger. Bit straight-laced, and a Tory, but we forgive our elders their misjudgements out of respect."

"You forgave no such thing. You two got into terrible rows when Thatcher came in—by which point he'd already lost a marble or two, so it wasn't a fair fight."

"There. You do remember something from before all the marbles rolled away."

"My mother is convinced that she brought this calamity on herself."

"How so?"

"Well, maybe my father really was devastated by losing Adelaide, because he didn't remarry until . . . I think it was 1936. He was a fine-looking chap in his day—trim figure, high cheekbones, that flaming head of hair he kept to the very end. My mum's job as a receptionist for his practice wouldn't have paid much, and marrying a solicitor seemed to offer a security she could only dream of. The only reason a single young woman like my mother would have worked back then was that her family hadn't the means to keep her—and her father was a hand-to-mouth shopkeeper."

"Spare us Maggie's humble origins routine, bab. Your upbringing was altogether prosperous, and you know it."

Back in the day, pompous Britons would lay claim to a distant relative with aristocratic credentials—a baroness, a duke—the better to bootstrap themselves up a social tier in the eyes of their fellows. More recently, the broadly middle-class populace laid pompous claim instead to relations who were coal miners or steel workers. But with a father employed first by Longbridge and then by British Leyland, Cyril the Brummie always won the contest over whose background was the more depressing—although he tended to play down the fact that by the time his father retired automotive workers were handsomely paid. Moreover, he'd invented all manner of explanations for why he'd rigorously erased his Brummie accent after shifting to London from Birmingham, but the real reason was simple: shame. Which made any rare regional residue like "bab," an endearment Cyril reserved exclusively for his wife, all the more precious.

"May I finish, oh salt of the earth?" Kay said. "In the mid-1930s the economy was still crap. And of course my mother was flattered by an older man's attentions. I think she did truly fall for him, but in that overawed way you get infatuated with an imposing professional who's your boss. He represented a port in the storm. The eighteen-year age difference must have seemed more an advantage than a sacrifice."

"Young people have no imagination," Cyril said.

"Exactly," Kay said. "She might have considered the consequences for their children—since for Percy and me, our father always seemed like an old man; little did we know how young he still was. Our classmates' fathers had all fought in 'the war,' and we tended to conceal the fact that ours had fought in the other one. Still, the last thing my mother would have calculated at her wedding is that when her groom turned eighty, she'd be only sixty-two, looking right smart for a woman getting on, and stuck with a basket case who suddenly can't remember who's prime minister. And since almost no one lived terribly long in the thirties, the very, *very* last thing my mother would have calculated is that when he finally died at ninety-flipping-four, she'd be seventy-six, with bad hips, after having squandered a decade and a half on toilet duty, cursed and vilified for her efforts, mind you—only to be looking at the next tranche of her life and wondering if the same thing is about to happen to her!"

"I'm not accusing you of being self-centred," Cyril said gently, touching her hand. "But are you crying for your mother, or for you and me?"

"Oh, I have no idea," Kay said, wiping her eyes, on this day of all days relieved to be crying over someone, if only herself.

"Are you by any chance also angry at me?" Cyril asked tentatively. "For not covering for you more often, with your father?"

"No, no, we've talked about this. Please stop castigating yourself. One of us had to be here for Hayley whilst she was still in school, and someone had to remember to pick up a loaf of bread. You surely remember that those few times you relieved me my father got dreadfully agitated. Maybe he perceived you as a rival for *Adelaide*'s affections. Besides, you run up to Birmingham to check on your own ageing parents practically every month. And who knows what will happen to my mother . . . I'm utterly wrung-out, and how much of this overseeing of corruption can we take? It's as if our full-time job in future is watching a fruit bowl rot."

Cyril waited a contemplative beat. "Should your mother also prove long-lived, I can see why you're worried about going through this all over again. After all, Percy has only lent a hand by planning the funeral once the truly hard part was dispensed—"

"And what a hash he made of that. He should have talked Mum out of the main sanctuary at St Mark's, which must seat five hundred people. It looked ridiculous. All my father's friends are dead. His siblings are dead. He'd alienated his nieces and nephews by going doolally, and most of them are also too old to attend a service in North

London without walking frames. No one was there. It looked less like a congregation than a tour group."

"I can also see why you're worried about having to take care of my parents," Cyril resumed patiently. "But my sister is bound to help. And I'll pay whatever it takes to keep them from living with us, because obviously you and my mother have never got on. So. If you don't mind. I'm much more worried about what will happen to *us*."

"In our early fifties, aren't you pushing the programme a mite?"

"Not at all. The time to consider one's options in old age is when one is still relatively young and fit. You've been terribly kind and given me a virtual free pass. But the real reason I avoided doing my part in your father's caretaking is that I found my comparatively brief exposure to his decline intolerable. He wasn't my father, so strictly speaking he wasn't my responsibility, a technicality I eagerly took full advantage of: I didn't take care of him because I didn't have to, full stop. I may have a few patients at the clinic who are also elderly and compromised, but the appointments are only ten minutes, they almost always attend with a relative, and I'm not expected to change their nappies or to decide fifty times a day whether to humour or correct their delusions. I've found these encounters discouraging and gloomy, but not incapacitatingly so. By contrast, your father frankly made me suicidal—or homicidal—or both. Half an hour in his presence passed like a mini ice age. He made me feel as if all of life is pointless and horrid. Politically misguided, yes, but Godfrey had always been well-spoken, well-educated, and well-kept, only to become worse than an animal. At least you can take real animals to the vet to be put down well before they reach a state that biologically scandalous. I will do almost anything to keep the two of us from acceding to such a fate."

"That's what everyone says," Kay said morosely, propping her feet on the opposite chair. "Everyone thinks they're the exception. Everyone looks at what happens to old people and vows that it will never happen to them. They won't put up with it. They have their standards. They value *quality of life*. Somehow they'll do something so their ageing will proceed with *dignity*. If they ever do die—not that most people believe in their heart of hearts that they ever will—they'll be wise, warm, funny, and sound of mind until the very end, with doting friends and family gathered round. Everyone thinks they have too much self-respect to allow a stranger to wash their private parts, or to incarcerate themselves in a care home that's either sterile and impersonal, or filthy and impersonal.

"Then it turns out that, lo and behold, they're exactly like everyone else! And they fall apart like everyone else, and finish out the miserable end of their lives like everyone else: either with some Bulgarian in the spare bedroom who despises them and sneaks their whiskey, or in a cynical institution that cuts corners by serving meat-paste sandwiches on stale white bread for every lunch. Yes, my father was once nattily dressed and erudite. If, back then, a Ghost of Christmas Future provided him with a vision of his life in his nineties, fleeing from a wife he imagines is an MI6 agent whilst streaked in his own waste, don't you think he'd tell that ghost that he'd rather be dead?"

"That's what I'm rounding on," Cyril said. "I've seen enough geriatric patients come and go to surmise pretty conclusively that very few people sustain that 'quality of life' we currently take for granted beyond about the age of eighty. The chronic conditions come thick and furious. Even if the mind doesn't go, the body implodes, and daily life almost exclusively concerns pain. Every advancing year entails a whole new set of things that you used to do and now you can't. Worlds shrink, nothing in the newspaper matters, until all you care about is lessening the pain, or at least not letting it get any worse. And possibly food, in the unlikely event that you still have an appetite. It's a good round number. So I fancy that eighty is the limit."

"At which point, what?"

"As a physician, I'm well positioned to obtain an effective medical solution well in advance. The key to not ending up like everyone else is to be proactive."

"Hold on. Let's be clear." Kay swung her feet back to the floor and sat up straight. "You're proposing that we get to eighty and then commit suicide. You didn't use the word. Anyone who concocts a plan like that shouldn't rely on euphemism and evasion."

"Quite right." Cyril recited, "*I am proposing that we get to eighty and then commit suicide.*"

"But assuming you're actually serious—"

"Deadly serious. For that matter, the flesh is heir to a thousand natural shocks at any age. We should really keep the means to a quick exit at the ready on principle. There are things one can experience over the course of ten minutes that would have either of us begging for oblivion well before the ten minutes were up."

"Is that a threat?"

"An observation. I don't have to remind you what we've both seen."

"But how would this pact work? You're over a year older than I am. So I watch you nod off after taking your nefarious hemlock, don't call nine-nine-nine—for which, in this fantasy paradigm of yours, I'm not arrested—and then I loiter about mourning your passing for the following fourteen months? At which point I'm under a contractual obligation to top myself."

"I'd rather we did it as we've done everything else since 1963: together. We could opt for my birthday, but unless you're ailing, which of course you might be, that would entail a small sacrifice on your part. So I would propose that I hang on, in whatever shape, and we wait for yours."

"Some birthday," Kay muttered.

"Our commitment would need to be fierce. Although it might comfort you to know that life expectancy in England and Wales for men is presently seventy-three, and for women seventy-nine. Your father was an actuarial aberration. A bookmaker would give us better than even odds of never having to make good on such a pact."

Only a few years later, anyone who rattled off the life expectancy for men and women in England and Wales would fail to impress, as eight-year-olds with access to a phone line would retrieve such statistics in seconds—like magic. A few years after that, eight-year-olds would carry in their hip pockets the means of retrieving such statistics from the very air—as well as the acreage of Micronesia and common treatments for corns—thereby rendering broad general knowledge nearly worthless. But at this time, Cyril could summon these up-to-date figures only because he was a general practitioner who kept up.

"What if I say no?" Kay asked. "Would you still do it?"

"Possibly. As a favour. A big favour, if your father is any guide."

"It might not feel like a favour."

"True kindness doesn't require credit."

At this juncture, Kay could have fobbed her husband off with a casual agreement that would get him off her case, and then they could have carried on as before. As the more vivid images of her father's decay began to fade, Cyril might forget all about his absurd pact. But she knew him better than that. He would not forget. She hadn't fostered a condescending relationship to her husband, and was not about to do so now. After twenty-eight years of marriage, Cyril would easily have detected any insincerity on her part. After twenty-eight years of marriage, Kay would have detected any insincerity on his part as well—any element of whimsy or passing rashness that he was bound to take back. He was a serious person, too serious, often, for her tastes, and she had sometimes found his idealism oppressive. Without question he had contemplated this matter for quite some time, perhaps for years. If he'd now gone so far as to put the proposition on the table, his resolve had reached a point of no return. The least she could do was consider his proposal in earnest and commit deeply, or just as deeply refuse.

So she told Cyril that he'd sprung this idea on her all of a sudden, and given the gravity of what was at stake she had to think about it. Rising to stash the sherry in the fridge, she was dismayed to discover that they, or rather she, had finished the bottle. Lord, at only seven-thirty-five p.m. she was already squiffy, with no enthusiasm for making dinner, and in this condition she shouldn't be trusted to operate a hot cooker anyway. No tipple before eight p.m.! Those rules of Cyril's might have seemed rigid and arbitrary, but a few immovable markers in life provided the structure for productivity and purpose.

Within a week of her husband's modest proposal, Kay was rummaging on the top shelf of the fridge in the confidence that they still had an open jar of mint sauce up there, when she encountered a small black box of sturdy cardboard nestled in the back left-hand corner. She recognized the container as the housing of a posh but ill-considered stainless-steel soap dish (stainless steel being an attractive material only when not mucked with bar soap), and in truth she'd saved the impractical accessory only for its classy box, whose top descended with a satisfying *pfff*. As Cyril had not yet accused her of being an agent for MI6, he had clearly not refrigerated a metal soap dish. Indeed, the moment she laid eyes on the box she was sure what it contained. It would be too strong to say that she was afraid of the box. She regarded it with a conflicted combination of curiosity and wariness, though the curiosity was not so intense as to move her to lift the top. She left the container undisturbed and resigned herself to opening a fresh jar of mint sauce.

That was spring. By autumn, Kay flung the same dark wool coat onto the Corian and dropped into the same kitchen chair. The reduction of her immediate family by one had not reprieved her altogether from Maida Vale, although these visits could now be scheduled in advance at seemly times of day. Cyril had Saturday hours at his clinic this month and had just arrived home.

"We've more or less concluded that Alzheimer's has a strong genetic component, have we not?" Kay asked limply.

"'Lifestyle' appears to be a contributing factor—a nifty thumbnail gaining currency in the NHS that conveniently blames our patients for their own misfortunes—but, yes, dementia does seem to have a heritable aspect."

"Because I found ten boxes of Weetabix in my mother's cupboards. She's always stocked her larder with the efficiency of an army mess. Now she says she goes to Sainsbury's and can't remember that she already bought cereal. As I refrained from pointing out, she also doesn't remember that it was my father who ate Weetabix for breakfast, and she only has toast."

"You're understandably fearful. Are you leaping to conclusions?"

"I'm less leaping than making a little hop. In the course of an hour, she told me about the same chamber concert at St Mark's three times. She kept asking how 'Cyril' is getting on at Barclays and how 'Cyril' likes his new flat, so I had to infer she meant Simon. Lastly, I found a stack of freshly laundered towels in her oven. That pact of yours, my dear?" Kay raised grimly. She hadn't alluded to her husband's macabre proposal since he'd first mooted the idea in April. "I'm all in."

Thus Kay and Cyril Wilkinson's deal was sealed in October of 1991. With the eternal arrogance of the present, the final decade of the twentieth century seemed to boldly advance into a brave new world, for the world is ever new, if not always brave. Like all the other eras before it, this one had the air of being terribly modern and full of astonishing innovations—computers cheap and compact enough that every household could have one—whose invention most people had played no part in, yet whose dazzling capacities appeared to reflect well on them personally.

Despite economic headwinds, it was a period of giddy optimism. In the UK, Michael Heseltine having poured cold water on his own party leader, the wicked witch had melted (although Kay had a soft spot for Maggie that she wisely concealed from Cyril). Mandela was out of prison and already forgiving what would have seemed the un-forgivable, whilst multi-party peace talks got underway in Johannes-burg. The six weeks of what was not yet known as the "first" Gulf War felt long at the time, yet soon cheerfully foreshortened to "only" six weeks. The Berlin Wall having crumbled to touristic souvenirs, tyrants in Eastern Europe were deposed or lynched, Germany was reunited, and a cascade of Soviet republics most Westerners had never heard of declared independence—all told, enticing a prominent polit-ical philosopher to posit "the end of history," which, with two world wars still within living memory, was an appealing prospect.

Britain's National Health Service was established when Cyril was nine, and the post-war cultural climate in which both he and Kay grew up was one of solidarity and sacrifice. Eager to take part in his country's grand new socialist experiment, he'd resolved to become a GP by the age of fifteen. Thus, despite scandals like the contam-ination of the national blood supply with HIV and hepatitis C in the 1980s and the headache of spiralling costs, his professional com-mitment to what politicians and punters alike sentimentally dubbed "*our* NHS" had been unwavering. His first residency onwards, there'd never been any question: Dr Cyril J. Wilkinson was an NHS lifer.

By contrast, Kay's decision to train as a nurse had been more a matter of opportunity. In the late 1950s, nursing was one of the few professions wide open to women. Yet she was not temperamentally suited to the job. She'd been squeamish as a girl, averse to needles, and was able to get past a perilous light-headedness when giving jabs only by imagining the patient's arm was a pork tenderloin. She was generous enough, but not self-abnegating, and covertly yearned for the personal recognition that the caregiving professions did not afford. Although entirely competent, and nowhere near a mere timeserver at St Thomas' Endocrinology Department, she'd never quite seen nursing as a calling. So she retired at the standard age of fifty-five and promptly enrolled at Kingston University in an interior design course. Reinvention meant overcoming fierce spousal protest. She was obliged to remind her husband how many times he'd admired her aesthetic eye, for she had single-handedly knocked their house in Lambeth into a fashionable shape that often drew comment. After graduation and licensing, her first jobs were for friends, but interior decoration advertises itself, and word spread. In due course, Kay forged a whole new second career. It was much more fun.

GPs were expected to retire at sixty, but Cyril hung on an extra five years—and perhaps he should have stayed on even longer, considering that any hint of indolence made him grumpy (he'd no interest in the garden). He had his reading, though the dry non-fiction tomes to which he gravitated served no purpose beyond his own edification— and who cared what subjects a superannuated physician had mastered? Even before his rants decrying another gratuitous Gulf War, he spent hours over the *Guardian* muttering about what on earth was the use of having a Labour government at last with a glad-handing, plastic prime minister who was a Tory in sheep's clothing? If only to fill out the day, he physically slowed, whereas Kay, ever a vigorous woman, had sped up. There was always a paint colour to choose, another estate auction to attend, a kooky kerbside love seat that begged for rescue and reupholstery before the council hauled it to the tip.

The couple rarely referenced their self-designated D-day. The "effective medical solution" remained in the same back left-hand corner of the fridge for years, and Kay never touched it. It was likely that Cyril regularly replaced its contents with fresher pharmaceuticals, though if so he never rejuvenated their supply in her presence. When their faithful John Lewis fridge-freezer finally peed condensation all over the floor like a trembling old dog about to be put down, Kay took responsibility for unloading all the mayo and marmalade and chucking the mouldy lemon halves at the bottom of the vegetable drawer. But when she came to clearing the top shelf, she found a crusty open jar of mint sauce, but no black box. Once the new Bosch was delivered, she began stashing the surviving comestibles, only to find that in the otherwise empty new fridge the black box was back, restored to the far-left corner on the top shelf. Throughout the turmoil that attends the failure of a major appliance, she'd seen Cyril approach neither the defunct one nor its replacement. Mysterious.

With pointed frequency, however, Cyril did implicitly allude to their understanding in the course of their animated but not always jolly dinnertime discourse. His idea of sparkling repartee ran to observations like, "Have you noticed that you almost never see animals in the wild which look visibly aged—which are stooped and balding and can barely walk? Deer, for example: they mature, they look roughly the same across a normal lifespan, and then they die. We get used to seeing very old people, but we're animals as well, and for creatures to survive in a state of advanced decay is unnatural."

He continued to track the steady rise of life expectancy in a spirit of dismay. "In news reports about our 'ageing population,'" he pointed out over chicken pot pie, "presenters no sooner mention increased longevity than immediately add, 'which is a good thing, of course!' The aside is compulsive. But it's not a good thing! We're not living for longer. We're dying for longer!"

Apropos of not much, he volunteered that since its inception in 1948 "the NHS annual budget has multiplied by four times! And that's in real terms, including inflation!" By the time Cyril retired in 1999 and Tony Blair was injecting cash into the "free" service as if prepping a turkey with hot butter, Cyril updated, "By six times!"

He kept his wife apprised of the escalating proportion of Britons over sixty-five, especially underscoring the increase in the "old-old" over eighty-five, whose manifold chronic conditions were fiscally ruinous, not to mention the stuff of untold private suffering.

"People our age," he observed whilst the couple were still in their mid-sixties, "cost the service twice as much as the average thirty-year-old. But by eighty-five, that differential is five-to-one! Five times as much dosh to keep alive some old coot who slumps half-asleep in front of *Come Dine with Me* all afternoon, compared to a taxpayer with young children who can still have a laugh on a fine day out and play a spot of footie."

He predicted to Kay jovially that the Queen, who personally signed birthday cards for all new centenarians, would soon have to relinquish the job to a computer, because so many Britons were living past one hundred that the kindly old dear would otherwise spend all day dispatching empty felicities and take to her bed from writer's cramp.

Cyril kept a running tally of the rising percentage of "bed-blockers" in British hospitals: elderly patients technically well enough to go home but too frail to be released on their own recognizance. What with the UK's patchy social care, they often remained in hospital for months, taking up places urgently needed for younger patients still capable of getting well. He seemed almost to celebrate the escalating rate of surgery cancellations that the wicked bed-blockers brought about, for often a patient would have the same crucial operation delayed at the last minute multiple times because there was no hospital bed available in which to recuperate. "Can you imagine?" Cyril regaled his wife. "You've seen it yourself: it takes a fierce girding of loins to prepare mentally for being carved up. Physically, too, you follow all these rules, like nil by mouth after midnight. Think of going through all that anxiety, only to be told that very morning, sorry, the surgery isn't going to happen after all, so please go home. And then to endure the same build-up and let-down, over and over again? It's a scandal."

This ministerial holding forth recalled the born-again evangelists on Speakers' Corner in Hyde Park, except what Cyril seemed to be hawking wasn't the promise of eternal life, but quite the opposite. His apparent grudge against the aged could seem uncharitable, given that all these poor people had done wrong was hang about. Yet as time ticked on, Kay was moved to note, "You'll soon have to stop banging on about 'them,' my dear, and start banging on about '*us*.'"

As they age, most people grow muddled in the course of organizing their affairs, being understandably unclear on precisely how many years these affairs are being organized for. One makes somewhat different decisions in the instance that four decades lie at one's disposal, versus the next four days—which is why it's surprisingly commonplace for even quite elderly people to make decisions based on the default assumption they will live forever. After all, the alternative is to fully accept that at any second one might drop dead, leading logically to the ceaseless and perhaps annoying declaration to one's nearest and dearest of how terribly near and dear they are—whilst turning a blind eye to the paying of electricity bills, the filling out of job applications, and the scrubbing of toilets that should never be allowed to despoil one's final moments on this earth. The alternative, then, is to sit in a dark room, unemployed, with a rank loo.

Yet unusual certainty about the maximum extent of their shared existence enabled Kay and Cyril to plan, most crucially in regard to finance. They were in accord about the children. Simon made scads in the City, and hardly required a handout. Hayley's degree in performance art from Goldsmiths hadn't, predictably, led to a lucrative career, but her youthful flamboyance had snagged her a husband with a solid professorship in linguistics at University College London safely before her mesmeric volatility slid to ordinary neurosis and self-involvement. An inheritance of any size would only increase their daughter's undermining sense of dependency. As for Roy, he was the one child who needed money, since he was up to his eyeballs in credit-card debt. But whether or not Hayley was right that the younger of her two brothers had an intermittent drug problem, Roy had dropped countless degrees mid-course, left a string of girlfriends in the lurch, and habitually appealed to his parents to bail him out. Give that boy a nest egg and he would suck it dry enough for painting by the following Easter. Cyril didn't believe in inherited wealth anyway, and for that matter, given the knee-high ceiling on tax-free bequests, neither did the British state.

Thus when Cyril also began to draw his pension, they refinanced the house, extracting multiples more money in equity than they'd paid for the place. They established irrevocable trusts for the five grandchildren—just substantial enough to give the youngsters a start in life, but not so lavish as to make them lazy. To cover the fiscal ravages of Godfrey's care, Kay's mother Dahlia had also been forced to refinance the property in Maida Vale, and the subsequently reduced proceeds of selling the house rapidly vaporized from the charges of a rather posh care home; it had better have been posh, at £78,000/year, fees whose payment Kay and Cyril assumed in due course. They also installed a live-in private carer with Cyril's parents in Birmingham, as his younger sister could hardly be expected to shoulder the extra burden on a social worker's salary.

At least Dahlia Poskitt's decline was gentle and benign, exhibiting none of Godfrey's latter violence and personality change. Having never accepted that the care home was where she lived, she arose daily convinced that she was just "visiting." Thus, when interacting with her fellow residents, Dahlia made the gracious inquiries after their health and despairing comments about the weather that her generation expected from English women of some position when accepting hospitality. Elaborately deferent and keen to be no trouble, she refused to choose between the lemon posset and the sherry trifle when there was plenty of both. In contrast to her late husband, she remembered the bloom of her marriage in full, whilst blessedly forgetting its final fourteen years of torture. Neurological rewrite had also neatly edited any reference to "Adelaide" from her husband's biography. Her primary lapse was an inability to remember that Godfrey had passed. Eventually, out of kindness, Kay stopped reminding her mother of her father's demise, because the news always hit afresh and plunged the poor woman into raw grief. It seemed easier all round to instead submit that Godfrey was waiting for her back home once she finished "visiting." When she finally died at eighty-six—it was presumed from dehydration, because she was too anxious about straining her host's generosity to ask for water—Kay actually shed a tear or two, like a real daughter.

As for Cyril's parents, his mother died with little warning at seventy-nine. Although Cyril was suitably sorrowful, his grief exhibited a curious overlay of what Kay could only identify as *approval*. Betsy Wilkinson had expired at the perfect knell of female life expectancy in England and Wales, and she hadn't set a poor example by wetting her feet in his personal Rubicon of her eightieth birthday. The onset of viral pneumonia was rapid, her fatal illness brief: ergo, she had not unduly burdened the sacred National Health Service with a drawn-out decline, only to meet the same fate in the end at many times the price. In her son's view, Betsy Wilkinson had proved a model senior citizen. As she'd been wont to observe a bit too often herself, she had suffered her life's travails without complaint. (*Ha!* thought Kay. With barely suppressed resentment, more like it. Betsy's unsparing disapproval of her daughter-in-law's continuing to work at the endocrinology unit whilst raising three children, and the vinegary old woman's undisguised derision when Kay enrolled in the interior design course at Kingston, was all a blind for envy. When after the outbreak of the Second World War the Longbridge automotive plant converted to munitions, she'd joined the workforce for the duration of hostilities, and she'd never felt as bracingly useful since.) Betsy had produced a demographically spot-on two children. As a considerate, frugal subject of the realm, Cyril's mother left the world on time.

Cyril's father was another matter. More robust than his arthritic late wife, Norman didn't really require help with his shopping but still kept on the live-in carer for companionship—although Kalisa, an upbeat, ardently Christian Jamaican, was now getting on herself. Less wading than hydroplaning across Cyril's strict Rubicon of eight decades, he remained a famous raconteur at his local, continuing to rewire lamps and refurbish vacuum cleaners for his neighbours, whilst railing against "yampy" modern mechanisms that weren't designed for repair. "Plastic!" he'd despair of contemporary Dysons. "One tab broke, and that's it for the whole blooming thing!" (*Thing* with a Brummie's hard G.) He wheeled his own bins to and from the kerb, and by ninety-two was still holding his own with Cyril regarding Britain's new prime minister, a Tory toff whom Norman derided as looking like an "overfed teddy bear."

For Kay, given Cyril's fondness for his boisterous dad, her husband's detectable ambivalence about his father's hale constitution struck an odd note. To his son, Norman's unlikely mental and physical sturdiness seemed almost an annoyance. Yet it wasn't as if she and Cyril had reason to resent paying the caretaker's modest salary. Unlike the rest of their cohort, they'd no need to keep a packet in reserve in case they themselves contributed to the Queen's writing cramp by living past a hundred. (At this rate, the indestructible royal would soon be sending a birthday card to herself.) The problem, then, wasn't financial drain. Rather, Norman was spannering Cyril's worldview. As a specimen of the "old-old," Norman should have been miserable, costly to the public purse, and better off dead. Yet so little was he faltering that Norman might also sail gaily beyond one hundred. In that event, were they to follow through on their undisclosed vow, Cyril would subject his elderly father to sudden, devastating bereavement. Kay was fairly certain that putting his father through the trauma of an only son and daughter-in-law's joint suicide would present itself as a bridge too far. Cyril was an ideologue; he wasn't a monster.

Meanwhile, with the small measure of their savings remaining after supporting their parents, two ample NHS pensions, and a dribble from freelance decorating, Kay and Cyril had taken a series of exotic holidays—to Malta, to Australia, to Key West, to Las Vegas, to Japan. Other than delving enthusiastically into the details of competing health care systems, Cyril merely endured these adventures, within a day or two pining to get back home (to do *what*? Kay always wondered). Kay had a reliably glorious time, for she easily made new friends on the fly and hadn't yet lost an appetite for novelty, be that for new words, new venues, or new food. "I make a rather grand old bag, don't you agree?" she'd exclaim merrily, twirling a parasol on a boat to an island off the coast of Queensland known for its gnarly mangroves. Cyril would smile tightly and wait a seemly amount of time before complaining, again, about his back.

For his part, Cyril Wilkinson was finding old age less than enchanting. It was making the expected inroads on his pleasures: his voice got too craggy to keep singing in his men's choir; his joints grew too painful to keep accompanying Kay on her brisk Sunday walkabouts along the South Bank. But in addition to vigour, something more crucial was waning: how much he cared—and not just about the state of the NHS, but about whether the Lib Dems would sufficiently constrain the Tories in coalition, whether Simon and his family were coming for Christmas, even whether the M&S focaccia from last night was still fresh enough to stretch to a second dinner. He felt, in a way he couldn't seem to control, a dwindling sense of investment—in events, other people, his own day-to-day contentment. The single matter in which he remained as invested as ever was his pact with his wife.

He theorized to himself that all lifetimes trace a distinctive energy arc, and Kay's and his were out of sync. She'd always been such a busy bee; were she a clockwork toy, the key at her back would still be chuntering at a stable rate, whilst his own wind-up motor was starting to stutter. Hence he kept watch on his wife with leeriness and even a touch of dread. It wouldn't have done to waste the time they had left together by focusing solely on the point at which they would be together no longer, and it was all to the good that she didn't reference their contract with morbid frequency. Yet it made him uneasy that by the time the countdown forever ticking in his head notched to a single decade, his wife had gone from mentioning their plans seldom to not at all.

Cyril remembered from his own youth that the steady succession of New Year's Eves didn't strike younger people as remarkable, much less as hard to believe. One took the year of one's birth as a given, and the years immediately thereafter seemed numerically nearby and alto-gether likely. Those so-called millennials, for example, would hardly have viewed as inconceivable an arithmetic turn of the wheel for which their generation was christened. But for helplessly older people like Kay and Cyril, the relentless advance of Anno Domini had pro-gressed from the expected to the surprising, from the surprising to the implausible, and then onward to the incredible, until the date in the left-hand corner of their daily *Guardian* became a manifestation of the impossible. He found it a peculiar experience to be living in 2010 itself whilst simultaneously convinced that such a year belonged exclusively to the realm of science fiction.

For if, as Cyril submitted over that fateful sherry in 1991, young people had no imagination, neither did the middle-aged. Back when Kay signed onto their mutual treaty to spare family, friends, and most of all each other the anguish and disgrace of extreme senescence—a commitment he'd never have accused her of having made lightly, but perhaps her acquiescence had displayed an element of impulsivity all the same—even the year 2000 had still sounded fanciful, all rather Arthur C. Clarke. At fifty-one, she'd been adept enough at elementary maths. Born in the nice round year of 1940, she'd have readily calculated that her eightieth birthday would land in 2020. It would have sounded like a ridiculous year, an unfathomable year, the stuff of late-night films with spaceships and dying suns that drive the human race to colonize other planets—and so clearly, she must have blithely assumed, it would never arrive.

2

The First Last Supper

In the approach to the twenty-second of January 2019, Cyril went out of his way to insist that the family *not* organize a big do for his eightieth birthday. With a ferocity intended to nip in the bud any prospect of a party, he stressed his ardent desire to mark the occasion by having an intimate dinner with his wife. Best to condition the family to regard the couple's landmark birthdays as private affairs. Way back when, he and Kay had agreed that, unless a diagnosis or faulty ticker intervened to spare them, they'd wait until she, too, turned eighty before acting on their pledge. His own eightieth was therefore a trial run.

The ominous symbolism of the threshold he was crossing wasn't lost on Kay, whose demeanour on waking on the twenty-second was dolorous and reserved. At Cyril's urging, this evening they planned to stay in, and Kay would make a small effort: a homemade steak and ale pie, cauliflower cheese—common fare, but well prepared. He far preferred British classics to the sea foams and thin trails of venison reduction that passed for gravy at the chic eatery where Simon had sponsored their fiftieth anniversary bash in 2013. At lunchtime, Kay suggested that maybe they should give a cake a miss this year, since at their age they should be keeping a lid on sugar.

"Whatever for?" he asked in disbelief. "In order to prevent what? Bake a cake, for heaven's sake!"

He didn't, really, want the cake. He wanted her to stop making sacrifices for a long term that had become perfectly synonymous with the short term. As their personal D-day loomed, he craved some regular indication on her part that little by little all the old rules didn't apply.

"All right, never mind diabetes," she'd said. "But you know how people worry about having a car accident in dirty knickers? I don't want to be found on my death bed *fat*."

There was little danger of that. As she brought out the pie that night wearing the embroidered birds of paradise kimono they'd picked up in Kyoto, he caught a glimpse of the Registered General Nurse he'd fallen for at Imperial College London. If anything, she was thinner, and the candlelight gentled the frown lines in her forehead and the scores on either side of her mouth. He was never sure whether she looked astonishingly young for her age or he could no longer see her as others did. In the most vital sense, he did see *her*, and he was reluctant to regard this essence-at-a-glance as a form of clouding. Now, for example, her face exhibited the subtle twitch and churn indicative of the fact that the quantity of thoughts in her head was at inverse proportion to the quantity of her conversation.

"I find it extraordinary," she announced once seated, "that we never talk about it."

The subject to which she referred was hovering so over this mirthless occasion that as an identifier "it" more than sufficed. However apprehensive about his wife's capacity for skittishness in the face of next year's official use-by date, Cyril was at least relieved not to be talking about you-know-what, a subject that at any British gathering had achieved that Basil Fawlty quality of don't-mention-the-war. The week before, their feeble prime minister had suffered the largest governmental defeat in parliamentary history. The whole business was such a horlicks.

"I thought you were the one who doesn't want to talk about it," he said.

"I'm not avoiding it exactly. I suppose I don't know what to say. It's still so unreal to me. *Sur*real."

He knew what she meant, as he had sometimes felt the same way, though he presently struggled in silence to put the absurdity of this sensation into words. There was surely nothing more *real* than what had sat sombrely on their agenda for over twenty-seven years: the final if hardly incidental item of a very long to-do list. Yet it was somehow typical of their species to perceive the starkly real—the, if anything, *hyper*-real, the real as sin, the real as real can get—as not real. As beyond comprehension and therefore as fake. The dissonance was on a par with people's bizarre compulsion to "feel alive" when that's precisely what they were.

"You haven't," she added, "ever faltered? In your commitment? You've never hesitated, thought twice?"

"'Never' might put it too strongly. You always criticize me for being rigid—"

"I admire the strength of your convictions. It can simply be frustrating to deal with a man who thinks in black and white when the world is shades of grey."

"I'm afraid this is black and white for once. Something we do, or we don't. The very first time we discussed this—"

"Meaning, the only time we've discussed this."

"You said everyone imagines they're exceptions and they'll surely arrange an early and merciful exit before submitting to the intolerable. And then they do submit to the intolerable. That's because, in order to retain agency over your own end of life, you have to be willing to give up some small portion of it that's not particularly rubbish. Otherwise, you go downhill, doctors and relatives take over, and you're apt to lose the very part of yourself that makes judgements and takes action. We have a narrow window in which to exercise control."

"We have no idea how narrow that window is."

"That's true, we don't. We're placing a high-stakes wager. But we're not playing a game of pure chance like roulette. It's a calculated gamble, more like blackjack. You remember, we studied the online guidelines in Las Vegas, which were roughly reliable, even if never drawing on a hard seventeen didn't guarantee that we'd win. We're working within fairly strict parameters. We won't live to three hundred."

"Yes, that's all frightfully reasonable," Kay said, her verdict withering. "But I can't overcome a certain perplexity that here I am contemplating suicide"—she paused to let the rawness of the rare mention sink in—"in a state of relative contentment. Now. You're the one pushing us to throw caution to the winds. So have another glass of this Barolo. It's top drawer."

Thereafter, Cyril felt guilty. Indulging himself an extra year and two months that he would deny his wife felt like cheating, or even theft. As this was time that he would have Kay herself discard—time by inference not worth living—he was tugged by a perverse urge to make his own bonus add-on of fourteen months appear as wretched as possible. He played up his sciatica, and sometimes winced, or limped on the stairs, when the pain was merely modest. (He'd been informed in his mid-seventies that the stenosis was operable. But why go through all that agony, and cost the NHS a packet in the process, when he didn't plan to benefit from the surgery for more than a handful of years?) He feigned a poor appetite when he might really have fancied a second helping, and in general avoided expressions of relish.

The one circumstance in which Cyril was unable to pretend to indifference—the one circumstance in which he failed utterly to cast this extra, stolen bit of life as a burden—was in bed with his wife. Sleeping with this exquisite woman (even if at eighty he was seldom, if you will, up for much more) was simply gorgeous, as it had been since their wedding night. He was taller than Kay, which gave him just the geometric extent to wholly wrap her back. He could honestly say that he could not remember ever lying around her, beside her, or intertwined with her in a position that was even slightly uncomfortable— that was, in fact, anything short of sumptuous. The earthy tones of his wife's natural scent hit a descant note of sweetness, and featured the same subtle complexity that Kay savoured in red wine; thus he loved nothing better than nestling a cheek on her shoulder to inhale at the base of her neck, where the heady smell was distilled. She didn't snore, but she did have an endearing habit of talking as she dreamt, which helped convey that the shifting and realigning of their bodies during the night were a form of conversation. Their sleep was best in winter and constituted the most winning aspect of the season (in comparison, sod Christmas), when they lowered the thermostat to 12°C and doubled the duvets, the air sharp and fresh in their lungs, their bodies in due course so indolently warm that it felt almost criminal. An instep cooled outside the duvet would slip bracingly against his calf; a hand warmed under the pillow would cup the side of his neck, making him feel not only safe and beloved, but more profoundly and perfectly present in the single beating moments of his life than he ever felt during the day. For any given night's repose comprised a sequence of accelerating ecstasies: from a glissando of descent, to the thick brown mud bath of deep slumber, to an early stirring and serene resurfacing, the return to consciousness as clean, smooth, and uplifting as those super-fast glass lifts in the atriums of modern high-rises, in which you can watch the greenery in the lobby foreshorten as you ascend, ears popping, to the eighty-ninth floor. The one element of his retirement that he cherished above all was the opportunity for lie-ins, whose sacrifice during his working years he regarded as his most personally costly tithe to the NHS. Accordingly, it was mornings, riding languid swells in and out of sleep, like rocking lazily in a boat at sea, that he experienced his greatest doubts about their treaty. The prospect of never again resting in his wife's arms in bed was enough to make him weep, as resting in her arms nearly made him weep as well, from pleasure.

As 2019 advanced, Kay agonized with gathering intensity over choosing to spend a given evening visiting one of the children, having a drink with her oldest friend Glenda, or dining at home with Cyril— their oft-repeated ritual of chopping, laying the table, lighting the candles, lingering, and efficiently tidying up having suddenly grown as precious as officially festive occasions like her graduation from Kingston. Frankly, she was starting to panic. This giddy, mind-racing rush to capitalize on time remaining reminded her of those low-budget reality shows in which contestants are let loose in a supermarket to pile as many preferably high-value goods as possible in a trolley in twenty minutes. Effectively, she was clattering down the aisles with one bad wheel whilst trying to remember the pine nuts and vanilla.

What was especially disconcerting? Nothing had really changed. Whether or not she and Cyril took the exact end date into their own hands or left it to chance, her life was always fated to wrap up after a countable number of nights. Accordingly, each and every one of those nights had been just as important as every other, and every bit as important as the abruptly prized 365 that apparently remained as of her seventy-ninth birthday. What was peculiar, then, was not this sweating over what to do on Tuesday, but the heedless caprice with which she had hitherto scheduled all the other Tuesdays.

This strange rising hysteria, which too often took the form of paralysis, went beyond what to do with her evenings. She would begin reading *The Week*, to which they had subscribed for many years, and seize in confusion over why she was reading a summary of seven days that were over. She could no longer identify why she should give a toss about high inflation in Iran. Suppose she were to take Cyril's proposition seriously for once (which, were she honest with herself, she almost never did, or . . . never did—why, she didn't take his preposterous plan seriously at all, not a whit; now that was sobering, perhaps even portentous). Presumably, nothing whatsoever that occurred after the end of March 2020 anywhere in the world—not only in the Middle East, but in Britain, London, Lambeth, at the Samsons' next-door—in her very own house—had the slightest bearing on her life. What life? There was meant to be no life to have bearing on. Therefore, did *The Week* contain a single item that should reasonably command her scarce and terrifyingly terminal attention? And if nothing in that magazine deserved her time now, had it ever?

It wasn't only *The Week*. She wasn't sure what had taken her so long, but she was finally beginning to intuit that the *Guardian* and the BBC's *News at 10* were lying—and not in the fashionable sense of "fake news." Most of the news was true enough, as far as it went, and she had every confidence that its purveyors were sincere in their pursuit of what they believed worthy of public interest. She had the impression of having been misled just the same. None of these journalists seemed to have been covering what mattered. It was anything but obvious what did matter, but she was increasingly certain that the gist, whatever it was, did not involve trade talks about chlorinated chicken, shadow foreign secretaries, or the divorce settlements of the superrich.

This crisis of . . . of value, of what to do with her life now that she didn't, or wouldn't in such short order, even have one (the crisis itself wasteful: still more scarce time squandered on flailing and confusion) came to a head over the one issue that had been the focus of an immoderate degree of emotion for the last three years. Not only was the fervour nationwide, nay, worldwide, but for Kay it had been a private obsession also. The fact that in the main her feelings were secret had made them only more intense. Yet as her looming private departure eerily mirrored the approach of a larger will-we/won't-we public one, she seemed to split in two. The Kay she had always been followed the fracas's every twist and turn with the absorption of watching one of those *Bourne* thrillers. Every media outlet, every dinner party quarrel, every shouty exchange on Facebook fed the version of events whereby this impasse constituted the most important historical juncture since the Second World War. It concerned the alignment of great powers and her nation's very soul. So exhaustive, and exhausting, had the debate grown by 2019 that most of her compatriots were attesting to total burn-out, claiming to have become so sick to the eyeballs of the whole business that they wished to talk about anything but. Yet these same people employed this very declaration of weariness as a preface for pontificating for hours on end about what they ostensibly could not bear even to mention. There were those who argued that this or that result would engender the ultimate test of democracy, the triumph of democracy, the death of democracy, or what was wrong with democracy, but in any case "democracy" got bandied about by both sides with the sort of frequency that makes you get a bit fuzzy about what the word means.

Then there was the other Kay, a new Kay, a woman she wished she had more time to get to know. This Kay didn't, it turned out, give a sod about "democracy" one way or the other. This Kay whispered seditiously that, however it was resolved, there was no better an example of mere bagatelle than *Brexit*.

Thus Kay Wilkinson awoke on her seventy-ninth birthday in a strangely schizoid state. By sheer coincidence, Kay was born on March twenty-ninth, the very date on which for the last two years the United

Kingdom had been slated to formally depart the European Union. As of a week previous, with no small sense of anticlimax, for the time being Britain would continue to stay put. The two Kays being at odds, she wasn't sure if she felt happy, sad, or indifferent.

"So I assume you're as relieved as I am," Cyril said. He had taken her to a little neighbourhood bistro. It was obscurely disheartening that he'd ordered the chicken. "Even if a mingy fortnight's reprieve isn't all that comforting."

"Oh, they'll push back the date again," Kay said dispassionately. She had toyed with making a confession tonight—what had she to lose, with only a year to go?—but decided abruptly against it. This was supposedly her last year, and she didn't want to mar it with recrimination and penance.

"Probably," he agreed. "That withdrawal bill is a dog's dinner, and I can't see it passing in this parliament even three-times-lucky. Theresa May is incompetent. But at least she's a Remainer at heart, and it's begun to show." Her husband spoke with his usual certitude. There were not two Cyrils. Ever since the referendum, he'd been perpetually enraged by their witless countrymen's confounding attempt at "national suicide." For the UK to top itself was an atrocity; for the two of them to do the same was an act of social generosity.

"You know, it's been a bit queer . . ." No one used that word to mean "strange" any more, but one of the few pleasures of living on Death Row was release from the linguistic tyrannies of the day. "Having people argue so vociferously all the time about whether to 'leave' or 'remain.' It's as if they're debating our personal quandary."

"Since when are we in a quandary?" he snapped. "We've made a decision and we're sticking to it. But as for Brexit"—he pronounced the pestilent neologism with distaste—"there's all to play for. The chances of a second referendum are rising by the day. It's the only way out of this gridlock. And the next time round, the knuckle-dragging

Neanderthals won't bludgeon us civilized Britons with clubs. Polly Toynbee got all that stick for observing the plain demographic facts: any number of addled older voters who opted for Leave in 2016 have now died, whilst more progressive young people have come of age, so in a re-run Remain would win hands down. The ruckus in response to that column was mental. As if she wished those older voters dead, or was happy they were dead—"

"For the sake of both her argument and her electoral convenience, I think she *was* happy."

"All that matters is that statistically Toynbee was right. Look at my father. I'm hardly celebrating, but it's one positive aspect of our loss: he can't vote for flagrant idiocy a second time."

Two years earlier, Norman's death at ninety-nine had doubly saddened Kay. She liked him, and not merely as Exhibit A for cogent, energetic old age. (He'd fallen from a ladder and broken his hip, after which his decline was swift. It was the perfect way to go: pruning an overgrown magnolia.) But she'd also treasured the way his longevity complicated the consummation of that 1991 covenant. If she was right, that Cyril would never bereave his dad, then so long as he survived Norman had provided an insurance policy of sorts. Now the policy had been cancelled.

"I wish you hadn't squandered your last few months together squabbling about the EU," she said, signalling a *third* time for a breadbasket refill. Throughout the last decade or so, in restaurants she and Cyril had seemed invisible. "For that matter, is this really how we're going to spend my birthday as well? Talking about Brexit? Because in case you need reminding, as of exactly a year from today, *we're* not voting in any second referendum, either."

"The People's Vote movement best get their act together pronto, then."

"But doesn't it . . . mean something to you," she said cautiously, "how much you still seem to care? As a Remainer, how passionate you still are? This involvement of yours, ever since 2016 . . . I didn't want to say anything and just make you feel worse, but for a time there you'd got draggy and cranky and cantankerous, like a proper old man. You tried to humour me, but it was obvious from the very start of a holiday that you were counting the days before we'd go home. You seemed to be losing interest in everything. You let that new iPad Simon gave you sit for nearly a year before I bullied you into learning how to use it, and there wasn't much more to it than turning it on. You even started to leave the *Guardian* half unread. So you may rail against it, but that referendum gave you a new lease on life. You've got back your old energy, as if you're closer to sixty than eighty. Even your voice sounds stronger. You've stayed home from my constitutionals for years, but nothing stopped you joining that massive Remain march to Parliament Square last Saturday. Honestly, with that back of yours, I was worried you might get trampled."

Cyril ripped the last bread roll savagely. "Fury is a tonic."

"I'm simply saying . . . You're so fully engaged now . . . So determined to personally help reverse this thing . . . Whose consequences you're not even expecting to suffer . . ."

"Out with it, wench."

"It's just—you don't seem like a man who's anywhere near ready to let life go!"

"Well! I suppose I'm not, quite. As you said, we've a whole year left, God willing, and I intend to put it to good use. I aim for us to go to our maker after having helped safely restore this country to the good graces of the European Union—that alliance being one of the greatest historical achievements of the Western world. Speaking of which, I've assessed our finances, and we've undershot our spending goals a bit. So I made a sizable donation to the People's Vote campaign. We'll still have enough left over to cover basic expenses for the next twelve months."

Finally the waitress arrived—with no bread—and sloshed the whole last half of their cabernet carelessly into their glasses, perhaps in the hopes that the doddering old dears would forgetfully drink up, and order another bottle.

Obligingly, Cyril picked up his glass and toasted. "Happy birthday, bab. Must say, it's nice to be able to celebrate two cheerful events in one, the birth of your fine self and an extension of Article Fifty."

"It has been peculiar hearing broadcasters make incessant reference to 'March twenty-ninth.' As if Radio Four has been planning my surprise party."

"Mark my words, this is the beginning of the end for those Leaver louts." Once again sounding far younger than eighty, Cyril was so lively tonight that maybe they would order that second bottle. Well. Or at least a port.

"Do you ever consider," Kay inserted slyly, "moving our own Leave date? Perhaps just a smidgeon? By and large, our health seems to be holding, and neither of us has stashed the towels in the oven."

"Now, that's dangerous talk, bab. Apostasy!" He was joking, and not.

Cyril was right. It was indeed dangerous talk—just as he was also right that the purportedly hard-and-fast date for Brexit having been deferred at the last minute was prospectively fatal for the whole enterprise. As soon as you put off what is writ in stone, it is writ in water. During the whole post-referendum omnishambles, something about the prime minister's hectoring insistence that "Brexit means Brexit," an empty assertion echoed by the pressure group Leave Means Leave, had reminded Kay of her husband's implicit and equally intransigent motto, *Eighty means eighty.* For over the last couple of years, Theresa May's incessant repetition of her monotonous mantra had subtly backfired. Self-evident like all tautologies, the slogan had introduced an element of insecurity that, as last week's EU deferral to the twelfth of April demonstrated, was well founded. Since Brexit meaning Brexit

should have gone without saying, yet did not go without saying—
could not go without saying *all the time*—perhaps Brexit didn't mean
Brexit after all. Thus today's non-event introduced a ray of hope that
Kay's personal departure date could also be forestalled. Even one delay would throw the whole proposition up for renegotiation, because
then Cyril's uncompromising base-ten deadline (a piquant term in this
case) would be breached. For what was bound to happen before April
twelfth? Article 50 would be extended again. By inference, if Cyril's
arbitrary cut-off ever shifted by so much as a day or two, eighty could
become eighty-one could become ninety-three and a half. That's why
the Leave camp was so crushed today, and why, irrespective of her political propinquities, Kay was rather uplifted. What can be postponed
once can be postponed indefinitely.

Kay's salmon was dry, and in compensation she ordered that port.
In fact, she ordered two, and at eleven twenty-five p.m. the invisible
old fogies in the corner banquette closed the joint. After all, Cyril had
called her tentative proposal to stick around just a smidgeon longer
"apostasy." So assuming that she didn't tragically stumble from being
so tipsy on the walk home, this was the only remaining birthday that
she was guaranteed to live all the way through.

To say that the following year went by quickly would be an under-
statement.

Kay was well aware that despite the rejuvenating effects of Remainer indignation her husband was playing up his physical infir-
mities. His back gave him legitimate grief, but he was the one who'd
refused the surgery. He often left his hearing aids out on purpose, because making his wife repeat, "Do you want another piece of toast?"
four times made his company seem more geriatric. Believe it or not,

he was still fairly spry. (How curious, that by convention an adjective meaning "agile" applies exclusively to old people. She'd looked it up once, and the strict dictionary definition had nothing whatsoever to do with the unfeasible leaping about of the decrepit.) Yet he deliberately slumped when he read, deliberately fell behind when they walked along the pavement, and deliberately vocalized moments of discomfort with groans and cries of dismay, although after stubbing his toe as a younger man he'd been stoic. He sometimes requested that one of the children give him a hand doing chores like stashing the outdoor furniture in the tool shed in the autumn that he was perfectly capable of dispatching by himself.

For every action, there is an equal and opposite reaction. So stiff did Kay's upper lip become that it was doubtful she could use a straw. In truth, her right shoulder had developed a fierce pain whenever she raised her arm higher than about forty-five degrees, but she merely popped discreet overdoses of ibuprofen when Cyril wasn't looking. She was constantly tortured by nocturnal leg cramps, which she walked off in silence after slipping from the bedclothes without waking her husband. Her joints and spine made a cacophony of sinister noises, although the internal snap, crackle, and pop wasn't that audible to other people, and she let the advert for Rice Krispies broadcast its continuous loop without remark. The arthritis in her toes, of all places, had become so agonizing that a Sunday walk along the South Bank had become more grim discipline than refreshing jaunt, and she'd taken to lingering over a coffee at her turnaround, the better not to admit to Cyril that she'd cut her former distance in half. She concealed her GP's consternating verdict of high blood pressure from her husband, disguising the medication in a bottle that once held antacids. So whilst suffering the same insults to her physical person as anyone else on the cusp of eighty, to all appearances Kay Wilkinson was a model of functionality. (She was *spry*.) She refused to present herself to her murderous husband as a high-mileage, petrol-sucking jalopy in need of so many replacement parts that, rather than maintain the old girl, it was cheaper to throw the clunker on the scrap heap and buy a new car.

As the months flew by, she grew ever more dissociated. The split into two Kays now seemed perpetual, and she was wont to watch herself from a long way off, as if she were practising for being dead. It is commonplace to stare blankly into the refrigerator in mystification over whatever you're looking for, but Kay didn't stare blankly but fixedly, as she knew full well what she was looking for: the black soap-dish box in the back left-hand corner, which never accumulated the bits of food the other containers did, leading her to wonder if Cyril was reverently wiping it down when she was away at the shops. The rectangle seemed to peer back at her with a hint of smugness: such a small object, yet more powerful than its owners, whom it was poised to annihilate in . . . 184 days? No, the countdown was relentless: it was already 183.

The panic was now unabating. Was a documentary about loss of biodiversity in the Amazon really worth purchasing with the precious currency of her life, when she wasn't going to be around to mourn the extinction of the white-cheeked spider monkey? Probably not. Although even at her advanced age Kay had still been taking on small interior design jobs, mostly for friends, she abruptly bowed out of doing over Glenda's ground floor halfway through, at some cost to the friendship, owing to a sudden, frantic impatience amidst deciding on knobs-versus-rails for the drawers of the new kitchen island. Was determining whether the fixtures should be sleekly modern or hint at the Victorian really the way she wanted to spend her final year on this earth? No, no, no. Yet once any given activity was interrogated with sufficient rigour, no pursuit could pass the test. The answer to which activities were truly worth her time was absolutely none.

Meanwhile, Cyril threw himself into the campaign for a second referendum, leafleting and banging out diatribes on the social media he used to decry as background noise. He helped organize a petition by the British Medical Association protesting prospective restrictions or tariffs on drugs imported from Europe and the dangers this could pose for NHS patients. His further donations to the People's Vote campaign pinched their budget even if they were only eking through next March, obliging Kay to economize during a period they ought sensibly to have been loading up on smoked salmon, quails' eggs, and cognac. He conceived an outsize loathing for Boris Johnson, whom he'd always dismissed as a dishevelled, lightweight chancer and whom Cyril elevated, once the tousled pro-Leave Tory became prime minister, to a diabolical, double-dealing demagogue (alliteration itself being a signature Boris-ism). Cyril joined still another People's Vote march to Parliament Square that October, dubiously vaunted as one million protesters strong.

In tandem, Kay had grown so apathetic about the unending legislative impasse that she couldn't be bothered to get her head round some nonsense about parliamentary "prorogation" that was or was not "judiciable" and was or was not "unlawful," which for some reason wasn't the same thing as "illegal"; for pity's sake, in comparison deciding on kitchen fixtures was positively riveting. The spectacle of her husband throwing body and soul into a reversal of that stupid referendum bewildered her. For Kay and Cyril Wilkinson, whether the UK remained a member of the EU—or NATO, or the UN, or the Commonwealth—was perfectly on a par with whether the country entered the Eurovision Song Contest. In a handful of months, they were *planning to commit suicide*, at which point there would be no EU, NATO, UN, or Commonwealth, and no song contest. There would be no UK. There would also be no magpies, no skies blue or otherwise, no quails' eggs, no paperclips, no best friends with their noses out of joint, no cyberspace, no wellingtons, no household dust mites, no £6 discount coupons from Tesco if you spend £40 by 7/11/19, no scalp eczema, no elusive concepts like "populism," no such colour as "burnt orange," no words like "louche" whose definition she'd never quite pinned down, no emotion called "ebullience"—and not just the word for it but the very feeling of explosive joyfulness would exist no more. There would be no "supranational institutions"—not the names of them, not the overpaid, supercilious salarymen who ran them, not the ideas of them, not their acronyms or their unaudited finances. There would be no democracies and no parliaments, prorogued or unprorogued. In sum, there would be no Kay and Cyril, and therefore all these scraps that combined to form their perceived universe would vanish. She had the impression that Cyril didn't exactly *get it*.

To the best of her ability, Kay finally concluded that for her husband the country's death struggle over Brexit, of all things, was a priceless distraction from his own struggle. He was like their most feckless grandson, who locked himself in his bedroom playing video games when he should have been writing his essay on *Wuthering Heights*. At once, Cyril clung to the political crisis as a stand-in for all that in a short time hence he had vowed to give up: the arbitrary, transitory, irrational passions of the human world. She'd been exasperated by his lack of historical perspective (England as a nation had lasted for a thousand years and had been an EU member for only forty-six of them), but it was obvious that the last thing Cyril wanted was a sense of perspective. Brexit was intoxicating for its very status as a mania of the moment. The imbroglio had become his anchor to the present, which he gripped blindly like a lamppost in a gale. To "let go," as she put it on her seventy-ninth, of what currently so absorbed their neighbours was also to let go of everything else. He cared so much because the divisive issue of the day, which could very well appear negligible in fifty years' time if not in two or three, had come to represent caring itself.

Pointedly at first, that autumn Kay started planning their joint memorial service. Because Cyril wasn't the only one desperate for a source of attachment, the project soon became all-consuming. She combed through volumes of poetry, especially responding to the verses she'd been required to memorize at school—*Margaret, are you grieving / Over Goldengrove unleaving? . . . It is the blight man was born for, / It is Margaret you mourn for*—though the extraneous name "Margaret" might confuse congregants, and the poem's theme was a shade morose. She listened tirelessly to Spotify playlists from the late 1950s and early '60s, when she and Cyril had come of age and married—Roy Orbison, Shirley Bassey, the Everly Brothers, Tommy Bruce and the Bruisers—and sometimes the silliest numbers like "Itsy Bitsy Teeny Weeny Yellow Polka Dot Bikini" could move her to nostalgic tears. She paged methodically through a C of E hymnal, as more traditional churchgoers might appreciate respectfully sombre selections. Perusing the vast collection of family photographs that Hayley had kindly digitized, she searched for a suitable pic to put on the cover of the programme, and perhaps also to enlarge and prop on an easel before the altar. She was torn over whether to use a shot that included the children or a more romantic one of just the two of them. There was also the question of whether to use a recent (meaning depressing) likeness or an earlier photograph that captured their comely youth. (On the day they closed on the house in Lambeth, Cyril looked so triumphant holding the title aloft on the front steps. With a pang, she recognized the stylish frock with an off-centre, check-shaped collar that she had barely got away with wearing when four months pregnant with Hayley. Whatever happened to that dress?) She listed the order of service on an Excel spreadsheet, noting where the next-to-youngest granddaughter might serenade the loss of her grandparents, yet also display her budding prowess on the viola.

Kay spent hours on end composing her farewell from beyond the

grave, mindful not to leave anyone out, and therefore writing a per-
sonalized passage addressed not only to all three children and their
partners, but to each of the five grandchildren, her surviving cousins,
her brother Percy and his husband, Percy's estranged children and his
ex-wife, and Kay's four closest friends—then, worried that Charlotte
might take offence, making that the five closest.

Then she set about drafting an explanation for why she and Cyril
had chosen to take their own lives whilst still of sound mind and
body, trying to do justice to her husband's reasoning that in order
to exercise agency over one's own old age one had to sacrifice a small
bit that "wasn't rubbish." She submitted that Western society seemed
to promote longevity at any cost, whereas a shorter life vibrant to its
very end was surely more desirable than blighting a fine and fruitful
existence with protracted decay. She wrote about her father, and how
painful it had been for his memory to be overwritten by a violent,
paranoid lunatic, and she reminisced about her mother's gentler deterioration that had still turned a sensitive, intelligent woman into a
vacuous, killingly polite guest at an eternal tea party. She went on at
length about the NHS, researching the statistics online and laying out
for their friends and family what a terrible burden the escalating number of frail, elderly patients was placing on a health service to which
she and Cyril had devoted most of their working lives.

Alas, as enriching as the composition of these texts proved for her
personally, by the time she finished the valedictory it ran to thirty-one
pages, which took (she timed it) ninety-two minutes to deliver, and
that was before a single musical interlude or vaulting prayer. The exe-
gesis of their motives for the bulletin also grew as extensive as a small
book, and the printing costs alone would be exorbitant; she was reluctant to saddle the kids with stiff expenses, especially after they discovered that the better part of their parents' "estate" had already been
liquidated and that, beyond those token trusts for the grandchildren,

there would be no inheritance. Worse, on rereading the treatise, she realized that her message could be misconstrued as a castigation of anyone who chose to endure beyond eighty as short-sighted and selfish. The essay seemed intent on making the "old-old" feel literally guilty for living. She sounded hectoring, unfeeling, and fanatical. Only in a few wistful asides did her tone strike notes of sincerity.

At least one advantage to an early exit was that they could probably fill out a reputable number of pews in St Mark's. Their friends weren't all dead. They had loads of extended family. Many grateful patients would remember their long-serving GP. Kay still received Christmas cards from osteoporosis sufferers and patients with thyroid imbalances whose medication she'd managed at St Thomas'. Then there were all the satisfied customers whose lives she had brightened with sprightly new window treatments. She could ask the members of Cyril's old men's choir and the chatty fellow homeowners at their local residency association. For that matter, Cyril had made any number of new contacts through the People's Vote campaign. All told, compiling the invitation list—which would save the children such a headache, especially since she was helpfully including postal and email addresses—was gratifying. The couple had led full, useful lives.

Kay might have found the project engrossing, but getting Cyril to participate in the design of their memorial service was like pulling teeth—especially once Parliament finally acceded to a general election on the twelfth of December, and anything that didn't concern defeating Boris and his imbecilic Leaver henchmen couldn't hold her husband's interest for two minutes. "Just tell me," she prodded him. "Do you like Lonnie Donegan's 'I Wanna Go Home' for a processional, or would you prefer 'Save the Last Dance for Me' by the Drifters?" Cyril continued to bang away feverishly on Twitter, under whose soothing influence he'd grown convinced that not only was Boris headed for an ignominious loss of seats, but that Labour had a serious chance of attaining a proper majority. "And I was wondering whether it's too much of a stretch to invite our old dentist," she added. "I don't have his home address, but I imagine his former practice would forward a memorial announcement." Still no response. "Also, I'm sorry to nag, but it simply won't do for me to say goodbye to the whole family, and then for you not to leave behind so much as a fare-thee-well. You know the children would be hurt. So when do you think you can get around to drafting something? It needn't be exceedingly long, but it does need to be personal—"

Finally Cyril slapped his iPad shut. "Listen. You've been fretting about that service for weeks on end. I fear you may have forgotten one salient detail: *we're not going to be there.*"

On the evening of December twelfth, the Wilkinsons ate on the early side and hurried the washing up. Switching on the telly, Cyril settled himself in his regular armchair with a ceremonial bottle of ale and a festive bowl of barbecue-flavoured peanuts. "Even if it's a hung parliament after all," he announced with relish, "Labour and the SNP will have more than enough MPs to form a government, and that, as for Brexit, is that."

At ten p.m. on BBC One, the familiar chimes of Westminster tolled the hour. Sitting before an older picture of Big Ben without the scaffolding, the presenter gravely announced the results of the corporation's widely trusted exit poll: the Tories would win an eighty-seat majority.

The blood drained from Cyril's face. His posture collapsed and his limbs went slack. He looked his age and then some. The fact that his bottle was filled with *bitter* seemed horribly apt.

For the immediate future was a foregone conclusion. There would be no second referendum. Every Tory candidate had pledged to support Boris's tweaked withdrawal bill, which would now sail through Parliament like one of the crumbling building's many bats. The United Kingdom would depart the European Union at eleven p.m. on the thirty-first of January. There would be no further delays, and no appeal. The Remainers had lost. Kay was minded to take the eerie finality of the moment as an omen. There was such a thing as a deadline, a hard-and-fast deadline, a deadline that truly came due.

After that night, Cyril was lifeless. His dependency on the seemingly ceaseless political drama had bordered on chemical. Kay was reminded of the film *Awakenings*, in which comatose patients were given a drug that made them walk and talk like real people again, until the drug wore off. For Cyril, as of the worst result for Labour since 1935, the drug had worn off.

The UK left the European Union at the end of January with little fanfare. When the prime minister addressed the nation that evening, major broadcasters including the BBC refused to carry the speech in full. There was some boisterous flag-waving around Parliament Square, though the poor revellers weren't even allowed to drink. Relieved to see the back of the whole business, Kay was already disconcerted why membership of a trading bloc had ever seemed worth fighting over. The whole country seemed to be sheepishly recovering from a feral childhood tantrum. On both sides, everyone acted slightly embarrassed to have got quite so purple-faced over who got to play with the stuffed bunny.

On the heels of the devastating general election, Kay had worried that Cyril would arrive at her red-letter birthday on March twenty-ninth irretrievably unravelled. But as the first two months of 2020

inexorably advanced, he progressed from dismal, to pensive, to ele-
giac. Maybe it was for the best that his crusading high had subsided.
He had used the diversion of Brexit to avoid thinking about their own
exit—Cyrexit, if you will; Kayexit—and to approach such a Gethse-
mane without pause for contemplation would have reflected poorly
on his intellect.

Understandably distracted by the imminence of making good on
a suicide pact, Kay was slower than most Britons to pick up on mur-
murs about some illness in China. She paid the business no mind at
first; taking care not to blight her last winter on earth by lying febrile
and abed, she'd had her flu shot in the autumn. As infections began
to spread, to Seattle, to Lombardy, they seemed to have nothing to
do with her, even when the WHO declared a pandemic. Surging and
subsiding across the globe all her life, communicable disease constituted yet one more travail in the conduct of human affairs that she
would soon gladly leave to others.

Up against a stark final reckoning, Kay had zero interest in going
anywhere further away than Waitrose—making her wonder whether
their previous beaverings to foreign destinations had been diversion-
ary, and if so, a trip to Malta had been diversion from what? Yet her
less introspective compatriots continued to rush hither and yon, so it
was inevitable that this highly contagious pathogen would eventually
pop up in the United Kingdom. Indeed, on the first of March, the
Today programme cited that the number of confirmed cases in Britain was five. On the second of March, the same presenter announced
there were thirty-six.

Three days thereafter, the first British fatality was declared. By the
eighth of March, the fatalities had risen to three. While the Wilkinsons theoretically regretted anyone's demise, the couple had more
pressing matters to ponder. What had the sum total of their lives
come to? Had they left anyone in their extended family or social circle

feeling injured or neglected, and might amends be made before it was too late? And hold on a minute: was this pact of theirs flagrantly barking?

Yet if the spouses were unperturbed by three British fatalities and under three hundred cases, the rest of the world seemed to care a great deal. At the beginning of the second week of March, something unpleasant happened to the London stock market. Luckily for Kay and Cyril, the big advantage of having no more money was perfect imperviousness to its loss.

During the same week that the FTSE crashed, at the beginning of which the Wilkinsons had exactly twenty-one days to go before lights out, Kay received her first social cancellation. That Thursday, she and Glenda had planned to hit Borough Market to score some early wild garlic, meander to the Tate Modern, dander across the Millennium Bridge, pop into St Paul's, and saunter along the Strand to end up at The Ivy in Covent Garden for a well-earned fish supper. It was an engaging route they'd traced before. But on that Wednesday, when the Bank of England lowered its baseline interest rate from almost nothing to as-good-as-nothing and total UK deaths from so-called COVID-19 had reached eleven, Glenda begged off. Kay burst into tears.

"Sweetheart, why ever are you taking such a minor disappointment so hard?" Glenda puzzled. "It's just, this coronavirus does seem to have it in for us oldies, and Boris is discouraging us from socializing. I'm not a nervous Nellie, but staying put does seem sensible. We can reconvene when the excitement subsides and enjoy our outing twice as much for the wait. The weather will have improved as well."

"But how long do you think it will take for the 'excitement to subside'?" Kay whimpered.

"Oh, heaven knows. A few weeks? Goodness, a fortnight or two of Amazon Prime Video? You'll hardly die."

At that point, Kay grew inconsolable.

Within a day or two (as the FTSE plunged again in its giddiest drop since 1987—what a joy to have liquidated all those shares), every appointment Kay had meticulously scheduled for their final month, including benedictory evenings with all three children, was also cancelled. Friends and family alike backed off for the couple's own good, because anyone over seventy needed to be "shielded" from a disease whose fatalities had an average age of over eighty—leading Cyril to remark, "I have to say, that virus has good demographic taste."

"Maybe we needn't touch that black box in the fridge after all," Kay said, the direct mention so rare that it felt risqué. "We can simply run out in the road on my birthday and inhale."

"Now, given our circumstances," Cyril said from behind her at the kitchen sink, "why in heaven's name do you keep manically washing your hands?"

"Oh." Kay had already begun a mental rendition of the happy birthday song, which Boris had urged all Britons to sing to themselves twice before concluding this vital hygienic prophylaxis. But Cyril was right. Avoiding fatal infection in order to commit suicide was inconsistent to say the least.

"I suppose it's all those adverts on the telly," Kay said with a wan smile, drying her hands. "Propaganda works."

Cyril had been laconic and inward for months. The coronavirus didn't altogether alter that demeanour. But he spent all day online on his iPad, and the energy that emanated from his hunched figure had changed frequency. It hummed in a higher register. However poorly timed any spanking new enthusiasm, the contagion was right up his street.

The following week, Boris gently discouraged his countrymen from dining in restaurants and going to the theatre. The pound dropped to its lowest level against the dollar since 1985. It was announced that all schools would shut by that Friday. The Bank of England lowered its baseline rate once more, this time from as-good-as-nothing to no-longer-pretending-to-be-anything-but-nothing. To widespread popular horror, the BBC stopped filming *EastEnders*.

The whole experience was dizzying. Over the course of a mere ten days, the entire political and cultural landscape transformed, as if someone had pressed fast-forward on the country's remote. News presenters ceased utterly to mention the word "Brexit," which overnight was no more likely to arise in everyday conversation than "suit of armour" or "mead." In a final gesture of dividing the old era from the new, as if loudly lowering a rattling metal shutter between the gritty present and all the fluff and whimsy of the past, Boris U-turned on the cajoling and brought down the hammer. Pubs, theatres, gyms, cinemas, and restaurants would close—indeed, all "inessential" businesses. Addressing the nation, the prime minister announced that every Briton was ordered to stay home, unless they were fulfilling four specific purposes and only these purposes. The wholesale lockdown entailed the most extravagant curtailment of British civil liberties since the Second World War, during which, if Kay and Cyril weren't mistaken, it had still been legal to walk out your own front door.

"So I'm to spend the last six days of my life under house arrest," Kay said, after turning off the PM's address. "I have to confess I feel resentful. It isn't merely having all those dinners cancelled, our last opportunities to say goodbye, even to our own children. I feel sidelined. Diminished. As if the climactic conclusion of our lives has been summarily overshadowed and trivialized. With all those numbers on the news every night, who's going to notice if two more elderly Britons snuff it?"

Not having roused from his regular armchair, Cyril was scowling into his hands and didn't respond.

"And it's irrational, but I feel oddly left out," she continued. "Such a snowballing cataclysm, or so it would seem, reminds me, a bit painfully I'm afraid, of the extraordinary degree to which the world will carry on without us . . . Are you going to say anything? We don't have much time left to say anything at all to each other."

Cyril announced cryptically, "It's disproportionate."

"What is?"

"This shut-down. I've studied the data. That weedy, doom-mongering computer modeller at Imperial College London who predicted five hundred and ten thousand British deaths without draconian intervention—he has his head up his backside. The ponce may have Boris in his thrall, but Neil Ferguson has overestimated the lethality of this virus by at least an order of magnitude. And there has to be a reason we've never before responded to contagion by closing down the entire country: because it's not a good idea."

At least their final week would be tranquil. Traffic was sparse. Birdsong dominated the garden. Aeroplanes seldom scarred the sky.

When Kay discussed the details of their Last Supper, Cyril was kind enough to take an interest in the menu. "I love your bangers and mash," he said, with the tinge of sorrow that had coloured his discourse for days. "Let's have that."

An easy request to fulfil, you would think. Yet Kay returned from her first trip to Sainsbury's empty-handed. "It was like Venezuela, or the Soviet Union," she told her husband in bewilderment. "All the shelves bare, fresh food and non-perishables alike. Everyone's gone mental. As if it's the end of days. I wanted to scream, *You don't understand! My husband and I really are facing the end of our days—this very weekend!*" Fortunately, by that Friday, special shopping hours for the elderly were installed between seven and nine a.m.—during which the supermarket was jam-packed. As a crowning testimony to the gentrification of what was once a dodgy, down-at-the-heel neighbourhood, by seven-twenty a.m. the shop was already stripped clean of penne and pesto. But Kay was at least able to get her mitts on a packet of sausages.

Weaving in and out of sleep that final Sunday morning was so delectable that they didn't arise until noon, and then with reluctance. Being eighty years old was nothing like she had imagined many years ago. Various bits hurt, but otherwise she did not feel appreciably different now than when she was ten. As of the week before, it was officially spring, and for once the weather was cooperating with the conceit. Parting the bedroom drapes to let in the sun, she noted that the middle edges of the maroon velvet were light-bleached. So entrenched was the custom of planning for the future that she reflexively vowed to replace the drapes with more modern blinds—in canary yellow, she determined. Budding camellias in the back garden glistened; wings of butterflies flashed. Kay felt almost mocked.

"Happy birthday," Cyril said, nuzzling her neck with only his shirt on.

"Will it be?" she wondered aloud.

"At least we haven't to worry about the kids clamouring to help celebrate your eightieth," Cyril said. "If they did throw you a birthday bash, they could be arrested."

"You know, the clocks changed to summertime last night. We've lost an hour." Horribly, it was not noon, but already one p.m. "That doesn't seem fair, does it? Of all the days to be cheated."

"You never really 'lose' an hour, any more than you 'gain' one in the autumn. Time is constant. It can't be borrowed or gifted."

"Pedant," Kay said affectionately.

Cooking that afternoon achieved an ecclesiastical aspect. It was not a chore. Kay was sorry when all the potatoes were peeled. The tubers seemed harder and rounder and more resonant under a blade than ever before; the Bramley apples for their crumble also seemed crisper, tarter, and somehow more forcefully in the world, insistent on taking up their rightful space on the cutting board, pushing back against her knife. The smell of butter and cinnamon from the topping was heavenly. The menu was deliberately "ordinary," for it transpired that all along they'd not dined on Cumberland sausages and hearted cabbage for the sake of their budget, but because that was what they'd both grown up eating and that was what they liked. Truth be told, she'd never really fancied smoked salmon.

Hayley and Simon rang to wish her a "safe" birthday—safety having been mysteriously elevated of late to the highest of virtues. She hadn't the heart to tell them that, despite the government's good intentions, remaining "shielded" behind closed doors with her own husband was the most dangerous thing she could have done today. Both children seemed consternated when she kept them too long on the phone. Later they'd understand and be grateful, but in the moment their mother would have seemed clingy. Roy didn't ring, and perhaps in due course that would cost him. Or not.

Taking a break late afternoon, she sat on one of the patio chairs that Cyril had brought from the tool shed and wrapped herself in her favourite grey woolly jumper, for the air was still sharp. The sun had held and the light had goldened. She did not read *The Week*. How rarely she registered that sitting, looking, and thinking were activities in and of themselves, and rewarding activities at that. Cyril came out also and cupped her shoulders from behind, as they both beheld the azaleas, just coming into leaf.

They hailed from a generation still given wedding china. Laying out the elegant plates, with plain cream centres, solid emerald borders, and a glint of silver on the rims, Kay was pleased that she'd had the good taste in her youth to choose a simple pattern of which they would never tire. They should have used the good china more often, if not every day. They owned a service for twelve, and she had a sudden urge to smash one of the surplus plates like a heedless Greek, purely because she could. She didn't, but the notion was bracing.

"What is it?" she asked casually, pressing fresh candles into the holders, though the old ones still had five inches left to burn. "What's in the black box, exactly?"

"Quinalbarbitone," he said just as casually. "Aka Seconal. You remember, it was that insomnia medication taken off the market because of the dangers of overdosing."

"Is it painful?"

"Certainly not. Fatigue, a spot of dizziness or blurred vision. It's very quiet."

In the sitting room, Kay put on one of the 1960s playlists she'd located whilst planning their memorial service, turned down to a level low enough for them to talk. They partook of pre-prandial sherry, again dry Amontillado with a twist of lime, along with two strong cheeses and savoury biscuits so thin that they didn't crack but shatter. They could gorge themselves silly tonight without fear of getting fatter, but Kay inclined instead towards nibbling the tiniest smears of Ardrahan on the corner of a biscuit, then popping a single pea-sized Niçoise olive and sucking the pit.

"Oh, I love this song," she said when Otis Redding's "(Sittin' on) The Dock of the Bay" came on, and she sang along. Cyril joined in; he should never have quit that choir, with such fine pitch. The simple melodic line was so infectious that she hopped up to play the song a second time. They danced on the reprise. Ridiculously, on her eightieth birthday, she felt like a girl. Her swaying floor-length dress was a virginal white: the variety of garb in which women were both married and laid out. She'd done a good job on the sitting room, she concluded as the trailing-orchid wallpaper swirled about her. Those not-quite-matching end tables were just right.

They dined. The cheese had quickened her palate, and despite the nature of this occasion, which might have cast rather a pall over matters, Kay was hungry. The whipped potatoes were better with that extra double cream. The sausages had a nice crust without having burnt, and the hearted cabbage with butter and shards of sea salt was still bright with a slight crunch. In fact, all the colours were heightened—in candlelight, Cyril's face framed by the bookcase looked like a Rembrandt—as if she had taken tablets of a very different sort than the kind in the fridge.

So this was life without consequences. She'd have expected to have to gird herself, to make promises inside her head (*Come on, spit it out, this is your last chance to come clean!*), to at least need to take a breath, but the confession came out effortlessly over a second sausage. "I've meant to tell you something for a while now, my dear," Kay said, sawing off a crispy end piece. "I voted Leave."

Cyril's cutlery froze. "Is this a joke?"

Kay laughed. "In a way. What's not a joke now? Darling, I'm positively wounded if you can't finally find it funny. And amidst the chloroforming of the entire UK during a global pandemic, I am astonished—perhaps even impressed—that you still care. Goodness, all your dire warnings about how Brexit was 'committing economic suicide.' Now the UK is committing *real* economic suicide by putting a 'Gone Fishing' sign on the whole flipping country. Continuing to hyperventilate over whether a few goats can scamper unimpeded across the Northern Irish border seems incongruous to say the least."

"But the referendum seemed to matter monumentally in 2016. What in God's name got into you?"

"Something impish. It was a spur-of-the-moment thing at the polling station. I simply marked the X in a different box. The whole experience was terribly refreshing, like a tall drink of water on a hot day."

"You threw your country's future in the toilet on a *whim*?"

"My dear, we don't want to get into a row tonight of all nights. It wasn't a whim precisely. I did it because I knew I wasn't supposed to. Sometimes I wonder how well you know me after all. I don't like being told what to do. Including by you. Maybe especially by you." But she made these assertions lightly.

"Our countless conversations . . ." His expression gave human form to the "recalibrating!" declaration of their GPS when you took a turn in defiance of its officious instructions. "I always assumed you were testing our arguments the better to strengthen them. Playing devil's advocate."

"Honestly, I've long found those haughty, patronizing bureaucrats in Brussels hard to take. They're the same authoritarian sort who've imposed all these bossy stay-at-home orders."

"So all along this household has had a fifth column." He looked gutted.

"Yes, and all those insults you pitched at the 'ignorant bigots' and 'pathetic Little Englanders' you were hurling at me!" she said gleefully. "But I'm truly fascinated that right up to the brink you're still holding onto your umbrage over *Brexit*."

"First I discover that more than half my compatriots are self-destructive, small-minded louts. Next I discover that they're also sheep—'freeborn Englishmen' who will accept indefinite house arrest without a bleat of protest. Who blindly embrace as gospel the wild, unfounded forecasts of one maverick, historically alarmist epidemiologist at our alma mater, because after all this time they apparently still don't know how to use the internet on their own. Maybe it's easier to leave behind a country I no longer recognize."

"And a wife you no longer recognize?"

He reached to clasp her hand across the half-eaten mash; she'd made too much. "Nothing makes that easy, bab," he said, and his eyes filmed.

All day, Kay had been lifted by a peculiar floating sensation, as if she were drifting two or three inches above the floor, the way a hovercraft glides across the waves without touching water. This giddiness and detachment and lack of seriousness were dreadfully inappropriate considering, as if the guiding principle for all their major decisions for decades were merely a fanciful leg-pull. As she sipped the last of the champagne, this feeling of fizzy levitation intermingled with the refreshing spritz of bubbles on her nose, but the buzz wasn't from the wine; she felt as if she *were* the champagne, rising into the air, *pip, pip, pip*. This whole evening, she should have been consumed with dread and anxiety, and instead she couldn't remember a night in recent memory when she and her husband had had a better time.

"You know, after all the threats of disaster from the IMF, the CBI, and the Bank of England?" she mused, rising to open a pricey bottle of cabernet that she was damned if she'd leave for Roy. "I'm a bit disappointed that now I'll never learn whether leaving the EU turns out to be a calamity after all. Since we're still in the 'transition period,' the first results won't be in until next year. And now this coronavirus deep freeze introduces such a confound that the separate impact of Brexit may never be known. For that matter, I'm also intensely disappointed not to be able to see to the other side of this pandemic. Will millions die? Will the world economy implode into a dog-eat-dog depression? Why, we still don't even know whether Boris will make it." Boris had just tested positive, along with the Minister of Health and Prince Charles.

"That buffoon biting the dust could be one of the only good things to come out of this disease."

"Now, you don't really mean that."

"Of course I do," Cyril said irritably.

"Oh, never mind Boris. My point is—well, I find it surprisingly easy to stop *caring* about what happens—that is, I can readily let go of my attachment to a particular outcome—but I find it infernally difficult to stop being *interested*. I feel as if I'm in the middle of so many stories, and suddenly it's time to return all these unfinished novels to the library. Doesn't it bother you that now you'll never find out whether Donald Trump is re-elected?"

"Not especially," Cyril said. "Trump's not our problem. And if that charlatan does keep squatting in the White House, maybe I'm better off spared the news. Besides, something's bound to be up in the air, whenever one bows out."

"Sorry. Even amidst the end of the world—ours anyway—needs must!"

Kissing Cyril's top knuckle and giving his palm a squeeze, Kay slipped off to the loo—within whose privacy she felt a surge of the same last-minute fickleness, fecklessness, mischief, and caprice that had drawn her hand to the "wrong" box on the ballot paper in 2016. She was suddenly sorry she hadn't smashed that plate when the peculiar urge had been upon her, if only as an expression of the very agency that Cyril expected them to exercise before the night was through. As an efficacious substitute for shouting *Opa!* and pitching her wedding china against a wall, she withdrew her phone from her pocket and tapped the messages icon. There was no guarantee that the gesture would be availing, but Cyril had claimed that they were making a "calculated gamble," and in the spirit of a poker game Kay was introducing a wild card.

This moment of impulsivity came at a cost, for when she returned to the table the saturated colours of the tableaux had coarsened from Rembrandt to Hockney.

"We were talking about Trump!" she recommenced with a renewed zestfulness, returning her serviette to her lap and recharging both wine glasses. "I might rather know what happens to the git. In fact, I'd like to get to the last chapter of all manner of stories. Will the coronavirus peak and subside like any old bog-standard outbreak, or is civilization as we know it finished? Will the European migration crisis resume? Will the UK's potentially ruinous commitment to 'carbon neutrality' by 2050 make the slightest difference to climate change? Will the climate change after all, but quite differently than we imagine? And what is it that will surely happen in the next twenty years—doubtless something terrible—which no one today has even thought about?"

Cyril regarded her with a new wariness. This every-day making-conversation was surely disconcerting. It was getting late. Sombre summary pronouncements about two lives well lived and a long, loving marriage would have seemed more suitable than cant about climate change.

"Shall we clear up?" Kay proposed.

"Why on earth?"

"We always clear up."

"Tonight is the end of always."

She arose and carried the leftover bangers to the counter beside the fridge. "It wouldn't do to let this food spoil."

"Why not? Who's going to eat it?"

"Well, maybe one of the children—"

"*One of the children* is going to discover both parents overdosed on Seconal and then scavenge the fridge for potatoes?"

"Probably not Hayley, she's too theatrical," Kay conceded. "But Simon is very practical—even if he's become a bit snobbish for leftovers—and Roy is always hungry."

"You're forgetting about two large pieces of meat which are bound to go off," Cyril said brutally, "and spoil any visitor's appetite."

"Yes, I was wondering about that," Kay said, sealing cling film over the cabbage. "How long do you think it will take for anyone to notice we're not out and about? Especially with all this 'social distancing' and 'shielding'? Because I took on a design job once where an old man had died, and they'd only found him after a neighbour complained to the council about the reek. The smell lingered interminably, and halved the property's market value."

"So? We barely own this house any more. It's mortgaged to the hilt."

"But I do worry about giving one of the children a fright. It seems inconsiderate. Hayley would claim to have PTSD for the rest of her life. So I wonder if we might pop to the post box across the road and drop an advisory note to the police."

"After privatization, Royal Mail's got so rubbish, not to mention the Met after all those Tory cuts. When Hayley and Simon can't rouse us on the phone, one of them will drop by, or contact the authorities themselves. I doubt a note would work any faster than leaving it to chance."

"Oh, you're probably right." Kay collected the plates and slotted them into the dishwasher. "I know it seems silly to tidy up. But I like order, and I like our regular ritual, and I don't want to spend my last night on earth surrounded by grot."

This was an explanation Cyril seemed to accept. He put away the mustard and, as he'd always done, wiped down the counters.

"Port and crumble?" she proposed once the kitchen was spotless. As Cyril fetched the bottle, she glanced at the clock. It was already ten fifty-five p.m.—the literal eleventh hour—and she had a feeling that her husband would be a stickler about the exact conclusion of her eightieth birthday. Even arguing for an extra hour after having been cheated by the clocks' changing wouldn't likely wash; it would introduce the same possibility of infinite delay as last year's pushing back of the EU withdrawal date.

When they retired to the sitting room, Kay's mood sank. She might have prepared the meal that afternoon in a meditative swoon, but she'd been inattentive. The crumble topping was slightly burnt, the apples were overcooked, and she really should have forced herself to whisk up the custard from scratch. This poor showing was destined to be her last pudding ever? And granted, their daughter lived conveniently nearby in Borough. But Hayley did sometimes make a fashionable gesture of independence from the screen, Kay recalled morosely, and turned off her phone for days.

Kay's printed-out directions for their memorial service were arrayed on the coffee table, along with a flash drive with the digital files for the family's convenience. But so much for liking order; the papers looked neat, but their contents were a shambles. She'd listed well too many musical selections, and before dinner had even scribbled "Dock of the Bay" onto the hard copy, as if twenty-three songs needed a twenty-fourth. When she'd tried to trim her farewell address, she kept thinking of indispensable additions, and the document had grown only more bloated. In kind, when she'd tried to soften the chiding self-righteousness of the essay to accompany the order of service, she merely managed to sound condescending (*we're* responsible, but it's too much to ask for *you* to be responsible). Besides, when Cyril had finally got round to writing his own farewell, he refused to be "sentimental" and instead pontificated about the same costs to the NHS, the looming "economically unsustainable support ratio," and the "burden on younger taxpayers" that she'd cited in her own essay, so the compositions were redundant. Worst of all, during the coronavirus lockdown, which could prospectively last for months, funerals were restricted to a handful of mourners spaced two metres apart. No one would sing anything or read anything or even be there, and the couple would be cremated as carelessly as this crumble.

Alas, whilst she was fretting over the disappointing pudding with its lacklustre commercial custard, Kay's motions became so jagged that she knocked over her port glass, splashing fortified wine onto the printouts and using up three or four minutes of the twenty-eight that apparently remained of her entire life on mopping up the spill. Port had also splattered her lovely white dress. Although she didn't want to waste even more time changing clothes, being found covered in ruby stains seemed déclassé.

Cyril fetched her a refill, but when he returned with a tray it also held a pitcher of water and two tumblers. He set the tray in the middle of the coffee table with the stern priestly air of serving communion.

"It's taken me ages to realize that I still don't understand what this *is*," Kay blithered. "I mean, it's difficult to quit something when you've no idea what you're quitting. I may be eighty, and perhaps that really is as much time as I deserve, but I still can't get my head round what it means to be alive in the first place, much less what it means to die. I don't know what this place is, I don't know whether it's even real, much less whatever it was we were supposed to do here, and if I've wasted my time I still can't tell you what I should have done instead. I've no more idea what matters than I did when I was five. I keep having this feeling that there was something I was supposed to come to grips with, and there's not much chance of my grasping the nettle in"—she checked her watch again—"fourteen minutes!"

Cyril had just launched into some *Jonathan Livingston Seagull*-style pap about only being able truly to understand what you have once you're in the process of losing it when the front door banged open and slammed. Hayley burst into the sitting room. Kay couldn't stop herself thinking what a pity it was that at only forty-eight their daughter had grown awfully dumpy. She'd been just a slip of a thing at university.

"Mum!" Hayley knelt and took her mother's face in both hands. She was wearing a kooky homemade mask whose fabric was incongruously covered in smiley faces. "Look at me! Have you taken anything? Tell me, quick, whilst you still can, if you've taken something, what is it?"

In their daughter's clutch, Kay could just catch Cyril's face in the corner of her eye. His expression communicated in an instant that he could indeed distinguish between a mere difference of opinion on a political matter and full-on personal betrayal. He had never in their marriage shot her a look that cutting. "You *told* her."

"Sweetheart, please stop slapping my cheeks like that," Kay implored over sirens *wah-oo-wha-oo-wha-oo*ing terribly close to this house. "I'm quite awake, we're both fine, and no one has consumed anything untoward, unless you count an underwhelming crumble." Just then she wished that she had indeed popped upstairs to change, because the splattered white dress conveyed the very derangement that Cyril's scheme was designed to avoid.

Impatient pounding sounded on the front door.

"Whoever's that?" Kay said.

"Who do you think, Mum?" Hayley said. "I obviously rang nine-nine-nine!"

"Emergency services!" More pounding. "Open up!"

Kay realized that she was still foolishly clutching the stem of her port glass, which with all Hayley's patting and shaking had spilled yet more fortified wine on her dress. When she reached to put it on the coffee table, a sharp, excruciating pain in her right shoulder was another reminder of the corruption that Cyril would have spared her. As she attempted to scurry to the door, just rising from the sofa was slow going, and one didn't "scurry" with arthritic toes. Hayley hurried ahead to let in the ambulance crew.

"We got a call-in about an attempted suicide?" a male voice boomed.

"My mum claims she hasn't taken anything," Hayley said, "but I'm not sure I believe her."

When Kay arrived in the foyer covered in port, which they might have mistaken for blood, she didn't make for a very credible witness when she protested again that neither she nor her spouse had imbibed anything more poisonous than watery Sainsbury's custard. There was a hullabaloo about pumping her stomach anyway or at least taking her to hospital for observation.

"Hayley, it's true I was having second thoughts, and on balance I'm glad to see you," Kay said. "But we needn't trouble these fine paramedics, who must have far more urgent situations to attend to during a national emergency. I don't want all this fuss!"

"Madam," one of the medics said through his mask and from behind a Perspex facial shield, in a tone that denoted anything but respect. They were both wearing not only blue surgical gloves, but full-body protective suits, as if en route to outer space. "Can you please inform us if the household contains any firearms?"

"Of course we weren't planning to use a gun," Kay dismissed. "What a messy business that would be."

"Mum, if you're telling the truth about not having taken anything yet, then where's the bottle? Where are the tablets?"

"I'm not sure I prefer to tell you," Kay said stiffly. "I might care to stick around a bit longer, but it's our business if we—"

"Mum!" Hayley violently shook her mother's shoulders; this scene would surely satisfy the girl's keen appetite for high drama for weeks. "*Where are the tablets?*"

That right shoulder was now screaming in such pain that it might have been dislocated; if only to make her daughter stop, Kay capitulated. "In the fridge. A black box, top shelf, back left."

Hayley returned from the kitchen glaring and empty-handed. "It's *not there.*"

"Then ask Cyril. He's the master of ceremonies."

"You mean Dad is the homicidal maniac, from the sound of it!" Hayley exclaimed. "Another Dr Kevorkian! Or Harold Shipman! He's

obviously brainwashed you into going along with one of his blinkered, fanatical socialist fixations! This whole nonsense is so like him
I could be sick!"

Yet when they returned to the sitting room, Cyril had vanished. So
had one of the tumblers. It was a large house, much larger than the
couple needed with the children gone, and by the time they finally
located his body in the tool shed, it was too late.

In the immediate aftermath, Kay couldn't bear cooking for herself,
and when the casserole from the Samsons ran out she actually ate
most of the leftover bangers and mash—which kept quite well, as the
cream in the potatoes had been fresh. But she didn't have the option
of a long, inert bereavement, because their savings were shot, and her
pension couldn't cover the massive remortgage. By mid-May, property transactions were allowed again, and moving house was a useful distraction—although Roy was most unpleasant about the sale,
whose proceeds he'd been counting on to finance a protracted disso-
lution after his parents' passing. Disposing of most of their things was
painful at first but a relief in the end, and shifting into an efficient
one-bed flat in Kennington allowed for meeting the divorcee next-
door—who on hearing the story of her widowhood (a story she might
have deployed with a trace of manipulation; it made her interesting)
declared appealingly, "I'm not sure what impresses me more: him going through with it, or you not." To her own surprise even more than
the children's, she took up with Ellis within the year, because at their
age an extended courtship was a long walk on a short pier. The new
relationship was neither better nor worse but different; you couldn't
replicate a long-standing marriage of fifty-seven years, but Ellis was
less, as the kids said, "controlling," and let her take the lead, even

when she made the radical proposition that they knock down the wall between their flats. Her high blood pressure became more challenging to manage pharmaceutically when it began to alternate erratically with low blood pressure, but she learnt to have a lie-down when she felt faint, and one of the liberations of age was not having to worry about the underlying reasons some system of your body was on the fritz, because if that didn't go wrong then something else would. The right shoulder grew worse, but she got surgery, which was largely, if not altogether, a success. The toes were a more enduring torture, but it turned out that those mobility scooters were a right laugh, and she and Ellis conducted races down the halls of their tower block, becoming even peskier tearaways than the youngsters on trick bikes in the car park. Attempting to make a light at Elephant and Castle one afternoon—witnesses tsked that the pedestrian signal had long before turned red, but Kay on her scooter had become a proper daredevil—she chanced her arm once too often and was sent spinning into a lamppost by an archetypal White Van Man. The end wasn't "quiet," as Cyril had once promised, but it was quick. She was ninety-two.

3

White Van Man Redux

Kissing Cyril's top knuckle and giving his palm a squeeze, Kay slipped off to the loo—within whose privacy she felt a surge of the same last-minute fickleness, fecklessness, mischief, and caprice that had drawn her hand to the "wrong" box on the ballot paper in 2016. She was suddenly sorry she hadn't smashed that plate when the peculiar urge had been upon her, if only as an expression of the very agency that Cyril expected them to exercise before the night was through. As an efficacious substitute for shouting *Opa!* and pitching her wedding china against a wall, she withdrew her phone from her pocket and tapped the messages icon. There was no guarantee that the gesture would be availing, but Cyril had claimed that they were making a "calculated gamble," and in the spirit of a poker game Kay was introducing a wild card.

Yet, thumbs poised, she remembered how Hayley herself had expressed exasperation with her mother's marital passivity during the girl's childhood. The two had conducted fruitful heart-to-hearts about the fact that, as a member of the dismally christened Silent Generation, Kay hadn't been gifted with the self-respect that women Hayley's age took for granted. It was thanks to her daughter's encouragement that she'd stood up to Cyril when she wanted to enrol in that degree course at Kingston. (Her husband had considered it a dereliction of duty to retire from the NHS at fifty-five, and strenuously urged that she stick out ten more years. He'd dismissed interior design as "frivolous." It had been quite a showdown.) Tonight, placing her fate in the hands of fortune—effectively tossing a note in a bottle into the cybersea, on the off chance that a passing beachcomber picked it up—was no more dignified than leaving the decision entirely to her husband. After all, what punchy slogan won the referendum for Leave? *Take back control.*

"Now, listen here," Kay said back at the table, pushing the cork back in the unfinished bottle of cabernet and giving the stopper an extra party's-over shove for good measure. "This evening has been great fun in its way, but it's also a complete nonsense, and I'm calling time."

"Sorry. What are you on about?"

People often employ incomprehension not as a means to clarify what you did say, but as a demand that you say something else. "This is a charade and a ridiculous charade at that. This pantomime of ours is made all the more daft by the pandemic. Here we are playing at poison-pill-popping, whilst the world outside our front door is battened down in terror that they'll all get sick and die. Supposedly this dismal lockdown is expressly to protect the so-called vulnerable, meaning old people *just like us.* Ignoring younger people's sacrifices on our behalf and popping our clogs on purpose—well, it seems ungrateful. It would be one thing if we were in agony, or were facing the lingering horrors of a terminal diagnosis, or had turned into gibbering idiots like my father—"

"In which case, we wouldn't have the mental wherewithal—"

"Yes, yes, Catch-22, but we're *not* demented. I misplace keys or have trouble remembering who wrote *The Go-Between*, but I had the same lapses in my twenties. We've our share of aches and pains, but nothing that merits suicide, for heaven's sake. Which is dreadfully hard on survivors, even if the deceased are long in the tooth. This isn't fair on the children. It isn't fair on us, either. It certainly isn't fair on me."

"We both made a commitment. No one forced you."

"You had an idea, and I went along with it. As usual."

"Not that again."

"I love you dearly, but you can be bossy."

"And you can be reactive. Which isn't any more independent-minded than slavish obedience. You made it damnably clear that you voted Leave to spite me."

"Are you ever going to let that go? Because for once we're talking about something more important than *Brexit*. I've no idea what happens after you die, but the odds are frightfully high that nothing does. The sole upside to death is the end of suffering, but we're not suffering—or at least our incidental suffering can't compare to the grievous kind that you and I so often witnessed in the NHS. You characterized this plan of yours as a gamble. Look at the two bets we could place in terms of the cold statistical logic of a professional high-roller, then. One wager would win—maybe win only a bit, maybe a great deal: more wine, more buttered crumpets, more pretty sunsets, along with watching our two youngest grandchildren grow up and the odd mediocre mini-series. Like those scratch cards that guarantee that you'll always win something, if only a quid or two. What's the other wager? Lose, full stop—lose everything, our whole stake. Win something, or lose the lot? As the kids say, *duh*."

"You've no idea what we might end up paying for a few more sunsets—"

"This was never a realistic proposal," she cut him off, whisking the corked wine to the counter, "and I'm sorry I went along with it as long as I did. There's something childish about it, and one of us has to go back to being a grown-up. I've no plans to overdose tonight on anything more deadly than a burnt crumble." Kay collected the plates, suppressing a wince from her shoulder.

"And I thought for once in our lives we might get out of washing up," Cyril quipped. It was his idea of lightening the mood.

"I don't mind washing up," Kay said, putting the cutlery in the dishwasher tines up, though Cyril always pointed them down. "I find it satisfying. That's part of what this whole business is about, isn't it? I enjoy life more than you do. That's especially been the case since you retired. I think you've resented the fact that I went on to have a whole second career, in which I've distinguished myself and had a delightful time. Meanwhile, you've glowered over your *Guardian* and constantly looked at the clock—in the hopes that yet another burdensome hour will have been dispatched. So you contrived this levelling exercise, whereby I get dragged down to your negativity and nihilism."

"That's neither kind nor true," Cyril objected. "When I proposed our private final solution, I was full-time at the clinic, where I worked for another, what, thirteen years. You were still at St Thomas', with no second career at that time for me to, quote, 'resent.' Your uncharitable explanation for my motives is sheer fabrication, and not very well thought through."

"I don't even care. Because you know what? I'm enjoying expressing myself and saying whatever I like. Even having this argument beats hands down swooning on the sofa in 'fatigue' whilst I begin to experience 'blurred vision.' I don't even mind saying things that aren't true or aren't nice so long as I get to say something. I may never have appreciated it before: talking, simply talking, is a joy."

"Are you making this summary decision for the two of us? Because working myself up to this moment has taken *years* of concentration, contemplation, and resolve."

"Yes, I believe that," she said. "This morbid project of yours has substituted for doing something more positive. I may have done the cooking, but tonight was supposed to be your crowning act of creation. A passion play of bravery and nobility. But real bravery and nobility entail losing everything you love by degrees like everyone else, and taking what comes like everyone else, and dying when you least expect it and when you don't want to, like everyone else."

"I can't remember when you were last such a chatterbox."

"It's the reprieve. Like in those old black-and-white films, when the phone finally rings in the penitentiary at two minutes to twelve. They don't show it, but I reckon the fellow with the commuted sentence who's already strapped in the electric chair is suddenly a chatterbox, too." Cupping the flames, Kay blew out the candles, then licked her thumb and forefinger to extinguish the glowing wicks with a tiny *ch-shsh*, the benedictory sound of another splendid dinner done. The aroma of the wax mixed with the singe from the wicks was heady.

"What if I still want to go through with it?" Cyril said.

"That's your business. Though I'd strongly prefer that you didn't. Besides, admit it: without my following suit, you'd lose the symmetry, and the grandeur of the gesture. You'd appear to be just one more old man who'd got isolated and a bit depressed. The stunt would look small if not pathetic, or even silly. I would have to tell Simon, no you can't speak to your father, because he just took his own life for no good reason. Your passing would still be sad, but you'd seem batty. You wouldn't make a forceful statement. You wouldn't set an example. Because—sorry—there'd be no media coverage, not when so many men your age are already dropping like flies from COVID-19. So you can forget this notion that thousands if not millions of your fellow socialist utopians will follow your heroic lead when they reach eighty, and the elderly's mass self-sacrifice will prove the salvation of the NHS. Think I don't know what kind of overblown fantasies circle that grandiose head of yours? In sum, my dear, keeping to plan wouldn't reflect well on you. And I'm afraid my memory of you would be tarnished. Any nostalgia would be compromised by annoyance and disappointment. I'd remember your churlish, bloody-minded insistence on having your way, your refusal to change your mind or to listen to reason—listen to *me*—as a desertion, a betrayal, and an insult."

"But if I did . . . Would you ring nine-nine-nine?"

She considered, washing the champagne glasses, which didn't go into the dishwasher or they'd etch. "Probably, yes. And then there'd be the possibility of not coming out the other side in tip-top shape."

"Were you ever going to go through with it?" he asked mournfully, still slumped in his chair.

That pulled her up short. "I'm not entirely sure. Some days, probably. This morning, almost. And I've loved the holidays, spending all our money. I've quite fancied the proposition that I'll never have to face getting any older than I am today. I've fancied the *denial*. Why not? Worrying about getting old doesn't make it easier." She leant into his ear as she cleared off the potatoes. "Tonight, you may even have given me a gift, whether or not you meant to. I'm happy to be alive. As I should be." She kissed his forehead. "It's my birthday."

But it was only when Cyril finally pulled himself up and began to wipe down the counters that Kay exhaled with relief. She put away the food. There was just about enough left over of every dish for tomorrow night's dinner.

The next morning at breakfast, Kay was still relishing the rare sensation of sitting in the marital driver's seat—not to mention the sensation of sitting anywhere at all. She'd had to run out for provisions, because before a certain change of plans she'd had no reason to stock up; to the contrary, she'd made a concerted effort to systematically run down the larder to a cup or two of sugar, an impulse-buy tin of red bean paste from the Asian supermarket near Elephant, and a bag of dried red lentils (which so disappointingly lost their colour when cooked). But thanks to the morning's hasty excursion to the M&S Metro, whose shelves weren't yet entirely emptied by hoarders, these crumpets were extra fresh.

"Now, I'm not saying we have to toss the tablets in the toilet," Kay said, waiting for the butter to melt into the perforations. "We could still face some medical calamity and require a resort. They can stay where they are. I'm accustomed to that box, and I find it a useful reminder to try to enjoy the day."

Cyril had seemed sheepish since they got up. Having begged her for a few extra minutes of embrace in bed, he didn't seem to wish he were dead any more than she did. "Dear me, I just remembered," he said. "Whilst you were in the loo last night, I slipped out the front to pop a note to the Met in the post box. It told them where to find us and that we'd be—you know."

"Why alert the police? The smell? Or to spare the children?"

"To spare the house. I informed the police that the Samsons have a key. You picked out such a corker of a new front door, with all those fiddly diamonds of leaded glass. I couldn't bear the peelers smashing those panes with a battering ram."

She was touched. Cyril might have been resistant to her second career at first, but in time he'd grown proud of her good eye. "Does that mean they'll be letting themselves in at any moment? As I picture the scene, it's *awkward*."

"That post box is collected on weekday mornings at eleven o'clock," Cyril said. "I don't imagine the police will get my note until tomorrow or the day after at the earliest. Gives us time to head them off, or at least to figure out what to say. 'Sorry, we're scaredy cats'? And then we're on the public record as a danger to ourselves. That won't look good if Roy ever gets a mind to section us in some hellhole against our will and sell the house."

"Yes, it would certainly be Roy," Kay said with a sigh. "But it's still only ten forty-five. Why don't I try and intercept the postman—or *postperson*? She's always seemed sweet, and I might talk her into giving the letter back."

Kay positioned herself by the red pillar-box a few minutes before eleven. Sure enough, the pretty young Somali who'd delivered their post for the last year showed up with her mail cart and key right on time. She was wearing blue Latex surgical gloves and a paper mask on her chin.

Kay wasn't about to divulge the real story, so came up with an elaborate tale about having become convinced that the couple had been victims of fraud (which happened so often these days; the number of pensioners cleaned out by unscrupulous scammers was a scandal). But husband and wife simply hadn't been communicating, and the charge Cyril had put on their credit card—for her birthday, which was yesterday, and yes, thanks so much for your good wishes—well, it was perfectly valid after all . . .

The story didn't make much sense. Obviously, you didn't write to the police about fraudulent card charges but contacted Visa directly. Happily, a young person would readily assume that the decrepit were procedurally clueless. Besides, the girl wasn't really listening, another advantage, in this case, of the petitioner's advanced years, and she seemed eager to get away from an old woman, because the elderly had already acquired an ominous air of contagion.

Kay pointed. "There! That's it. The light blue one, with *Mr and Mrs Cyril Wilkinson* embossed on the flap." Even if the girl didn't recognize the wizened woman whose post she delivered daily, the distinctive envelope made Kay's claim to its ownership credible. Only oldies would purchase engraved stationery.

Mumbling something about interfering with posted mail being technically illegal, the girl reluctantly capitulated, probably just to get the rabbiting old biddy off her back.

Exhilarated by her successful mission, and perhaps exhilarated full stop, just because she was still feeling the spring breeze on her cheeks, still looking forward to a second buttered crumpet, and still, despite his infernally programmatic approach to complex problems, in love with her boneheaded husband, Kay raised the envelope high with her more functional left arm and rushed across the road to their house on the corner without looking. An archetypal White Van Man knocked her ten feet into a lamppost, and that was that. She was eighty years old and a day.

4

Cyril Has an Unexpected Change of Heart

"It's taken me ages to realize that I still don't understand what this *is*," Kay blithered. "I mean, it's difficult to quit something when you've no idea what you're quitting. I may be eighty, and perhaps that really is as much time as I deserve, but I still can't get my head round what it means to be alive in the first place, much less what it means to die. I don't know what this place is, I don't know whether it's even real, much less whatever it was we were supposed to do here, and if I've wasted my time I still can't tell you what I should have done instead. I've no more idea what matters than I did when I was five. I keep having this feeling that there was something I was supposed to come to grips with, and there's not much chance of my grasping the nettle in"—she checked her watch again—"fourteen minutes!"

Cyril had been patient throughout the insensible monologue, clearly the product of hysteria. "I doubt any of us can understand what life is until the moment we lose it," he said soothingly, stroking her hand. "Maybe a full grasp of life is only possible in the act of sacrificing it. Whatever you think you're supposed to 'come to grips with' may elude you until the final epiphany."

Kay frowned. "To live, you have to die?"

It was a crude translation, when he thought he'd put his philosophical formulation rather poetically for a medical man. There was something heartbreaking about the way his wife kept starting and seeming to prick her ears at the least sound from outside—a far-off siren, the screech of a fox—whilst continually darting her eyes wildly in the direction of the foyer, as if she were expecting rescue by an angel from the great beyond at the last minute. Perhaps it's impossible to foretell how one will react, up against the ultimate unknown, and Kay's reaction was panic—which was probably standard.

Yet Cyril himself felt calm and lucid. He was experiencing the sense of presence that visited him so often when sleeping with his wife but that seldom returned during the waking day. It was a deeply enjoyable sensation of being cohesive, unified, of a piece, and his thoughts, frequently clamorous, were still.

As he sucked the top from the black box, it made a satisfying *swoosh*, like the release of an air lock. He shook the tablets from the bottle inside and lined them up in a neat grid on the coffee table. Kay regarded his arrangement, which looked as if he were setting about a travel game of Go, with abject terror.

"What are you afraid of, bab?" he asked gently.

Emitting only the faint buzz of an incandescent lightbulb filament, she was trembling nonetheless. "Of making a mistake."

"But this is our fate. It's everyone's fate. So it can't really be a mistake, unless the design of the universe is in error."

"Maybe it is in error." She was stalling for time. He'd rarely felt so eloquent, yet he knew that expression on his wife's face: annoyance.

"You should experience only a soft, slow decrescendo," he said. "Nothing to fear. I would never do anything to hurt you."

She shot another desperate, inexplicable glance at the entrance to the foyer.

"This is the best possible way out," he intoned. "On our terms, in our home, when we're still sane and recognizable to each other. When we're able to embrace and say goodbye. Before we're put through untold degradation and indignity. Before we cost our compatriots a mint whilst surviving as grotesque parodies of our younger selves, or as mere vessels for affliction. We're exercising control over our own destinies. Remember what happened to your parents."

"That was decades ago, so I suppose their decline has grown less vivid. And I don't want to remember it. Why would I?"

"For the time being, you don't remember their woeful deterioration because you don't want to. Soon you could neglect to remember it because you can't."

"Oh, maybe you're right. As you are about most things, of course. I mean, I'm sorry about voting Leave. I'm not sure what got into me. I dare say it *will* be bad for the economy, and you know I never imagined in a million years that Leave might win—"

"No more Brexit," he abjured with a smile, brushing her cheek. "Not during our last few minutes on this earth."

"Sorry," she said in embarrassment. "Distracted chatter. Maybe that's all that palaver ever was."

"Shush. You're still talking about it. Talk about now. Think about now. That's all that's left."

". . . At least we're doing this together, right? Which makes all the difference, to me anyway." She ran her hand up and down the thigh she had stroked, squeezed, and traced lingeringly with a forefinger on the way up to more intriguing anatomy for fifty-seven years. "It doesn't make it easy, but easier—much easier."

"And this way, neither of us has to live without the other, even for a short while," he said. "I've always been anxious that if anything happened to you, I'd fall apart. Not be able to eat, wash, or shop, much less sleep. I've pictured myself as one of those widowers in a brown moth-eaten cardigan and slippers with crushed heels—who stares into space for hours on end. Who smells."

"It really doesn't hurt?" She sounded like a child.

"No."

Something seemed to give—to collapse, to release, to let go. She dropped her shoulders, took a breath, and looked straight into his eyes with a trust that made Cyril feel obscurely guilty. "I've been lucky so far, but I do have wretched genes, don't I? And I can't bear the prospect of ruining your life, the way my father ruined my mother's—until you come to hate me and can't remember anything good. We had a lovely dinner, didn't we? And a lovely life."

She kissed him deeply, the way they used to kiss for hours when they were courting, and withdrew from his lips at last with the same reluctance he remembered from those days as well, when they had to get back to their medical studies. That kiss sent a tingling shimmer through the entirety of their lives together, as if their marriage were a crash cymbal whose rim she'd just hit deftly with a felt mallet.

She poured the water from the pitcher herself. She held out her palm, leaving it to Cyril to decide how many. She bolted them all at once and drained the tumbler.

"Will you stay with me?" she asked. "Promise to hold me till it's over."

"I promise," Cyril said, drawing her to his shoulder and putting an arm around the birdlike bones of her back. However ironically, he felt fiercely protective of her. He would wait to take his own dosage until she was safe, or until the concept of safety no longer pertained. It was a kind of absolute security, when you thought about it: to achieve a state in which no one could do anything at all to you, no matter how dreadful. He had just rescued his wife from every insult under the sun.

"I hope Hayley doesn't think it's her fault," Kay mumbled before nodding off. It was the drug. She was confused.

The moment was technically peaceful, but that was not the word he would have chosen to describe the point at which he instantly sensed that she was no longer there. Even his slight wife's body felt heavy—burdensome, cloying in its weight, like something he frantically wanted off him, and the corpse—that is what her beloved body had become, a *corpse*—didn't exude a becalming serenity, but energized him with horror. As a GP, Cyril had seen plenty of people die, but they were patients, kept at a necessary clinical remove, and none of their passings had felt anything like this.

He lifted her under the arms with all the tenderness he could muster, given that the physical exertion required to hoist *dead weight* was considerable. (The lexicon of lethality suddenly pulsed with meaning; he had the thought, especially absurd for a physician, *So this is what they were talking about*.) As best he could, he settled her in a slump on the opposite side of the sofa, trying and failing to close her mouth. If not altogether formulated, the idea had floated in the back of his mind that letting Kay go first would inspire him to go second. He wasn't so simple-minded as to imagine himself rushing to meet back up with his spouse on some harp-strewn cartoon cloud, but presumably he would welcome the offer of instantaneous escape from grief. He loved his wife, and that tidy array of tablets on the table would reprieve him from experiencing the desolate world without Kay in it for any more than a few minutes.

But that wasn't what happened. And something did happen: a great welling up from a place in himself with which he was little acquainted. This force arose unbidden; so involuntary was its eruption that the closest comparison he could contrive was to vomiting, although the sensation was not so unpleasant. This—quantity, this—substance, this—enormous, formless *thing* wasn't outside of him, or alien to him; it *was* him. It was what had always been there waiting and watching from within, a sort of under-seer whom he'd rarely had need to consult. In the grip of this larger, stronger, more primitive entity that he had apparently inhabited all along, Cyril looked at the pitcher. Then he looked at his hand. But he simply could not pour the water into the tumbler. The everyday task seemed a physical impossibility, as if the neurological connection between his brain and his arm were severed. Likewise, the notion of sweeping those tablets into an open palm and knocking them back was also impossible. Not merely unappealing, but *impossible.* With all his being, he *believed* in this contract he'd entered into with his wife, so he had not been disingenuous. It was his profoundly held conviction that to serve both his own and his nation's long-term interest he should keep a vow of three decades' standing to take his own life at the age of eighty-one.

He just didn't want to.

Dr Cyril J. Wilkinson was still a cogent, clear-headed retired professional who had accumulated invaluable insights into the strengths and, yes, failings of the fifth largest employer in the world. He was a fount of historical knowledge, anecdotal and otherwise, about the early and middle years of one of the greatest social projects a state had undertaken. Why hadn't he thought of this before, whilst wasting all that time gazing at mangroves in Australia? It was time he wrote his memoirs. He had never been entirely contented with the NHS trust system, which resulted in the much-derogated "post-code lottery": care in some regions well exceeded care in others. The service was too dependent on foreign staff, and attracting doctors and nurses from Romania, Bulgaria, Pakistan, and India deprived these countries of their own medics. The neglect of GP training was a scandal, for an inability to get appointments at the general-practice level was driving countless patients with non-urgent complaints to Accident and Emergency, far more costly than a clinic. The book he would write washed across his brain like a foetal hormone, and after thirty seconds it seemed the work was already composed and getting it down on paper would be a mere formality.

As for Kay, there was nothing for it. She had made her choice. Perhaps a prudent choice as well; her DNA was indeed riddled with dementia, whereas his own father, the old bastard, remained of sound mind to ninety-nine. He hadn't forced her. She had poured her own water and extended her hand for the tablets, which she'd swallowed of her own accord. This was nothing like a homicide, but a mere forking in the road of once-mutual intent.

That said, it was a great relief to Cyril that his wife would never know he changed his mind.

The ability to think methodically at such a juncture was nothing short of shocking, but he had already found out something about himself this evening that he hadn't known before. This capacity for calculation was simply one more door opening in a character whose floor plan turned out to include many more rooms than he'd imagined. He would need to notify the authorities in due course, though surely the tearful call could wait for daybreak. In the meantime, best arrange matters in such a way as to allay any suspicion of foul play. He could already hear himself bewailing to an abashed, mutely respectful officer, "It's true, for the last few weeks she's seemed depressed, but I'd no idea her spirits had sunk this low . . . She must have come downstairs late last night, as she sometimes does when she can't sleep, usually to read without disturbing me—though I've always assured her that I'm not bothered in the slightest if she keeps her bedside light on . . . And then I found her on the sofa this morning!" It wouldn't be a strain to appear upset, because he was.

Cyril rescued the remaining tablets from the coffee table and pipped them in the bottle, which he restored to the black box. The box he fitted back in its ritual location, the far upper left corner of the fridge—

who knows, he might still require an exit strategy at a later date—then occluded the box with Kay's 2018 thick-cut Seville marmalade (a vintage batch) and a darkening jar of mint sauce. He slid his clean tumbler back in the cupboard. He sponged the last sticky remnants of the spilled port from the table and scrubbed a few spots from the carpet. He slipped the flash drive with Kay's memorial documents into an upstairs mug of pens and pencils where it would never attract attention. He flipped through the printouts and removed his own farewell address, as well as Kay's essay on why they had resolved to slough off their mortal coils in tandem. These papers he set afire in their log burner, then shovelled out the black flakes and stirred them into the ash pail. He kept the order of service and her memorial farewell, which unambiguously established her dire intentions. The spatter of port on the printout's edges added a convincing touch of emotional disarray.

Yet he could not allow his beautiful wife to be pawed over by paramedics or policemen, perhaps photographed as well, whilst her becoming white frock was stained with ruby port. Lovingly, he unfastened the buttons at the back and worked the frock down her hips. Kissing her neck in apology for the impertinence—she was still warm—he removed her undergarments as well, taking a moment to gaze mournfully at the woman still comely in old age whose every square inch he knew as intimately as his own skin. Upstairs in her bureau, he located a pretty but modest nightdress—an old Christmas present from her mother, which in truth she never wore, because she and Cyril had always slept in each other's arms naked. From a hook on the back of the bedroom door, he also took a dramatic robe he'd found her on eBay that she adored: a black satin number with a crimson sash and bold 1940s shoulders that would have suited Joan Crawford. Getting the gear on her body was awkward, and however he arranged it the robe still looked askew, but she looked ever so much more presentable— and more as if she'd left him behind in bed to read downstairs.

Lastly, he washed up their crumble dishes and put the remainder of the pudding in the fridge, along with the open carton of Sainsbury's custard.

"You're the one who's a fanatic. So why aren't you dead?"

It had struck Cyril as ominous that after all the other guests who participated in the Zoom memorial service had sorrowfully logged off (the ban on gatherings being still in force), Hayley had remained on-line. Ever since receiving the terrible news, his daughter had seemed not only furious, but bulging with some undisclosed knowledge, like a cat who'd eaten the canary and the cage to boot.

"I realize this loss has been very difficult for you, Hayley," he said, as ever careful to keep from reclining onto the side of the sofa where he had arranged Kay in her robe. "But you should take heart that your mother led a full and wonderful life. It's just that she had started, you know, to forget things . . . After dementia ravaged both Grandpa and Nanna Poskitt, I can only assume she wanted to spare us—"

Hayley didn't seem interested in the pat explanation he had generated for the memorial's other virtual guests. "Her rambling 'so long, it's been nice to know you' thing that Simon read out on Zoom. Am I the only one who found it freaking weird that Mum remembered to say goodbye to her fourth-best friend, but not to her own husband?"

"Well, she'd have regarded things between us as private."

"Besides," Hayley continued, "Mum wasn't losing it. She was totally on the ball."

"She was skilful at covering her lapses. It was worse than you knew."

"It was exactly the way I knew: she was sharp as a tack. And I don't appreciate you sullying her memory by pretending she'd gone all drooling and doolally."

"You're grieving. If it helps to take out your pain on me, I'm willing to oblige as a whipping post, so long as you always bear in mind that I lost her as well."

"Uh-huh. And why was that?"

"As I said, she was forgetting things! This conversation is getting circular—"

"Dad. One of the many things Mum did *not* forget was to text me that night. She was pretty explicit about your plans for after the pudding."

Hayley paused to let this sink in, whilst Cyril's feelings ricocheted between woundedness and horror. He was stricken that Kay would betray his confidence, and it injured him beyond words that the last night of her life included an act of such disloyalty. Yet her disclosure of their pact also put a different slant on events thereafter.

"I usually take my phone up to bed and set its alarm," Hayley continued. "But during the lockdown, John doesn't have to go into UCL, and we're sleeping in. So tragically, when we went upstairs to read in bed, I left the phone behind in the kitchen. That's where it was sitting when Mum's text pinged in. A stupid little change of routine whose consequences I now have to live with forever. So I repeat: why are you not dead?"

He bowed his head. "I couldn't."

"Mum was always braver than you."

"It's hard to explain, but I don't think the problem was being too fearful."

"Well, if it wasn't cowardice, then it was egotism. Which takes the biscuit, because the whole melodramatic proposition would have been your idea! The stroke of midnight on her birthday, the inflexible cut-off of turning eighty, the self-righteous fake altruism behind the reasoning—the whole ball of wax has got Cyril J. Wilkinson written all over it!"

Hayley had long displayed a hectoring side, and although Cyril loved his daughter, the badgering was not attractive. "You can at least take comfort that your mother wasn't alone in her final moments, but in my arms. She died knowing she was cherished—"

"I could tell the police, you know."

"Tell them what? I didn't break the law."

"You just admitted to me that you *watched her die*. That has to qualify as criminal negligence. Maybe it's not murder, but it's freaking close. Besides, you lied to the cops. You weren't upstairs in bed. She didn't overdose in secret. You *helped* her. And in the UK, assisted suicide is super illegal."

"Most of those cases are never prosecuted—"

"Honestly, what did you accomplish? You basically killed my mother. Now you're all by yourself. Is that what you wanted? Were you tired of her?"

"Don't be absurd. And there's no evidence of anything criminal. No one will be interested in pursuing an investigation, and you shouldn't be either."

"She texted me because she obviously wanted to be *rescued*. From my father, the zealot. Who didn't even have the decency to carry out his own dumb idea."

"You sound as if you wish *I* were the one who'd topped himself."

"Yeah, well"—Hayley's forefinger loomed towards the screen, poised over her red "Leave" button—"the truth hurts."

Even before agreeing to leave this world hand-in-hand on 29 March 2020, Kay and Cyril had long embraced the commonplace romance that if one of them died, the other would soon follow. After all, this actuarial mirroring in long marriages had plenty of precedent. The prospect of soldiering on single again, perhaps even continuing to have a pleasant time, had seemed traitorous. They'd a mutual understanding that either losing the other would also entail losing the will to live.

Yet it turned out that Cyril could live without his wife. He couldn't decide if this reflected on him poorly or well. The discovery that he was able to carry on alone was saddening in a way, as it threatened to cast the defining relationship of his life as ancillary or expendable. Still, it was worth remembering that he did not create himself, and so could not be held responsible for his own essence. Besides, his surprisingly unshakable determination to endure did not reduce to petty selfishness or, as Hayley put it, egotism. From an early age, Cyril was naturally possessed of a ferocity—also not of his concoction—that could be directed towards ill or good. In the main, he had aimed the energy at his long, distinguished medical career, throughout which he had helped thousands of ordinary people to experience less pain, enjoy greater functionality, and overcome disease. The same ferocity had also sent his wife hurtling towards a D-day of her husband's design.

Looking back, Hayley was right: the grand scheme had accomplished nothing but tragedy. Perhaps the proposition had always been a bit too high-concept. The trouble was that on reaching the improbable year of 2020 neither spouse had been ailing. Such a hard-and-fast deadline might have been feasible had everyone else in the country also agreed to reach the knell of eight decades and call it quits. But everyone hadn't. The eccentric protocol was therefore fragile. Admittedly, Cyril had always been bloody-minded, and now he didn't benefit from the moderating, cajoling influence of a more flexible companion. Kay had been more given to caprice; good grief, consider that absurd impulse to vote Leave. Thus he'd little doubt that had he implored her to abandon their plans rather than pushing their original agenda that fateful birthday, she'd have popped the Seconal cheerfully back in the bottle and washed her teeth.

His life as a widower was not as warm and not as fun. The chill wind that blew through his days was made the colder by the fact that Hayley, predictably, could not keep her gob shut, and now all three children blamed him for their mother's death. Furthermore, their filial attachments had probably skewed in the maternal direction to begin with. Even once the lockdown was lifted, visits from the kids and their progeny were sparse.

He quickly came to appreciate that Kay had more than pulled her domestic weight—lightly, reflexively, without complaint. But the mundane tasks he'd imagined would grow insurmountable proved a salvation. Laundering his clothes, tidying the kitchen, and shopping for provisions filled and ordered his days. He grew to resent the intrusion of these monotonous chores only once his memoir got underway.

The project soon absorbed him to the point that he was even able to put out of mind his precarious (which was to say, disastrous) financial position. After taxes and his daily expenses, the whole of his monthly pension couldn't service the enormous remortgage that had paid for the couple's charitable contributions, generous parental support, and holidays. The state bereavement payment bought him some time, but once the pittance was extinguished he allowed the bank notices to pile up unopened. Living under the assumption that there was no future had become a habit.

Cyril was no Luddite, so he was hardly buffeted by stacks of spiral notebooks jagged with crimped, manic printing. Nonetheless, the size of the chapter files on his computer burgeoned. He was at least able to constrain the reminiscences about his wartime childhood and ascetic adolescence. (Rationing lasted until 1954. Now, *that* was "austerity," a word much abused during the twenty-teens. He was no fan of the "bedroom tax," but at least housing benefit claimants penalized for a spare room could still buy butter.) British television had long wallowed in the history of this era, and he was loath to further feed the nauseating nostalgia for plucky, resourceful, stiff-lipped England. But once he hit his professional years, his views on what did and didn't work in the NHS consumed his hard drive like yeast eating sugar.

Under the working title *Fit for Purpose*, the manuscript might have remained marginally under control—although Cyril was already contemplating two volumes—when at around the 200,000-word mark he veered into Brexit and fell in a hole. He imagined that he could write himself out of it, filling the pit with his fecund opinions and scrambling up the other side. Thereafter, he planned to delve into the poor preparation, carelessly alarmist epidemiology, and disproportionate public hysteria that contributed to the coronavirus debacle. Finally, he would divulge to the reader the pact he'd entered into with his wife, then explore the many reasons why quitting life at eighty was so sensible (the case somewhat hampered by the fact that the author making it was eighty-two). In the closing pages, he would reveal the sorrowful outcome, thereby ending the memoir on a poignant and confessional note. But in order to reach this climactic bare-all, he had to claw through his exasperation with British intransigence in trade talks, the sentimental overvaluation of the fisheries, and the terrible yet ineffable spiritual loss of exile from the European Union.

Flailing through this digressive "chapter" that after reaching 120,000 words still showed no sign of having exhausted itself, Cyril began putting in longer hours, hunching over his computer with a cold bacon butty at elbow until two or three a.m. It was in the vicinity of this witching hour that he felt an odd palsy on the right side of his face, whilst his right forefinger had an unaccustomed difficulty reaching the Y on the keyboard. The print on the screen danced, and his extensive elucidation of the many challenges facing the European continent that could only be tackled through concerted supranational action—migration, terrorism, further outbreaks of contagion—no longer quite made sense. Arising for the eternally futile cure-all of a glass of water, he stumbled dizzily and landed on the floor. He had a splitting headache. Doctors seldom regard the copious advisories they dish out to their patients as having anything to do with them person-ally, so that if anything Cyril took longer than mere punters would have taken to conclude that, yes—it was an insult to a medical man who should have earned himself out of the squalid, quotidian ail-ments that afflicted the hoi polloi—he was having a stroke. But by that point he had lost command of his limbs, and he was nowhere near a phone.

"I figure we should pull the plug."

"That may be a bit hasty."

"Well, what's the prognosis? Is he ever going to recover?"

"These things are idiosyncratic. Though at your father's age, the chances of significant improvement are slim. The damage was sub-stantial."

"It sounds like you think we should give it some time. Wait until he's completely stabilized."

"Wait? Wait for what? You heard the bloke. Chances are there's fuck-all to wait for. In which case, get it over with. Pull the plug."

"This is totally what he was afraid of. Like, it's almost poetic. In some ways, this is the perfect revenge. Way better than him dying. Just lying there forever with nothing to do but contemplate his sins."

"I'm sorry for what must seem like my sister's cold-heartedness, Dr Evans, but there's something of a *backstory*. She has her reasons."

"Well, there's no need to make any big decisions right away. So I'll leave you to spend a few minutes with your *loved one*."

A door closed.

"He was being sarcastic, right? He was totally being sarcastic."

Cyril's eyes fluttered open. There was a spot of water damage on the ceiling the shape of Norway. On the one hand he was curious what else his children might say when they thought their father was insensate; on the other, maybe he was better off not knowing. Yet croaking, "You know, I can hear you!" was clearly impossible whilst he was intubated.

Instead, Cyril waved an arm frantically to indicate to his visitors that the patient was awake. Correction: wave was what he intended to do, but in truth the limb continued to lie motionless, and the kids kept talking. He attempted to turn his head so that at least he could see his family, but that didn't happen either. It was consternating to marshal the neurological commands one was never, ordinarily, even aware of issuing, and then to have them blithely ignored. The loss of authority was vertiginous. He might as well have been the President for Life of a small, cowed country who'd been abruptly deposed, and suddenly the terrifying dictator whose every whim had been slavishly executed on pain of death was a pathetic, no-account convict in dirty underwear whose edicts roused nothing but laughter.

"How long is that doc going to make us wait before deciding Dad's completely vegged out?" Roy said. "Probate can take a while, and it would make a big difference to my *circumstances* to get the estate settled and the house sold off. Must be worth a couple mil by now."

"Hate to break it to you, little brother," Simon said. "But I swung by Lambeth the other day, just to check on the mail and that. Turns out they refinanced, and Dad hasn't kept up with the payments, either. He hadn't opened the envelopes, but he's in the process of being evicted."

"How can you be evicted from your own house?" Hayley asked in horror.

"It isn't his house. It's the bank's house. And there's more. I poked around his statements, and all his accounts are either down to spare change or in overdraft. In sum, Roy, there is no estate."

"*Motherfucker!*" Roy exploded.

A wad of bunched-up bedding was poking uncomfortably into Cyril's upper back, but he was powerless to rearrange it. His right hand seemed to regard the request to scratch a raging itch on his bum as positively hilarious. Experimentally, he made a concentrated effort to wiggle his toes, but when the sheet didn't brush against them he could tell that they weren't moving.

"The other thing I found," Simon said, "was this huge, incontinent manuscript on his computer."

"Incontinent" my foot! Cyril raged silently.

"The story of his life or something," Simon continued. "You know, it was long enough to make a Karl Ove Knausgaard novel seem like a travel brochure. Though the section onscreen when he collapsed was like, believe it or not, hundreds of pages about the European Union."

Hayley groaned. "*Gawd.* As if anyone wants to talk about the *EU* any more."

"Still, I was wondering if we should rescue the files," Simon said. "This magnum opus is the last thing he left behind. It might be of historical interest . . ."

"Well, it's certainly of no interest to me," Hayley said. "You can't honestly imagine that any of us would ever read it."

"Go ahead and print it out," Roy said. "I've finally used up my lock-down stockpile, and I'm running low on loo roll."

"What a typical vanity project," Hayley said. "It's so like him to go on and on like that—doubtless in the expectation that this turgid, self-aggrandizing tome will be published, and glowingly reviewed, and go on to become not only a bestseller, but required reading in medical schools. Maybe he was right in the first place, planning to bite the big one at eighty. He makes a crap old man. Being elderly is all about stepping aside and accepting you've had your day. In his whole life, Dad hasn't experienced actual humility for five minutes."

"Listen, do you think he left a living will?" Simon asked.

Of course there's a living will! Cyril screamed. *Middle drawer of the filing cabinet in the study, in the red flexi-folder at the front!*

"Ordinarily, you'd think so," Hayley said. "But he and Mum were expecting to do that whole theatrical double suicide thing, before it morphed into *murder*. He probably didn't bother."

"Bloody hell!" Roy exclaimed. "He's blinking."

The three ingrates gathered round their father's bed and peered down. However under-affectionate his middle-aged progeny, it was a relief to see something besides Norway. Cyril blinked frenetically.

"Do you think that's involuntary?" Hayley said.

"Hard to say," Simon said. "It could be a twitch."

Cyril blinked hard; stopped; blinked frenetically again; then stopped and stared. He was new at this, and unsure of the protocol for "appearing to blink on purpose."

"Figure there's someone still in there?" Roy said.

"Wow," Hayley said. "That is sick."

"Dad?" Simon said. "Is that you?"

Blink-blink-blink-blink-blink.

"Dad?" Simon said again. "If you can hear and understand me, blink once for yes, and twice—or cancel that. Blink twice for yes. Obviously if the answer is no, you're not going to answer at all."

Blink-blink.

"I know it sounds cruel," Hayley said. "But there's something, like, delicious about this. If he's really with it, that is, and not in a comatose fog. I mean, you can *really* contemplate your sins now, can't you, Dad?"

Cyril had never known that it was possible for time to pass so slowly. A mere half hour presented a vast temporal desert; he pictured himself dragging over dunes weighed down with equipment and wearing boots full of sand. Aside from occasional visits from nurses, and far more occasional visits from Simon, the most dutiful of the three, he lived without markers—that is, the firm junctures of an ordinary day that gave one purchase on its passage. Fed intravenously, he ate no meals. Hydrated by tubes, he sipped no bracing breakfast coffee or four p.m. tea. They'd installed a catheter and colonic irrigation bag, and he'd never appreciated before the welcome punctuation and purposeful urgency of visits to the WC. He could only sleep with drugs, and then only for three or four hours. Morning, afternoon, and evening were abstractions. Weather was irrelevant. A nurse sometimes turned on the television, but because he couldn't control the channels or even turn it off, the drivel rapidly decayed into one more torture.

Back in the day, he had savoured opportunities for reflection—sitting in contemplation on the Tube and deliberately choosing not to read, or enjoying an unexpected break in his workday when one more patient was a no-show and he could be alone with his thoughts. But now being alone with his thoughts had become his full-time job. Keeping something circulating through his head was a burden. Having once fancied himself something of an intellectual, he grew deeply disappointed by the limits of his mental athleticism, for his cerebral workouts resembled less Olympic gymnastics than clumsy clambering on a climbing frame. It was official: he didn't have a creative mind. (*There*, he yearned to tell Hayley. *How's that for humility?*) He could resort to memories of emotional occasions, but even highlights like Kay's acceptance of his marriage proposal or the rousing tributes at his retirement party were fragmentary, like old silent films with jagged motions, silly captions with too many exclamation marks, and flecked film. He doubted that his powers of recall were unusually

weak. Human memory was atrocious. At best he could vividly conjure only instants captured in still photographs. Not only did he rapidly tire of the few photos on his private hard drive that he could
mentally double-click, but the images began to distort, until faces in
his wedding pictures looked leering and grotesque.

Why, on examination, his precious recollections of his wartime
childhood didn't stand up to scrutiny either. During Operation Pied
Piper in the autumn of 1939, his mother had evacuated to Kent with
Cyril as an infant. When for months on end the sky didn't fall, she
returned with her baby to Birmingham. By the time German ructions
began in earnest, the newly intrepid Betsy Wilkinson was leaving
her firstborn with her younger sister during the day, the better to
help manufacture munitions. Although the bombings in Birmingham were ferocious, she chose aiding the war effort over the safety of
her family and refused to evacuate a second time—a decision Cyril
had always lauded. Yet his jumbled images of that period were full of
anachronisms; in one much-revisited snippet, whilst on leave from
the Italian campaign, his handsome uniformed father put a reassur-
ing arm around his son in the sitting room as they watched *television*.
Why, Cyril had even fancied that he retained flashes of that original
evacuation to Kent—he'd stored glimpses of hurried kisses on a train
platform, a gracious family waiting with chocolate biscuits on the receiving end—but for pity's sake, he'd only been eight months old.
His vivid "recollection" of his mother's insistence on dragging her
unwieldy yet beloved sewing box to the air raid shelter in the middle
of the night had a female voice-over: what he remembered was being
told about it. All the Blitzy crashes, booms, and dust in his mind had
been constructed from family lore, embellished with every retelling.
The bombings had been real enough, but his memories of the assaults
were fraudulent.

He went through a period of walking ritually around the floor plan of every house or flat in which he'd lived: the two-up two-down of his childhood in Birmingham, the larger house the family had shifted to when he was sixteen, the residence halls of Imperial College London, his first bedsit in Rotherhithe with Kay . . . With concentration, he could summon a floppy green sofa from the early years of his marriage that he hadn't pictured in decades, or the rose-patterned wallpaper of his childhood bedroom. He rehearsed the interiors, bodies, and controls of every car he'd ever owned—the Ford Cortina when they married, the Morris Minor Traveller when the kids were small . . . Having never been a dandy, he surprised himself with his keen recollection of his clothing through the years, from the funny corduroy shorts with the blue braces looping around brass buttons that he'd worn in early primary school to the streamlined pinstripe three-piece with a classic red tie that he'd worn professionally in the 1980s. During another phase he thought about foods, cycling his mother's shepherd's pie and Kay's famous cauliflower cheese on a loop like an automated cafeteria. Yet he'd never cared much about food, and he always circled dolefully back to the bangers and mash of Kay's final birthday. He had exhausted his thoughts on the NHS whilst writing his memoir; besides, it didn't matter a jot what a silent lump in a bed thought about the health service. He could presumably muse about the purpose of the universe, but he wasn't a philosopher, and any contemplation along these lines degenerated into a muddle of rage, resentment, and despair that made Kay's soliloquy on her last night—"It's taken me ages to realize that I still don't understand what this *is*!"—seem like Shakespeare.

Yet he was not quite mind and only mind, like one of those brains suspended in a jar in the mad-scientist labs of 1950s science fiction films. That would be hellish enough, but perhaps preferable to continuing to inhabit a body over which, eyelids excepted, he could exert no control. By contrast, the torture chamber of the body still exerted control over him. Thus a muscle would cramp, yet he couldn't stretch to release it. His lips grew dry, and he couldn't lick them. The temperature in the hospital would drop, and he couldn't pull a coverlet to his chin; the temperature would rise, and he couldn't kick the coverlet aside. He could blink, but couldn't tease sleep from his eye. A stray housefly was a catastrophe; it could crawl his face with impunity. What an unwelcome discovery: how vital it was to be able to readjust one's legs in bed. Even the ability to discreetly pick one's own nose was revealed as the height of luxury.

Technically, Cyril was not altogether deprived of the ability to communicate, but the farce that passed for conversation was wholly dependent on someone else being inhumanly patient with the Esperanto of the eyelid. The nurses were accustomed to asking lacklustre yes or no questions like, "You okay, sweetie?" but the new hires and short-termers often forgot whether it was one or two blinks for "no" even if they bothered to watch. They'd all been informed that he was conscious, but so little power did he possess to impress that awareness upon the staff that in practice most of them talked over him to one another as if he were a dinette set.

Early on, he did toy with the idea of resuming the composition of *Fit for Purpose*, as it would have been theoretically possible to blink out one letter at a time with the assistance of the alphabet board. But the sedulous selection of N . . . (blink) H (blink) . . . S (blink) recalled the hair-tearing tedium of searching for "Panorama" in the iPlayer's on-demand television app: inputting letter by agonizing letter on the onscreen keyboard with the directional buttons of the remote. Besides, a return to his memoir could only have been facilitated by some saint prepared to slowly trace a finger back and forth across three rows of alphabet in order to reap a single W, and who would that be? His children had been brutally clear about just how fascinated they were by the textual culmination of their father's career. The chances that any of them would see the work through to publication were vanishingly slight. The problem wasn't only logistical, either. Resuming the manuscript would have required a force of will that was seeping away. In retrospect, he was incredulous that he'd squandered the twilight of his physical competency on the EU. It was no longer faintly obvious why a large bureaucracy in Brussels had ever mattered to him in the slightest.

The one matter that could wholly absorb him was mental rehearsal of Kay's eightieth. Having dodged a full reckoning with that night ever since, he had probably plunged into his memoirs as a flight from coming to terms with what he had done. What Kay had done? What he had done. So perfectly deprived of distraction, he finally came to recognize that he had been living in a permanent state of searing self-excoriation from the instant the dead weight of her head had sagged against his shoulder. From that moment forward, he'd been hating himself far more ferociously than his children had ever done. However unacknowledged, the verdict had been instantaneous: if he'd not killed his wife outright, he might as well have. He'd not only been missing her, but grievously ruing the fact that he had allowed dogma to take precedence over the love of his life.

No one would ever witness a none-too-subtle reordering of this version of events. Lying supine and motionless, lonely and suffocating, the ventilator tube raw in his throat, Cyril not only forgave himself, but thanked himself. Oh, yes, he missed her, all right. But he had spared her. Now Kay would never lie for an eternity staring up at a water spot the shape of Norway. Tipping those tablets into her waiting palm had constituted his purest act of altruism. For when he envisioned his wife slack in his arms, he no longer felt guilt, but envy.

This epiphany onwards, Cyril's sole purpose became getting his life support withdrawn. Achieving this aim was impeded by the fact that Marshall Evans, the lead doctor on his case, was one of those wet sorts forever trotting out that muddy metaphor, the "slippery slope." A Catholic tritely attached to the "sanctity of human life," the neurologist had already been queasy about taking his patient off the ventilator even back when Cyril appeared to have lapsed into a persistent vegetative state. Once the patient's blinking established that someone was home, his hallowed "human life" became all the more sacred. As a GP, Cyril had encountered plenty of Evans' ilk—the type who lobbied to keep flagrantly unviable infants alive for as long as medically possible, when the babies were doubtless in pain and were going to die anyway. It was the same type who spent tens of thousands of pounds at the vet on a fifteen-year-old arthritic dog. Besides, Cyril detected in his physician an unhealthy professional fascination with a rare waking coma that the doctor had read about but had never before encountered in practice. Evans wouldn't readily relinquish such an interesting specimen. With this chap, even passive assisted suicide was going to be a hard sell.

Consequently, Cyril left no room for ambiguity. As a nurse trailed her finger across the alphabet board and transcribed each letter that elicited a blink, he instructed Dr Evans starkly, P . . . U . . . L . . . L . . . [] . . . T . . . H . . . E . . . [] . . . P . . . L . . . U . . . G . . . [.] Yet all too typically keen to emphasize his status as a former colleague in *our* NHS, he made the mistake of elaborating: M . . . Y . . . [] . . . C . . . A . . . R . . . E . . . [] . . . I . . . S . . . [] . . . C . . . O . . . S . . . T . . . I . . . N . . . G . . . [] . . . A . . . [] . . . F . . . O . . . R . . . T . . . U . . . N . . . E . . . [.] . . . I . . . [] . . . A . . . M . . . [] . . . A . . . [] . . . B . . . E . . . D . . . [] . . . B . . . L . . . O . . . C . . . K . . . E . . . R . . . [.] From this perfectly rational concern, one that any advocate of a sustainable national health care system should regard as paramount, the neurologist concluded that the patient was suffering from the "low self-esteem" indicative of clinical depression. (*Who would NOT be clinically depressed when buried alive?*) Cyril was therefore in no fit state to make life and death decisions on his own behalf.

Consultations with the family were no more availing. If he didn't stand to benefit from an inheritance, Roy wasn't fussed either way. Simon was the most decent of the lot, but as a bean counter for the City, and a bloody Tory to boot, he wasn't a deep thinker; simplistically, he didn't want to assume the ethical responsibility for patricide. Hayley was a sadist who wanted to keep her father in living hell for as long as possible as punishment for her mother's "murder."

Stroke victims with locked-in syndrome did not commonly live longer than about four months. Yet if Cyril qua person had lost the will to live, Cyril qua organism was unusually robust. He lived to ninety-three.

5

The Precautionary Principle

"In the course of an hour, she told me about the same chamber concert at St Mark's three times. She kept asking how 'Cyril' was getting on at Barclays and how 'Cyril' likes his new flat, so I had to infer she meant Simon. Lastly, I found a stack of freshly laundered towels in her oven. That pact of yours, my dear?" Kay raised grimly. She hadn't alluded to her husband's macabre proposal since he'd first mooted the idea in April. "I'm all in."

Thus Kay and Cyril Wilkinson's deal was sealed in October of 1991. Yet, a scant two years later, Kay had a close call with an archetypal White Van Man—who as she advanced into a zebra crossing swerved only at the last minute and crashed into a lamppost, himself much the worse for wear. So near was the miss that it brought home the finality of what her husband planned for them both, should they be so lucky as to make it to the preposterous year of 2020.

"I'm still shaking," she said, staggering to a seat at the kitchen table. "He cut so close he restyled my hair."

"Can I get you something?" Cyril solicited. "A glass of water?"

"I don't want a glass of water! Why are people always offering you a glass of water?"

"Why so irritable?"

"I'm not irritable, I'm traumatized. If I'd stepped off the kerb one nanosecond earlier, I wouldn't be here. When a different future is that vivid—or when a lack of future is that vivid—it splits off into a parallel universe that's nearly as real as this one."

Cyril poured her the too-early dry Amontillado that now, it seemed, ritually accompanied their frank discussions of mortality.

"I'm not sure I can drink that. I feel a bit sick."

He left the glass. If memory served, its contents would evaporate in due course.

"Listen, my dear, I've been thinking," Kay said. "We never talk about it, as if the whole business is done and dusted. But I'd like to revisit your disagreeable plans for my eightieth birthday."

"They're not my plans. They're our plans."

Kay squinted. "Mmm. That's not altogether the way it feels."

"I can't change the fact that it was my idea. I'd hate to think that my proposal is permanently tainted purely for the fact that it was my proposal."

"But of course you're the one who would concoct such a scheme. It's absolutist. It's uncompromising. It's an abstract, arbitrary, and overly tidy attempt to head off an unknowable future that's bound to be messy, complicated, and horribly down to earth. I understand that you don't like uncertainty, but the alternative can't be a certainty that's off the beam."

"I don't apologize for trying to organize our lives with intent, and in concert with our beliefs. We don't want our avoidance of awkward, unpleasant subjects, and a consequent lack of forethought, to accidentally end up costing the health service perhaps millions of pounds, all lavished on misery—"

"Oh, put a sock in it."

"I thought you liked the idea of getting our affairs in order beforehand—"

"That's exactly what I've been thinking about," Kay interrupted, and took a slug of the sherry. "My mother has deteriorated precipitously, and we've had to make all these arrangements on the hoof. Scurrying round trying to find a facility that doesn't reek and where staff don't torture the dementia patients for sport, only to discover that one more care home in Surrey has suddenly closed after we drive all the way down there. It's all so last minute, as if it's a big surprise that she's old, which anyone could have predicted who can count. What you and I need to do is what nobody does: plan for decay. Stop pretending we're going to live forever, and stop indulging the standard conceit that we're frightfully special, so all the wretched things that happen to other old people will never happen to us."

Kay laid out a series of practical measures that entailed some sacrifice, but of a more modest nature than the drastic one that her husband had contrived. Cyril was impressed.

"I've never told you this," Kay added, "but for a while now I've been considering taking retirement two years from now and then qualifying as an interior designer. I really do think the conservatory turned out smashing. I've quite enjoyed doing up this house, and I think I'd be a dab hand at doing up other people's as well."

"Retire at fifty-five!" Cyril said, recoiling. "That borders on freeloading. And in comparison to addressing this country's escalating rates of Type 2 diabetes, selecting curtains seems awfully lightweight."

"Presently, they're more likely to be blinds. But don't get your knickers in a twist. I said I've considered it. In light of this discussion, I think not. A second career would be a risk, with no guarantee of panning out financially. It's probably better for me to put in ten or twelve more years at St Thomas'. Giving interior design a miss makes me sad, but it's sensible. And no, thank you, no more sherry, not until eight o'clock—which is sensible, too. I should get going on dinner. And whilst I'm at it . . ." She scanned the open refrigerator and rose on tiptoe. "We won't be needing this." With a clang, she dropped the black soap-dish box unceremoniously in the bin.

At that time, Kay and Cyril were both still under fifty-five, which made their purchase of long-term care insurance more affordable; most people waited until their sixties, by which point premiums skyrocketed. Nose to the grindstone even longer than she'd promised, Kay continued to work in the endocrinology unit until she was sixty-eight, whereas Cyril stayed on at the clinic in Bermondsey until he turned seventy—the minimum age, he argued to anyone who would listen (i.e., pretty much nobody), until which everyone would need to keep working if the economy in future was not to go belly-up. Putting off drawing down their pensions would increase their payouts when the time came.

They also made substantial contributions to private pensions. After taking a hit when the dot-com bubble burst, they rebalanced in a more conservative direction, which helped protect their portfolios from devastation when the monster Great Recession arrived in 2008. Continuing to rise in value, the house in Lambeth could prove the ultimate nest egg if either lived long enough to receive a birthday card from the Queen.

They took no exotic foreign holidays. Kay had wistfully hoped someday to visit Japan or Australia, but such lavish expenditures were imprudent. Instead they took day trips to Brighton, visited the cathedral in Salisbury, and spent the odd weekend in Scarborough. The holiday destinations of their native land were perfectly pleasant, even if these expeditions didn't sponsor many surprises and it was nearly always cold.

Meanwhile, penny-pinching was the most painful in relation to their parents. The less than luxurious care home they found for Kay's mother didn't smell like pee or anything, but it had the atmosphere of a budget hotel—all plastic chairs and curling fake-wood laminate. Even so, when the money from the sale of the house in Maida Vale was used up, Kay insisted that her brother Percy pitch in his share of the fees. Objecting that his aggrieved ex-wife had secured an outrageous settlement in the divorce and his husband was a skint journeyman actor, Percy was resentful, which turned the siblings' relationship frosty.

Once Cyril's mother died of viral pneumonia, they also made the painful decision to let the jovial live-in Jamaican go. Kalisa might have become one of the family, but Norman could manage mostly on his own, and Cyril's sister Fiona, who lived nearby, could regularly pop in to check on her father. The economics of the decision were cut-and-dried—a full-time salary year after year quickly adds up—but Fiona didn't appreciate having the responsibility dumped on her by merit of proximity, and she was understandably convinced that her father's care fell solely to her because she was the girl. That sibling relationship didn't prosper, either. Worse, although Norman had seemed to manage the loss of his wife with impressive resignation, losing his cheerful Christian companion—who sang whilst she worked, and served up not only a mean plate of plantains but a better than passable sausage lasagne—was more than he could bear. He needed Kalisa more than they realized. Weakened from losing weight, he fell prey to flu and died at eighty-one—which was beginning to seem young.

The Wilkinsons did extensive research on assisted living facilities, which varied enormously in quality, availability, and solvency. At last they settled on a high-end outfit in Suffolk, just outside Aldeburgh—close enough to London to easily visit friends and family so long as they were still able to travel. Journey's End was on the coast, which would allow for leisurely beachcombing during the period they remained ambulatory. Its amenities were flash: a gym, a pool, a games room with two snooker tables, a common area with pneumatic, attractively upholstered sofas and colourful cushions. The dining room for functional residents was kitted out like a restaurant, and its menu, as various as The Ivy in Covent Garden, catered to all manner of dietary requirements. They tried it out for lunch, and Cyril was impressed with the steak and ale pie, whereas Kay found it a good sign that they made their chips fresh from proper potatoes.

Typically for the posh establishments, residents progressed through three tiers. To begin with, if you could dress, wash, and feed yourself, and you were not incontinent or noticeably away with the fairies, you could live in a private flat, to which you were welcome to import your own furniture, wall hangings, and knickknacks. As medical needs escalated, you shifted to a more hands-on situation with greater assistance, and then finally to full-time nursing care. Residents in the last tier were not, Kay noted, trotted out to meet prospective customers. Their tour guide merely opened a door and closed it again, eager to move rapidly on to the in-house cinema.

Talking up Journey's End as if it were a swanky country club, the more independent residents they met tended to be highly educated professionals or successful entrepreneurs, so the social situation seemed promising. Though the fees were eye-watering, there was a waiting list—to which, putting down a substantial deposit, the Wilkinsons added their names.

To Hayley's consternation (their youngest was loath to lose free childminding in London), the couple took Journey's End's advice and shifted to the facility well before being hit by any major health crises at the ages of seventy-one and seventy-two. Early admission allowed them to take advantage of amenities like the rowing machine that might later merely taunt them. Arriving in good nick also allowed them to be admitted at all—for the facility did not accept new residents already wearing nappies or previously diagnosed with dementia. Cyril was grumpy and standoffish at first, but Kay threw herself into the wine tastings, book groups, and lectures by visiting artists and academics. She grew popular. Anyone with energy was at a premium—that is, anyone who could induce the illusion, however briefly, that they were somewhere else.

Five years in, the national referendum on the UK's membership of the European Union generated its own energy, since residents were divided, and arguments in the dining hall grew fierce. Naturally Cyril was vociferous, so much so that he was taken to task by a staff member who chided that deriding his companions as "cretinous dunderheads" and "knuckle-dragging bigots" was unacceptable. Kay focused on helping other residents attain and fill out their postal ballots, whichever way they voted. Never daring to tell Cyril, she flirted with the idea of voting Leave, but inevitably came round to the more level-headed position that keeping matters just as they were was surely the safer course. In that she had imagined the British people as similarly small-c conservative, the referendum result was a shock. Perhaps the calculated caution that had characterized the conduct of their own lives for the last twenty-three years had made risk-taking of any kind inconceivable. Fair play to the narrow majority of the electorate willing to go out on a limb, then, so Kay put her foot down: Cyril was forbidden from making a rashly sizable contribution to the campaign to hold yet another referendum, as if the state could bludgeon the people into delivering the "correct" answer by making them vote over and over until they surrendered from exhaustion. Whatever happened to the UK either way, Kay argued, in due course they weren't even going to be here, and they had to safeguard their resources for extortionate care-home charges that their flimsy insurance didn't begin to cover.

Assisted living wasn't all perfume and roses. To their surprise, they rarely made the trip back to London even in the early years, and after a while they didn't return at all. Something about the enclosed, hermetic atmosphere of Journey's End made the city seem vastly further away than it looked on a map. Moreover, back in the days when they both beavered hither and yon—popping in the supermarket after work, swinging by B&Q to pick up tiles for the eternally unfinished conservatory, giving Hayley a lift to netball practice—a state of constant motion was the norm. When shopping, cooking, cleaning, and laundry were all seen to by oppressively helpful minions, the most minor exertion came to seem like too much trouble. Apparently the less you did, the less you cared to do—an irony that inexorably accelerated until you sat all day, every day, in a chair.

Within the facility, Kay was unsurprisingly the more sociable of the two, which sometimes entailed submitting to a digressive, hour-long explanation of the "just in time" delivery of parts in the automotive industry—for these particular care-home residents were rarely people she'd have chosen to befriend. Living at Journey's End was a cross between jury duty and summer camp, save that the trial would never arrive at a verdict, and it was never time to tearfully exchange phone numbers and hit the back-to-school sales. Worse, given the nature of this cohort, new "fast friends" were often just that: suddenly whisked to the grimmer end of the facility after a coronary and never seen again by the healthier residents, or carried off on a stretcher and never seen again by anybody.

Despite remaining physically active and passing on the dining hall's chocolate cheesecake, both spouses were still subject to the steady medicalization of life that now tyrannized even the old and fit. Along with a growing mountain of tablets to be choked down multiple times per day, ceaseless check-ups, blood tests, urine samples, colonoscopies, hearing tests, eye exams, weigh-ins, stool smears, ECGs, and MRIs were the apparently mandatory price of overstaying your earthly welcome. Whilst professionally they'd seen tens of thousands of patients, in times past they'd both gone for years at a go without seeing a doctor themselves. The only medication either had taken for decades was multivitamins, and even those they ditched when research verified that the supplements were worthless.

By contrast, nowadays Kay's vacillating blood pressure was proving fiendishly difficult to control, and physicians were constantly tweaking her prescriptions, each of which came with a new raft of odious side effects. A steroid injection in her right shoulder provided relief for only a couple of months. She would have to opt for surgery or resign herself to chronic pain—and after Cyril's only partially successful spinal surgery at seventy-four, followed by a full year of exacting recovery, the optimal choice seemed anything but obvious. The arthritis in Kay's toes first kept beach walks short, then ruled them out. From the moment they left their house in Lambeth, Cyril's vigour had palpably waned. Though the referendum had seemed to get his juices running again, once the country left the European Union in early 2020, his former piss and vinegar drained right down the plughole. He blamed his irascibility on his back, but the problem was more global than stenosis.

Strictly speaking, the couple achieved Cyril's prime purpose. They'd planned for the future. Financing their care privately, they were not a drag on the public purse and solely burdened hirelings handsomely compensated for the imposition. No younger workers would have their pay packets taxed to peanuts in order to repair a certain old lady's rotator cuff. The NHS might have been teetering on collapse, but no one could justly have claimed that this precariousness was even fractionally the Wilkinsons' fault.

Kay put a brave face on it, because that was her nature, and she probably resisted the entropy of end-of-life institutionalization better than most. But there was no getting round the fact that they were both irrelevant. They had sidelined themselves, perhaps prematurely.

The grounds were landscaped, the buildings hygienic, the staff com-passionate, but Journey's End still constituted an exile—like one of those open-air prisons for white-collar criminals convicted of insider trading. Whilst they were technically at liberty to leave, freedom was tantamount to incarceration if you never took advantage of it. In-deed, the infectious agoraphobia of the care home's culture induced a kind of locked-in syndrome: with the best of intentions, Kay had buried them alive.

After making a stab at writing his memoirs, Cyril abandoned the project fifty pages in. No one would ever publish the wandering re-flections of a doddering old coot, he said, and Kay never thought she'd see the day when she'd feel nostalgic for her husband's grandios-ity. She sometimes posited that they had prepared for decline too well. They'd given in to the same crazed prudence of arriving at the airport five hours early, where there was nothing to do but suck on sweets that furred your teeth, order coffees that would make you pee, and try on glasses you weren't going to buy at the Sunglass Hut. Perhaps her own game plan for old age and Cyril's more dramatic exit strategy were not so different—except that Cyril would have had them die cleanly at a cliff edge, whereas Kay had them die by degrees down a long messy slope of scree.

It was darling of Hayley, Simon, and the grandkids to occasionally drive up, but there was agonizingly little to talk about, and both par-ties were relieved when these halting visits concluded. As the hysteria over COVID-19 gathered speed, their family seemed a bit too eager to avoid contact with elderly relatives "for their own protection."

Belonging to the cohort at the greatest risk of a lethal response to the disease, their fellow residents were petrified. Before visitors were disallowed altogether, every grandchild or local plumber was soon subject to the full-on folderol of sanitizing gels, face coverings and visors, plastic gloves, and disposable gowns. The facility was frantically cleansed multiple times per day—every railing, countertop, and snooker ball. Nevertheless, the social atmosphere at Journey's End recalled "The Masque of the Red Death," and even long-time confederates regarded one another with wariness. Well before Boris announced his national lockdown, the residents were rooting for one. As far as this affluent, erstwhile prominent contingent was concerned, the whole country could not be shut down too severely or for too many months. Years, if necessary—as long as required to produce and disseminate a vaccine that was a hundred percent safe and effective. For the coronavirus was a plague. Having ravaged the residents' contemporaries in Italy and Spain, it was now gunning for the venerable pillars of the community sheltered outside of Aldeburgh, who regarded this grave international catastrophe as threatening the very survival of the human race.

The pandemic having provided a new talking point, it briefly revived Cyril's inclination to opine. Yet whilst he had spearheaded the majority view during three and a half years of Remainer revanchism, he garnered less support—more precisely, no support—as a coronavirus contrarian. His "sense of proportion" was not well received. As fatalities soared both domestically and abroad, Cyril Wilkinson's poohpoohing was widely deplored as in poor taste.

"All these 'lockdowns' are an overreaction," Cyril announced in the dining hall, whose denizens fell silent and glared. "Every resident here is old enough to remember the Hong Kong flu in 1968, which killed eighty thousand Britons whilst the rest of the country got on with their lives. For that matter, fifty-eight million people died worldwide last year. A few hundred thousand extra is a drop in the bucket."

"If you were one of those drops in a kicked bucket," the former software engineer at the next table snarled, "you might not be so cavalier."

"I'm eighty-one and I've had a full life," Cyril said. "If I pick up a bug that doesn't agree with me, that may be a pity, but it's not tragic."

"You're disrespectful of the victims of this crisis!" the female ex-CEO at the opposite table charged. "I've a sister in Durham who's already at death's door, and if she gets infected that door will swing wide open. You've no regard for human life!"

"I've plenty of regard for human life, Carol," Cyril said calmly. "For example, last year one and a half million people died from TB, as well as over six hundred thousand of malaria, and world leaders didn't close a single newsagent. The developing world lives with lethal endemic disease as a matter of course, and we don't care because it's *Africa* and they're supposed to suffer."

"What a load of posturing rubbish," the software engineer muttered.

Cyril's voluble concern that a recession or even depression resulting from a sustained economic deep freeze could produce even higher casualties than the virus somehow translated into wanting to kill all the old people, despite him being a card-carrying codger himself. By the time the lockdown was declared, his fellow residents were practising "social distancing" of the old-school variety: sniffing pointedly and harrumphing to an opposite corner of the common room when he sat down. The cold shoulder wouldn't likely last—because his antagonists wouldn't last.

Marriages tend to involve a division of labour, and Kay's job as the upbeat one who knew how to savour life in all its piquant detail could become a tyranny. It didn't seem fair that she was obliged to be all very jolly hockey sticks the livelong day; surely getting down in the dumps was a human right. Why, it was a human right even on your birthday. Your eightieth birthday.

Journey's End never left residents to their own devices when such milestones came round. After all, nothing ever happened here aside from a novel diagnosis or another catastrophic fall, and even the appearance of new residents was facilitated by the disappearance of the old ones. Grateful for occasions of a more jovial variety, well-meaning but unimaginative staffers had planned a party for that night, when Kay could expect trite streamers, humourless banners, and bland cake with too much icing. At least there'd be wine. But she was dreading the evening all the same. None of these people cared it was her birthday really, and the only reason Kay cared she couldn't share.

At a private table in the dining hall at lunch that day, she slumped over a wild mushroom fajita that had long ago ceased to excite a sense of discovery. If this was a restaurant, it was always the same restaurant.

"I sometimes wonder if you had the right idea to begin with," she told Cyril glumly. "You know, live it up, spend the money down to the last fiver—and then go out in style, with music, and dancing, and tablets washed down with champagne."

"You're the one who chucked them in the bin," Cyril reminded her. "Why, would you take them now if we still had them?"

"Of course not." She gestured to the comely wooden blinds slatting the room with springtime sun. "This is fine, right? There's nothing wrong with it. You were bang on the money back when my father died. The only way to do it would have been to commit to the date massively in advance, as you proposed, and marshal our resolve massively in advance—"

"As I proposed."

"Because otherwise, it would always seem like a good idea to do *tomorrow*. Why, do *you* wish we'd committed to a firm exit date after all? If I hadn't tossed the Seconal, would you take it now? I mean right now, today, the way we planned to before I bottled it."

"No, but I'm not sure why not."

"The body is in control," Kay said. "The body wants to live, and the *body* will put up with anything. It has no standards. We get bored. Our bodies don't get bored. They don't even feel pain. *We* feel pain, but our bodies will never throw themselves off a bridge because they can't take it. The residents in this care home: I bet a lot of them, as people, don't want to be here any more. But their bodies want to be here. The body is so determined to keep chugging on until the last little valve sticks that it's amazing suicide is even possible. It's amazing that the body will *allow* you to lift an overdose of tablets to your mouth. Or to squeeze a trigger with a gun to your head—you'd think the finger would refuse. That hackneyed old survival instinct—it's bigger than we are, bigger than reason or desire, and it's astonishing that we ever get the better of it."

"Sometimes you still entertain me, birthday girl," he said with a kiss. "Good enough reason to hang about."

At least with medical attention at ready hand, the instant Cyril exhibited symptoms of a stroke the following year, he was rushed to the infirmary and administered tissue plasminogen activator, which substantially limited the brain damage. Full recovery was doubtful, but significant recovery was on offer if he worked diligently with the on-site therapists. Learning to wash his teeth, feed himself, and go to the loo all over again was a considerable demotion after having mastered these biological rudiments as a toddler. Yet glad for a project of any sort, Cyril made an effort.

He slowly learnt to speak again, though this time round his accent reverted to a Brummie brogue, whilst his vernacular returned to the idioms of his childhood. The hard Gs at the end of his gerunds were back. He'd reproach Kay for "clarting about," and now muttered, "I'm off to get my snap," as he shuffled off for lunch. (To begin with, he was barely able to shift his right foot an inch forward at a time with the help of a walking frame, but he was determined not to end up in a wheelchair, and one inch became two.) When frustrated by his progress in learning to hold a fork again, he exclaimed to the therapist in exasperation, "This ain't gettin' the babby a frock and pinny!" Kay was taken aback at first, for he didn't sound at all like her husband of nearly sixty years, but she was charmed in the end; his altered persona proved a welcome change of pace. He had more energy and optimism as a Brummie, and the return to his regional roots brought out his resemblance to his animated late father. Gesturing overhead in the hospital bed of their new Tier Two digs, he exclaimed in hearty surprise, "Well, go to the foot of the stairs!" And sure enough, she concurred, once he pointed it out: the water stain on the ceiling was the shape of Norway.

6

Home Cinema

"That post box is collected on weekday mornings at eleven o'clock," Cyril said. "I don't imagine the police will get my note until tomorrow or the day after at the earliest. Gives us time to head them off, or at least to figure out what to say. 'Sorry, we're scaredy cats'? And then we're on the public record as a danger to ourselves. That won't look good if Roy ever gets a mind to section us in some hellhole against our will and sell the house."

"Yes, it would certainly be Roy," Kay said with a sigh. "But it's still only ten forty-five. Why don't I try to intercept the postman—or *postperson*?"

"Oh, I shouldn't bother. Legally, once a letter is posted it belongs to the recipient. Besides, I just toasted another pair of crumpets."

It was the crumpet more than the legalese that persuaded her to stay put. The last of the packet, the spongy perforated pancakes were still hot enough for the butter to fully melt, and if she left to hang about the post box hers would be hard and cold when she got back. After the trauma of the night before, when they'd both edged to the very brink of the abyss, Kay was inclined to coddle herself. The police were so stretched these days. It was more than likely that a lone blue embossed envelope would get lost in the shuffle.

It's terribly rare that public servants are negligent when you want them to be, although they often oblige when you don't. Two days later, the front door pounded peremptorily, and what would prove the spare key from the Samsons slid into the lock. As Kay hurried to the door, a policeman walked in, and they both jumped.

The mask provided the officer an unaccountable anonymity, and the surgical gloves conveyed distaste. He was a big fellow, and although Kay had remained slender with some discipline, she sometimes experienced her size as a social handicap. The policeman was one of those towering specimens of a younger generation that had evolved effectively into a different species. He made her feel evolutionarily backward, as if in the classic Darwinian developmental sequence from ape to homo sapiens Kay was one of the hairy, hunched-over creatures two or three stages to the left. This bloke was further girded by the hardened stoicism with which one might prepare to confront decomposition. "Ma'am, we had a report of self-harm at this address."

When she identified herself, he seemed put out that she was not collecting flies on the floor. "I'm sorry *awfully*," she said. "I'm afraid this is my husband's idea of a prank. Perhaps a tasteless prank. You see, Sunday was my birthday, and he . . ."

"Ma'am," he said again, looming overhead. "Mind if I look round?" It was not a question. When he barged past her into the sitting room, he seemed to be sniffing the air. Regrettably, Cyril was out, which made it more difficult to demonstrate once and for all that she had not stuffed his body in a trunk.

The officer seemed rather a bully and insisted on poking about all three floors, as Kay cowered behind him blithering. Typically, the presence of law enforcement made her feel guilty, apologetic, and timorous. At once, the intruder gave rise to an indignation that she was obliged to repress, as if clapping her hand over the mouth of a child whose crying might give their location away as they hid from the Gestapo.

Back at the door, he withdrew a crumpled piece of blue stationery, on which Cyril had signed both their names. "Can you please verify that you and Mr Wilkinson originated this 'prank'?"

"Well, yes, but again, I'm so—"

Grandly, the officer withdrew his booklet of stencils and his all-powerful Biro. "I'm afraid I'm going to have to issue you a summons for wasting police time. A lenient magistrate might let you off light with a ninety-pound fine, but your offence is decidedly not small beer. It carries a maximum penalty of six months' imprisonment."

"Is that really necessary?" she asked. "This was merely a misunderstanding that got out of hand." Despite her efforts to stifle it, the indignation was surfacing. British police had clearance rates for theft, fraud, and assault at near zero, whilst some forces had not arrested a single burglar for months. They pushed around elderly taxpayers because frightened, compliant law abiders were easy pickings.

When the high-handed policeman demanded her details and got to the phone number, Kay drew an unprecedented blank. It was fairly commonplace not to recall your own mobile number, which one tended to communicate to others by texting or ringing up, and she'd misplaced her iPhone all morning (perturbing in itself). Of course she didn't know Cyril's; her phone knew Cyril's. Yet now she couldn't even retrieve the landline. When a selection of likely digits eventually danced in her head, she struggled to remember whether the last four numbers were 8406 or 8604. It is strangely difficult to locate your own phone number, and she excused herself upstairs to Cyril's study, rifling water bills and annual TV licences and finally scrounging a hard copy of a tax return from three years ago that included the landline. Aside from changes to the London prefix, they'd had the same phone number since 1972. Rattled, she no longer gave a toss about the silly summons, and when she returned to the foyer the officer, who when she'd suffered her so-called senior moment had seemed to vacillate between pity and contempt, had clearly made up his mind. He went with contempt.

The sure sign that the peculiar lapse bothered her on a profound level was that she did not tell Cyril. As time went on, there were other things she did not tell Cyril. She must have added the salt to her scone dough more than once; when she chucked the inedible batch, which tasted like colonic irrigation powder, she spirited the bag to the outdoor wheelie bin to conceal the fiasco. She'd have written off the botching of the baked goods as the kind of mistake any cook might make on occasion if it weren't for the other mistakes. She put capers instead of currents in her spotted dick and then lied about having been experimenting. After weeding the back garden for over an hour, she returned to the kitchen to discover that she'd left the hot water running in the sink. She heated four tablespoons of sunflower oil in a cast-iron skillet in preparation for making a crispy grated-potato cake and got distracted by a pile of laundered tea towels that needed folding. She was only reminded of the oil because of the smoke, and she was *really* not telling Cyril about that inattention; a minute or two later, the oil could have exploded. As a treat, she picked up a whole duck, but when she put the bird in the oven she left its plastic wrapping on. That slip she couldn't hide from Cyril, because the smell was horrendous, and her attempt to find the oversight comical failed. It wasn't funny.

As Kay had noted herself, people in their twenties also suffered from a sudden, inexplicable inability to recall the name of one of their favourite authors like L.T. Hartman . . . that is, L.*P.* Hartman . . . no, L.P. *Hartley*—and didn't conclude that their brains looked like Chernobyl. So when she got lost on the roundabout at Elephant and Castle on the way to Borough Market and ended up instead on Westminster

Bridge—after having driven this local route thousands of times—she reasoned that all the new development in the area had understandably made an already complex intersection unrecognizable. When she ordered ten bolts of cotton for converting her friend Lacy's library into a bedroom-with-half-bath for yet another live-in immigrant carer—when the window to be curtained was on the small side and one bolt would have more than sufficed—Kay could dismiss the error as the mere addition of an accidental zero. Why, anybody could misplace the odd decimal point.

Yet she went through a solid couple of days during which she couldn't conjure the name of the medical school where she and Cyril had trained. Chatting over the fence, she found herself avoiding the use of their next-door neighbour's Christian name, though they'd lived beside Whatsherface Samson for decades. It was one thing to be a bit hazy on the precise definition of "louche," quite another to pull out a stainless-steel bowl with many little holes in it and not know what it was called. Appalled, Kay placed the bowl-with-holes on the countertop and stared it down; she would not allow herself to proceed with dinner until after twenty minutes she finally produced "colander," a word that had never afforded her such relief. Yet her grasp of the syllables remained perilous, and forever after "colander" had a tentative, barely-within-reach quality. The word was changed. She couldn't trust it.

"Do you realize what you just said?" Cyril noted that autumn. "We need more 'Abyssinian foil.'"

"Not at all," she said. "I said we need more Abyssinian foil."

"You just did it again. It's aluminium foil."

"That's what I *said*." She was getting annoyed. "Abyssinian foil." She didn't care for the look on his face. The expression was something like—horror.

It was when she put two sponges in the toaster that Cyril announced he was taking over the cooking. She was consternated. Simon might have got all very cheffy, but theirs was a more traditional household, and the kitchen was her field day . . . her falafel . . . her fife and drum . . . her *fiefdom*.

"She's not a completely different person," Cyril said. "She just has to be watched very carefully."

"Don't be ridiculous," Hayley said. "My real mother doesn't put sponges in the toaster. For that matter, my real mother doesn't have to be 'watched very carefully.'"

They were doing it again, talking about her in her presence as if she weren't there and couldn't hear them.

"It's understandable that you're angry," Cyril told their daughter, "but it's not fair. You have to distinguish between there being something wrong with someone and her doing something wrong."

"I've had quite enough of your criticism!" Kay said, bustling about the kitchen and putting dishes away, though goodness knows where the utensils belonged; in desperation, she stuck the spatula in the spice rack. "I don't think I should be held to a standard that for anyone else would be unreasonable. We all have our . . . our . . . our moments of doing something strange. Why, just this morning I found the box for that stainless-steel soap dish in the fridge! How sensible is that? Rest assured, *I* didn't stash it there."

There was that look on his face again.

They wouldn't let her drive any more, and it wasn't lost on Kay that nowadays when Cyril was away there was always someone else underfoot: that vaguely familiar-looking woman she'd seen in the garden next-door, or Hayley, or Simon, or whatever his wife was called. Once, she was escorted home by a policeman, who was obviously persecuting her over that summons nonsense; she seemed to recall having sent them a letter, and this pettifogging officer must have been dogging her because the phone number under her address had been incorrect. The next time she decided to strike out on her regular South Bank constitutional, the front door was chained from the outside. From Kay's perspective, she had remained the same and all the people around her had gone insane. Yet some voice outside her whispered that the problem was quite the other way round. When she was petulant, this was the voice that informed her from overhead, "You're being petulant." When she grew exercised that her whole family was conspiring to convince her that she was cuckoo, this was the voice that said, "You're being paranoid."

That voice might have provided an anchor, but it was also a source of torture, for it was when she heard the overmaster direct, "You should know this" or "You used to know this," or press her sternly, "That is not an overweight stranger here to steal your wedding china; that is your daughter," that she was most apt to collapse into tears. Accordingly, little by little the voice shut up, and Kay felt fine. It was possible, of course, that she was sometimes misguided or in error, but heavens, so were most people.

Pleasantly, Kay entered a state of confidence and airy surety. Because everything had achieved a sense of surprise, the physical world was the source of eternal captivation. Picking at a hole in her favourite grey cardigan, she found that the threads could unweave into a fringe that was frightfully pretty, and eventually the hole was big enough to put her whole fist through, and how handy to have designed an extra sleeve. She darted her fingers in and out of the sunlight streaming through the parted crimson drapes in the bedroom, fascinated by how her hands kept going bright and then dark. Tiny maggoty grains on her plate could be arranged along the rim like a necklace, or pinged one at a time with her thumb and forefinger a quite astonishing number of feet, which made her laugh. A smooth soft white pile next to a sausage doubled as make-up, and she slathered the pale foundation over her cheeks, certain that the application would make her eyes appear less baggy—and a girl did need to look after herself. The red sauce in the plastic bottle with the small hole in the top was good for drawing on the table, and sometimes she squeezed it to make a volcano that went everywhere, and that was hilarious.

Then there was the brown stuff whose texture was so various, dense in bits and watery in others, though it wasn't entirely clear where the substance came from. It had a nice strong farmy smell, and could make intricate patterns on her ankles, like henna. She used the same paste to smear her hair from her forehead, streaking the strands back in a dramatic do. Perhaps it would be a nice change of pace to go brunette.

"Mum, for God's sake, that's disgusting!"

"Hayley, calm down. Believe it or not, she doesn't know what it is."

This rather pudgy woman shoved Kay into the shower and hosed her down roughly. She didn't mind the warm water, but the gruff mishandling seemed impolite.

For a time, Kay confided in a handsome middle-aged man, who suffered under the peculiar impression she was his mother. (Tired of correcting this extraordinary mix-up, at length she humoured the fellow—though she couldn't determine whether he was innocently delusional, or a fraudster.) She whispered in his ear conspiratorially that she was keeping a deep and devastating secret, which must at all costs be kept from her husband: *she was a Leaver.* This chap so fiercely convinced that he bore her some relation kept insensibly urging her to stay put.

"I'd urge my kids to come by more often," the middle-aged pretender said, "if she could keep her clothes on. It's not fair on Geoff to expect him to keep a straight face with her tits hanging out."

"It's unusual at her age, but she still has hot flushes," said an older gentleman who'd been making free with the house rather a lot. "So she breaks out in a sweat, and tears her top off."

"Listen, Dad, I'm afraid this is even *more* awkward," the scam-artist-slash-fantasist said. "After this collapse in the City—whatever they're telling you on the news, it's not just a recession this time, 'great' or otherwise—I'm not going to be able to keep subsidizing your mortgage payments. Our portfolios have tanked, and Ellen and I just don't have the dosh. You're going to have to downsize big time, like, to a one-bed flat—and maybe out of London. Sell off this monster, even if the timing could hardly be worse. You'll take a hit."

"Oh, it was good of you to chip in, but I've been expecting this," the old man said. "Maybe a smaller place would make it easier to keep an eye on Kay. Here, I'm always afraid she's going to burn the house down."

"To be honest, I can't for the life of me understand why you spent down your savings to the last penny and refinanced the house to the gills in the first place. Were a few foreign holidays worth it? I finally told Roy that he won't be inheriting two bits, and he's livid."

The older gentleman slumped in a dejected attitude that made Kay feel sorry for him. Whilst he could come across as strident, he still seemed like a very nice man. "Well, son, you're missing a piece of the puzzle. We didn't want to tell you kids in advance, because we didn't want you to try and stop us. And we didn't tell you afterwards, either, because we didn't want to cause you undue anxiety or to incite you to become interferingly protective. But in 2020 it was your mother's and my original intention to, um. Beat a mutual retreat."

"You mean, leave the country?"

"Leave the country and everything else besides."

"Why on earth would you do *that*?"

Kay didn't care for the fact that both these two gentlemen were visitors in her home, and yet they ignored their hostess. She herself was better brought up than that. Also owing to a proper upbringing, she often avoided pointing out that other people did not always make a great deal of sense. Here the strident chap wanted to find a missing piece of a puzzle, in which case they should all be on their hands and knees searching under the sofa. Which is just what she did.

"Well, both Grandpa and Nanna Poskitt met such a discouraging end," the older chap said, moving his legs out of the way as Kay patted the rug under the coffee table. "So your mum was afraid she might have inherited a susceptibility to dementia. On my own account, I also wanted to head off any sudden short-of-fatal stroke or something that might burden you kids with caretaking and burden the NHS with bills. It's not that unusual, Simon. When your mum and I spent that fortnight in Key West, we met a paramedic at a local bar who was vowing to get out of his line of work. What was the problem? The island has become a destination for elderly couples having a final fling— maybe arriving with diagnoses, maybe just falling apart. So emergency medical teams are constantly called to the scenes of messy double sui- cides, and the poor fellow found it all too depressing to bear."

"I can't find it," Kay said, sitting up on the floor.

"Find what, bab?" the nice old man said, though he didn't sound very interested.

"The piece, the piece!" Kay said. "You said you wanted it."

"Well, we all want peace," he said with a sigh, looking at the pre- tend son as if they had a special secret.

"It's like having a dog," muttered the middle-aged one.

"I assure you, it's considerably more difficult than having a dog."

"Mummy won't let me have a dog," Kay said, happy to join in. "But Percy wants one, too."

"Why didn't you and Mum go through with it, then?" the younger one said.

"Our health was roughly holding, and your mother changed her mind. She was still enjoying her life, and sticking to the plan myself would have meant abandoning her. But not long after that, she started to decline."

"Do you really want her into the Quality Street?"

Kay had discovered a tin of shiny packages, all twisted up like tiny presents. There was gold and red and blue. She smoothed the wrappings flat to lay out a tapestry, and then lined up the lumps inside as an audience on the rug.

"Oh, let her play with the sweets. Better the Quality Street than *treacle*," the nice old man said. "That was a right nightmare. She turned the whole house into a giant sticky toffee pudding."

The other one chuckled. "Though she used to make a cracking sticky toffee pudding, remember? That stayed in the bowl."

"I've inevitably wondered whether, that night she got cold feet, she'd have gone ahead with it after all, if she could have seen herself now. What a misery."

"She doesn't seem miserable to me," the fake son said. "*You* seem miserable. She makes *me* feel bloody well miserable. But look at her: *she* seems happy as Larry."

"Is this Larry fellow coming to dinner?" Kay said, meticulously peeling a purple foil from the clear sheet on top. "Should I set an extra place?"

"You said 'if she could see herself,'" the pretender continued. "But that's, like, the whole deal: she *can't* see herself. I may not care for that glazed look in her eyes any more than you do, but otherwise her expression is always either rapt or bemused. So maybe she makes *us* want to top ourselves, but Mum? She seems miles from suicidal."

"*Miles* from sui*ci*dal!" Kay repeated, delighting in the musicality of the phrase.

"Have you ever offered her the option of ending it?" the handsome one asked quietly.

"Oh, yes, more than once," the nice old man said. "But when I bring it up, she can't concentrate. She seems to understand what I'm talking about to start, and then bingo, she doesn't. She's been well beyond a capacity for consent for quite some time now. You can't offer tablets to people who don't know what tablets are or what they do."

Kay went to pains to impress upon these visitors who threaded inexplicably in and out that she had a terribly important appointment with a young woman named Adelaide, who was astonishingly lovely and wore long flowing dresses in sepia tones. Adelaide had been entrusted with Daddy's crucial work papers, which Kay was to deliver to her father before he went to the surgery tomorrow. Mummy was jealous of Adelaide, so Mummy had to be assured that there was nothing between Daddy and this poorly wisp of a girl, who was not long for this world anyway. Meanwhile, the nice old man seemed to have money problems, so they were all going on a trip. Kay loved to go on trips. The nice old man said she would like it where they were going, and Kay had no reason to believe otherwise. Kay liked it everywhere.

Oh, she experienced brief interludes of agitation. She'd quite an altercation with the nice old man, when she put her foot down that she was not leaving the house without her husband Cyril, who had obviously been kidnapped, perhaps even by the old man himself. But in time she accepted the geezer's dubious assurances at face value (whilst resolving at first opportunity to ring the police). When she insisted that Hayley had to have her breakfast immediately or she'd be late for school, the nice old man promised on a stack of Bibles that he would drive their young daughter to the school himself, with a parental note if necessary to explain the girl's tardiness.

Yet for the most part, the whole world of vexation had been miraculously neutralized, as former sources of annoyance converted to sources of merriment or absorption. Sitting for hours in a nearly stationary traffic jam was every bit as entertaining as whooshing along at seventy-five. She was as content to wait at a bus stop indefinitely as she was to get on if the bus arrived. She had defanged the eternal bugbear of "taxes" by neatly forgetting what exactly the word alluded to. On her every side, other people exploded with a host of complaints (she'd long ago stopped worrying about who they were; if they were so rude as to neglect to introduce themselves, that was their problem). They railed against telecom providers whose ignorant customer service personnel were all patchy English speakers in India, lamented the devastation of their pension funds due to some worldwide event to which Kay was under no obligation to attend, and forecasted Armageddon along a variety pack of vectors—*climate change, mass migration, fresh water shortage, food insecurity, unsustainable sovereign debt*—whilst for Kay these were mere sounds that came and went. The one certainty to which she cheerfully clung was that, whatever these whinge-bags were on about, it would eventually go away. Although it pleased her to spend a fair bit of time on the floor, her prevailing sensation was of floating overhead, looking down on all the little people and observing the paltriness of their supposed troubles. She felt very wise.

Kay was sometimes discombobulated, but the confusion passed, and who cared about being a bit at sixes and sevens anyway. Looking out the windows was a delight: so many people and shapes and cars and lights. The skies raced with clouds that formed faces, smiling as they passed by. And the inside of her head bulged with a fabulous grab bag of miscellany, like those big snarled bins in charity shops whose every item cost a quid. Suddenly that poofy green sofa in Rotherhithe would float across her consciousness like another cumulous cloud, and she would remember with a sly secretive grin what she and her husband had got up to on those pillows in the early days of their marriage. A funny little soap-dish box would loom in her mind pulsing with outsize powers, and the fact that for some reason the black box was always cold made it seem all the more excitingly sinister. She paraded before herself a sequence of her favourite frocks through the ages, as if putting on her own private fashion show— including an especially stylish dress with an off-centre, check-shaped collar in which she had waltzed into their first real home. Sometimes she imagined whisking up a roux for her famous cauliflower cheese or cutting lard into flour for a meat pie, and this whimsical style of cookery had the advantage of dirtying no dishes and never getting flour on your sleeves. There was sleep as well, of course, which afforded great sweeping vistas of Australian outback, gnarls of mangroves weaving like live snakes, swaying palm trees of the southernmost point of the continental United States, or the austere Buddhist temples in the mountains of Japan. She must have seen terribly much in her life to have stored such a boundless library of pictures that she could mix and match, though often the landscapes in her dreams were of her own contrivance—plunging with great chasms or rushing with mighty waters that she had never seen, even with all her journeys. Yet the mosaic of waking and the cinema of slumber tended to blend. A memory of the long flag-lined promenade of the Mall in the approach to Buckingham Palace melded indistinguishably with a faintly distorted facsimile of the boulevard in her sleep; the intermingling of confection and recollection didn't trouble her in the slightest. It was all just one vast glorious canvas of colour, texture, horses, and big pompous buildings. This undulating montage was every bit as transfixing as the grandiose epics she and Cyril had seen in Leicester Square: *Lawrence of Arabia* and *Doctor Zhivago*, which she could also project in eidetic sequences on the back of her skull. A young Arab's heartbreaking sink into quicksand until only a hand remained. The gallop of the sled across snow-covered hills with red-cheeked Lara and a soaring soundtrack.

Other times she sang: "Itsy Bitsy Teeny Weeny Yellow Polka Dot Bikini!" or "(Sittin' on) The Dock of the Bay." Some afternoons she serenaded the pelting British weather on the other side of a pane with scraps of poetry she'd memorized at school: *Margaret, are you grieving / Over Goldengrove unleaving?* When oftentimes she couldn't complete the verse, she made up the rest—*It's a flight plan for foreigners / Margaret is a porn star*—then moved blithely on to disconnected phrases that had scored themselves on her mind with uncanny insistence: *Eight out of ten cats prefer it! Every little helps! It does exactly what it says on the tin! The milk chocolate that melts in your mouth, not in your hand!* Or, if inexplicably, *Compare the meerkat dot-com!*

It was a bit concerning that the nice old man could sometimes be so forward. Though it felt nice and safe and close when he held her, she was worried that allowing him to touch her like that was disloyal to Cyril.

7

Fun with Dr Mimi

"Mum! *Where are the tablets?*"

". . . In the fridge. A black box, top shelf, back left."

Having dashed through the kitchen and scuttled up the back stairs, Cyril was crouched at the door of the master bedroom listening to his daughter's screeching below. He was quaking with rage. Imagine, not only had his own wife grassed their plans to the one child certain to make a maximum palaver over the disputable but much-touted *sanctity of human life*, but now Kay had given up the decades-long hiding place of their magic beans without a fight.

"It's *not there*," came accusingly from downstairs.

That's right, he thought, clutching the bottle in his pocket. *It ain't.*

"Then ask Cyril," Kay said. "He's the master of ceremonies."

"You mean Dad is the homicidal maniac, from the sound of it!" Hayley exclaimed. "Another Dr Kevorkian! Or Harold Shipman! He's obviously brainwashed you into going along with one of his blinkered, fanatical socialist fixations! This whole nonsense is so like him I could be sick!"

Cyril felt a great welling up from a place in himself with which he was little acquainted. The force arose unbidden; so involuntary was its eruption that the closest comparison he could contrive was to vomiting, although the sensation was not so unpleasant. This—quantity, this—substance, this—enormous, formless *thing* wasn't outside of him, or alien to him; it *was* him. And this deep very-self was affronted. How dare these *women* stand in his way? Should these weaker-willed creatures be allowed to defeat his plans of some thirty years? Should these soft, maudlin pussycats be allowed to hinder the courageous, honourable climax of an illustrious career? The consternation was blinding. He would show them what he was made of: fire, not their women's water. For they had *no right* to thwart him, *no right* to demand he, too, wither, crumble, and evaporate like every other addled old cretin clinging to the thinnest excuse for being alive, raging in hackneyed, over-cited poetry against the dying of the light. Those two had *no right* to compel Dr Cyril J. Wilkinson to implode into one more gibbering, palsied parody of his formerly formidable person, becoming one more burden on the state, one more burden on family, one more source of resentment, boredom, mockery, pity, and endless eyeroll. With all their sentimental wittering, they had *no right* to insist that he demean himself like all the others, conspire in his own ridicule, and obliterate all he had been and all he had achieved by growing witless, dependent, and enfeebled! He had the tablets and he had the power.

Yet amidst his flaming indignation, Cyril had not altogether lost his capacity to think methodically. In his panic of a few minutes before, he had hesitated in the kitchen, torn between fleeing upstairs and absconding out the back door to conceal himself in the garden. His choice of upstairs had made emotional sense, for he associated their bedroom of nearly half a century with safety, succour, and refuge. But, in practical terms, the unlit garden would have been more strategic. There was the tool shed, or he might have hauled himself over the back wall and into the great big wonderful world in which a freeborn Englishman could do with his own life whatever he pleased.

Yet it was too late for that Plan B. He could hear his "saviours" storming up both staircases. He might secure this door from the inside, but those meddlesome emergency personnel had the booming voices of bruisers. A cheap domestic doorknob lock—it wasn't a bolt—wouldn't keep them out for long. If he took the overdose now, they'd be sure to haul him off to A&E and pump his stomach. As a GP, he was familiar with standard procedure: he'd still feel unwell, he would not be dead, and they'd keep him in hospital under observation. They'd force him to see one of those lame, prying psychiatrists. He'd have to promise never to do it again. No one would believe him.

He was fucked.

Cyril stood as straight as his back allowed. Under the stern eye of the paramedics, he'd no choice but to relinquish the bottle of Seconal into Hayley's outstretched rubber-gloved palm, though he kept his gaze steely, and rather than look to the floor with a suggestion of embarrassment he locked eyes with his daughter. "That is not your property," he said, "and this is none of your business."

"I think it's very much my business," Hayley said primly. Her mask was adjusted so poorly that it wouldn't be doing any good, and that was dubiously assuming that any of those preening badges of purity and conformism ever did any good. "I'm the one who'd have had to clean up the mess if your warped scheme had succeeded."

His daughter was enjoying the whole drama enormously. She'd cast herself as the heroine of this tale, and that was not a role she'd frequent opportunity to fill as a neurotic, under-occupied housewife.

Once they'd all trooped back downstairs, Hayley assured the paramedics covered in protective gear that she had matters in hand. She promised to stay overnight to keep an eye on her disturbed, sadly diminished parents. When one medic provided her with the number of the local Community Mental Health Team, she tucked the slip of paper into her wallet with elaborate care, giving her bag a brisk zip.

After the young men left, Hayley marched to the downstairs loo, head held aloft in a posture of sacrifice and resolve. As Cyril eyed her from the hallway, she located a bin bag under the basin and proceeded to empty out the entire contents of the medicine cabinet. There went the ibuprofen, aspirin, antacids, cold-sore cream, anti-fungal toenail treatments, and constipation tablets with which her gaga parents could no longer be trusted. By the time Hayley finished child-proofing the two loos upstairs, they should have counted themselves lucky to have retained a spare toilet roll—and not because of the nationwide shortage due to hoarding, but because, theoretically, they might have looped the paper multiple times round the shower-curtain rail and used it to hang themselves.

Struck dumb by Kay's treachery, when the spouses went to bed Cyril couldn't bring himself to speak to his wife. Not one word. Once they arose in silence the next morning, it was as well that they'd no fruit or baked goods for breakfast. Their daughter had removed all the knives.

All day, they were effectively under house arrest—even more so than their compatriots, who could at least still go to the supermarket. That evening, Simon and Roy arrived; as the new head of household, Hayley let them in. Typically for a bloke who never got with anyone else's programme, Roy alone was not wearing personal protective equipment. Although Roy was just the type to contract COVID-19 and spitefully cough and sputter his way about town as a "super-spreader," Cyril gave their middle child begrudging credit for resistance to suffocatingly self-righteous social pressure. Once the parents were exiled to the sitting room, Simon went presumptuously upstairs; as the floorboards creaked overhead, Cyril could hear him nosing about the study and unashamedly slamming file drawers containing not a single document that should concern the boy. Thereafter, their children's collusive muttering round the kitchen table was punctuated by unkind-sounding bursts of laughter. The couple's situation recalled those movies in which Nazis invade a local's home, billeting in the bedrooms and making free with the wine cellar, all the while expecting the frightened inhabitants to be nice to them *or else*.

At last, the three siblings filed into the sitting room an ostentatious two metres apart, as *Boris* would have instructed. They rearranged the chairs in a "socially distanced" semi-circle around their misbehaved progenitors on the sofa. The pulled-back seating seemed to indicate less a consideration for the dangers of contagion than a wholesale withdrawal of familial warmth.

"We want you to understand," Hayley began, clasping her gloved hands piously in her lap. "We're all here out of concern, and we only want what's best for you. It's not like we're putting you on trial." Whatever people go out of their way to tell you that they are *not* doing is a reliable indicator of what they *are* doing. "It's obvious you're having emotional problems, like, depression and that. And maybe you're having trouble living on your own. Naturally you value your independence, but we can't elevate independence above *safety*. I'm afraid you'll have to consider this an intervention. You've clearly become a danger to yourselves."

If some children of geriatric parents found generational role reversal uncomfortable, Hayley wasn't one of them. Twisting in his chair, Simon was the one who looked uncomfortable. Cyril was accustomed to seeing his firstborn in nothing but the smart dark suits he wore in the City, but during this lockdown folderol he was trading from home; a shabby flannel shirt and ill-fitting jeans compromised the investment banker's usual air of authority. After all, the eldest ought logically to be presiding, but this was his sister's show. Roy was slumped with his signature smirk, tipping the chair back on its hind legs as if to remove himself from the festivities an extra few inches. He always placed himself outside the family unless he was looking for money. The trendy short beard he'd sported in recent years had sprouted in patches. A bald section on his chin was the shape of Norway.

"It's not as if we set the kitchen on fire because we can no longer tell the difference between vinegar and white spirit," Cyril said levelly, disliking the fact that in his own home with his own children he felt compelled to control his temper—and not to spare their feelings, but to protect his interest. He didn't care for the texture of this encounter one bit. "You interrupted the execution of a plan of many years' standing, made in a state of rationality at an age younger than Simon is now."

"Mum wasn't into it," Hayley said.

"If your mother was having second thoughts, she should have told me, not you," Cyril said.

"Yes," Kay said, looking to her writhing hands. "I should have put my foot down with your father myself and not dragged you into it, dear. I put you in an untenable position, for which I apologize awfully."

"That last-minute text was a cry for help, and I'm glad you sent it," Hayley said.

"The point is what we're going to do now," Simon said, clearly accustomed to meetings in which digressions had to be contained. "The three of us can't keep popping by to make sure you aren't trying to kill yourselves again."

"It's called being put on 'suicide watch' in the nick," Roy said.

"You should know," Hayley said curtly.

"Legally," Simon added, "we're not meant to be popping by at all."

"Indeed," Cyril said. "So however *delighted* we are to see our three lovely children, your well-intended 'intervention' entails the mixing of multiple households. Your best mate Boris, Simon, wouldn't approve a-tall, a-tall. In the nicest way possible, then, I'm going to have to invite you all to go home." This absurd and profoundly un-English lockdown was a time of hair-splitting legalism, line-toeing, tattle-taling, and censorious tsk-tskery. But Cyril wasn't above his own procedural pedantry if it served his purpose.

"To the contrary, I looked it up," Hayley said, pulling a Post-it note from her bag with the satisfaction of out-nitpicking a nitpicker. "One of the four legitimate reasons to leave the house is 'to attend to a medical need or provide care for the vulnerable.' Stopping two vulnerable people with mental health problems from topping themselves certainly qualifies as a 'medical need.'"

"We're *terribly* grateful for your concern," Cyril said. "Still, what your mother and I decide to do or not do is up to us. Thank you kindly for your offer of support, but we're of sound mind, and we don't require your assistance, or even your advice."

"Actually, I've been reluctant to say anything," Hayley said. "But Mum has become, you know, pretty forgetful."

"In what way?" Kay asked in astonishment.

"Just the other day," Hayley said. "You couldn't remember that author—"

"What, L.P. Hartley? That was a perfectly normal tip-of-the-tongue—"

"But it was the author of, you know, what's-it, one of your favourite books—"

"See?" Kay said. "*You* can't remember the title *The Go-Between* yourself—"

"It's not one of *my* favourite books!"

"I live with your mother," Cyril said, "and if she were becoming demented I would have noticed."

"Not if you were demented as well," Roy said. "You'd forget she was demented."

"It's impossible to prove a negative, so we can never conclusively demonstrate that we're not insane," Cyril said through his teeth. "Nonetheless, not only do I remember what year it is and who's prime minister, but I can recite every PM, in order, since 1945. Winston Churchill! Clement Atlee! Winston Churchill—!"

"You already said Winston Churchill," Hayley said with an eyeroll.

"Bloody hell, Dad, even I can remember Winston Churchill," Roy said. "Make it a bit harder on yourself."

"Anthony Eden! Harold McMillan! Alec Douglas-Home!"

"You've made your point, dear," Kay said, patting his knee.

She was right, this recitation was undignified, and Cyril pulled up short.

"I think we should cut to the chase," Simon said heavily. "We've decided it's in everyone's interest, especially yours, that you . . . get help. And we're not presenting that as a choice."

"What does that mean?" Cyril snapped.

Simon wouldn't look his father in the eye. "We're having you sectioned. For your own good."

"*What?*" the spouses said in unison.

"Under Section Three of the Mental Health Act," Hayley said officiously, "you can be detained if you 'pose a threat to yourselves or others,' even against your will. We all think it's the only answer."

"Hey, you haven't heard the best bit!" Roy said. "Then you qualify for this, whatever—"

"Section one-seventeen aftercare services," Hayley filled in.

"It's not means-tested!" Roy said cheerfully. "The state pays all your care-home fees and you get to keep the house! Fucking hell, you get to keep everything! Most of the time Hayley's bat-shit crazy, but this time she's come up with a corker."

"You have no evidence that would stand up in court," Cyril said.

"We have evidence up to the eyeballs," Hayley countered. "Mum's text. Your bottle of poison. Not to mention that lunatic memorial service. Mum's tearjerker farewell, which is longer than your average doctoral thesis. Two separate essays extolling the merits of self-euthanasia."

"And then there's the spending," Simon said with a sigh. "I've gone through your bank records, and your expenditures are almost manic. You'd paid off the original mortgage years ago. Why refinance? What happened to all the money? This degree of fiscal irresponsibility isn't going to look good to an AMHP."

The fact that these kids were already au courant with the abbreviation for the Approved Mental Health Professional who could put them away for eternity was not a good sign. Worse, Cyril remembered with a thud that their buffoon of a prime minister had revised the Mental Health Act earlier this very month to require one physician, not three, to sign off on sectioning. A backhander to a single quack, and your inconvenient parents could be disappeared.

"For one thing, not that it's your business, son," Cyril said, "we spent a great deal on keeping your Nanna Poskitt and Grandpa Norman comfortable and cared for."

"But you also made huge contributions to the People's Vote campaign. Look how constructive that turned out." Simon was a Tory Brexiteer and didn't even have the good sense to be ashamed of himself. It was a miracle that he and his father were still on speaking terms.

"At the risk of the self-evident, we earned our money," Cyril said. "So it's up to us how we spend it. Furthermore"—he was winging it, but starting to panic, and they needed every scrap of ammunition that lay to hand—"locking up a qualified GP during a national health crisis would be criminally wasteful. The NHS has already appealed to retired physicians to return to active duty and help keep the service from being overwhelmed—"

"Dad," Hayley said. "Please. You're eighty-one. Exactly the demographic most endangered by this disease. On the front line, you'd only be a liability. Wanting to put yourself in the way of a killer virus is just one more sign that you need protection from your own destructive impulses."

"But never mind that our money belongs to us," Cyril said, returning to first principles. "Our *lives* belong to us, whether or not we're your mum and dad, and it's up to us how we choose to end them. We may decide, in our wisdom, to stick around until a hundred and ten. Equally, we'd be within our rights to jump off Blackfriars Bridge tomorrow."

"That's not how the law sees it," Simon said, pained.

"And that's not how we see it," Hayley said triumphantly. "We promise to come and visit."

The council van in which they were bundled out of Lambeth had no windows—it was effectively a paddy wagon—which meant that Kay and Cyril had no idea where in the country they were driven to, giving this nominal adventure a Kafkaesque texture from the start. On their arrival at Close of Day Cottages, there wasn't a cottage in sight; the facility looked more like an Amazon warehouse or a Tesco distribution hub. In compliance with one of the many capricious but ironclad rules that would soon govern their lives, they were pushed to the administrator's office clutching their hastily packed bags in wheelchairs, though they were both capable of walking unassisted and carrying their own luggage. The hallway to the office was lined with elderly residents slopped to the side with mouths open, their unseeing gazes so stony that they might have been carved into the architecture like gargoyles. For Close of Day Cottages' newest admissions, a basket of emotions hit all at once: claustrophobia, horror, depression, and hysterical desperation to abscond by whatever means possible. Both spouses registered with a gut punch that being methodically determined to end their lives at a time and on the terms of their choosing and feeling genuinely, frenetically suicidal were chalk and cheese. At a stroke, involuntary institutionalization managed to induce the very urge to seek oblivion that sectioning was meant to cure.

"Well, now, what have we here?" The plump, fifty-ish woman behind the desk crisply stacked papers that didn't appear to need straightening, smiling with her mouth but not her eyes. She sported a bold statement necklace reminiscent of Theresa May. Her tight checked suit was a brand of ugly that only high-end designers can conjure, and she exuded a malicious cheer. "Kate and Cyrus! I'm Close of Day's director, Dr Mimi Mewshaw—though I don't stand on ceremony, and you can call me Dr Mimi."

"*Kay and Cyril* Wilkinson, thank you," Cyril corrected. "And are you a medical doctor?"

"I'm fully accredited, if that's what you're worried about, poopsie."

"I take that as a no," Cyril said. "*I* am a medical doctor."

"Sure you are, treasure," Dr Mimi said smoothly. "We have all kinds of super-important residents at Close of Day. Napoleon, Batman, and Jesus, to name a few. Now, I take it you two are sweethearts?"

"We're not 'sweethearts,'" Kay said. "We've been married for nearly sixty years."

"It's just that we don't have any double suites available at the minute, so I'm afraid you'll have to make do with singles."

"You mean we can't even sleep in the same bed?" Cyril asked, eyes popping.

"No, sweetie, afraid not. And you're one-seventeen council charges, meaning the compensation is quite inadequate—below cost, to be honest—so if a double does become available, we have to prioritize private self-paying guests. Beggars can't be choosers! But at your age, treasure, really. What does it matter? We find our clients sleep more soundly in separate beds anyway. Less chance of getting *agitated*." Dr Mimi turned to her computer screen and clicked away. She had one of those monster terminals that could have been twenty years old, which didn't speak well for the rest of the facilities. "I see here you're classified as in danger of self-harm? That's a special regime, but don't you worry. Safety first! Lance, could you search Kate and Cyrus's bags, please?"

The tall black orderly who'd been lurking by the door took Cyril's bag and splayed it open on a nearby table. The carefully folded button-downs and trousers with their creases lined up all got pitched willy-nilly in a rumpled pile.

"What is this, airport security?" Cyril asked incredulously.

"Medication," Lance announced, holding up one of the only bottles left in Lambeth once Hayley was through protecting her parents from themselves; the laxatives had been tucked away in Cyril's travel toiletry kit.

"That's only over-the-counter senna," Cyril objected. "Surely I can be trusted to manage my own bowels."

"We control all your medication," Dr Mimi said. "If you overdosed on that, think what a mess you'd make for our staff. Speaking of which, Cyrus—"

"I think I'd prefer 'Dr Wilkinson,' if you don't mind."

"Why, funnily enough, I *do* mind," Dr Mimi said, clapping her hands in delight. "All our stakeholders are on a first-name basis, and I'm sure you'll be with us long enough to get used to the friendly atmosphere! But like I was saying, treasure: when was your last poo?"

"I can't see why that's any of your concern," Cyril said coldly.

"I'll put you down for an enema, then," Dr Mimi said sweetly. So when she asked "Katie" the same question, Kay was quick enough to say, "This morning."

"Sharps," Lance said robotically. He'd found the Swiss Army knife, metal nail file, fingernail clippers, and corkscrew that Cyril had checked into airline holds for decades. The razor and razor blades got pitched on the director's desk, too. Yet the confiscations became less logical: felt-tip pens, a blank spiral notebook, his laptop, the iPad from Simon, a copy of the most recent *New Statesman*, and his hardback of Thomas Piketty's *Capital*, which being chained in Dante's nine circles of hell should at last have provided him the leisure to plough all the way through.

"I would like to request the return of my reading material, please," Cyril said, and this sadistically jolly glorified lollipop lady couldn't have appreciated the degree of self-control required to remain civil.

"We find militant political magazines and big, boring books about how terrible the world is, well," Dr Mimi said. "They're a wee bit dark for a self-harmer. The material might also get into the hands of other stakeholders, who could find it upsetting."

"So what are we supposed to read?" Kay asked with alarm, doubtless anxious about her copy of Margaret Atwood's *The Testaments*, which was definitely "dark."

"I'm sure you'll find our community activities so exciting, princess, that you'll be too knackered to read any old books. Katie, my poppet, I see here from your GP that you've been diagnosed with high blood pressure?"

Cyril shot Kay a look of surprise.

"Because that means we have to put you on a no-salt diet."

"I'm sorry," Kay said in a panic; she was very fond of olives and pecorino. "But according to more than one massive study, low-salt diets have significantly worse outcomes for coronary disease and stroke than diets with moderate sodium levels, and a *no*-salt diet would probably kill you."

That smile finally mirrored by a sparkle in her eyes, the director seemed pleased that fatally bland food would be received in the punitive spirit she intended.

"Contraband," Lance said in a monotone, having moved on to Kay's bag.

"Now, that was naughty," Dr Mimi admonished, reaching for the litre of dry Amontillado and placing it on the shelf behind her desk. "And suggestive of a dependency problem."

"No alcohol?" Kay asked meekly.

"Heavens no!" Dr Mimi exclaimed with the same genuine pleasure. "No caffeinated beverages; no smoking or e-cigarettes; no over-stimulating spices; no cream, butter, or full-fat milk; and no sexual relations amongst the stakeholders. We have an eight-thirty p.m. curfew, after which you're to retire to your private suite. Breakfast is at seven, lunch at eleven, dinner at five—and attendance is compulsory. If you're ever tempted to be babyish and turn up your nose at the fine nutrition this establishment provides, we reserve the right to force-feed. The council has placed your wellbeing in our hands, and we take our duty of care ever so seriously. Ordinarily, visiting hour is between one and two p.m. on Saturdays. But just to be extra, super-cali-fragilistic careful during the coronavirus outbreak, we've banned all visitors until further notice. Even if visitation rights resume, you poor dears shouldn't get your hopes up. We find that after a handful of token appearances, friends and family make themselves scarce. We're our own special village here, and outsiders can feel a bit left out. Oh, and lastly: participation in group activities is required. We don't want you turning inward. Socializing is in the interest of your mental health, and we all want to help you get better."

"Those people collapsed in the hallway," Kay said. "They're getting 'better'?"

Feeling compelled to assert himself as a person and not a human drool bucket, Cyril had meantime gone to Settings on his smartphone. "Mrs Mewshaw, could you give me the WiFi password, please?"

Dr Mimi chuckled. "Oh, poopsie, you won't be needing any password! But that does remind me." She held out her hand. "We have to confiscate your phones."

The brutal decontamination was justified, as so many tortures these days, by COVID-19. Perhaps the allusion was OTT, but Kay's associations with being led stark naked into a big cement room for a "shower" had inevitable associations with the Second World War, and the disinfectant with which they hosed her down left her skin reeking nauseously of bleach. The thin gown provided thereafter opened at the back and exposed her buttocks. Although she was assured that, *natch, cupcake*, her clothes would be returned after they'd been washed and pressed, she watched her smart navy frock tossed carelessly atop a snarled laundry cart with a forlorn presentiment that she'd never see it again. As she saw poor Cyril being led away for his humiliating enema, Kay was shown to her room. Down a dismal neon-lit corridor, the shrill perfume of cheap detergent vied with an underlying stench of excrement. "So," she remarked dryly to her minder. "Where's the pool?"

Her "private suite" was grey and confining, with a minimal toilet and basin, a flat mattress that seemed to have absorbed a whole Waitrose luxury assortment's worth of human effluents, and only one ornament on the walls: a digital display that declared, TODAY IS **WEDNESDAY**; THE DATE IS **1 APRIL 2020**; MY NAME IS **KATE WILKINGSIN**; I AM **HAPPY**. April Fool's Day. Too perfect.

The windowless room had neither a TV nor a radio. In all, the amenities were worse than Wandsworth Prison, which was at least awash in illicit mobiles and Class-A drugs piloted into the facility by the drones of organized crime. Surely crooks could have turned an even higher profit smuggling contraband into care homes. Just now, Kay would have paid hundreds of quid for that supermarket Amontillado.

Kay spent her first night tossing in self-recrimination. This debacle was all her fault. If she hadn't sent that text to Hayley, they'd never have ended up in Close of Day Cottages. What had possessed her to go behind Cyril's back and tattle? Why hadn't she simply stood up to him and said, "I'm afraid I can't go through with this"? For that matter, given the alternative of ending up here, why hadn't she simply gone through with it? Was she that much of a wuss?

And there was no discernible end to this incarceration. Of all people, Roy had volunteered to serve as their "nearest relative," whom statute designated as the sole person who could file a legal appeal for their discharge from detention. Per convention, the court had also awarded Roy power of attorney, which gave him carte blanche command of their finances, including their pensions. Why he might ever be motivated to release his parents from this purgatory was not altogether evident. Chillingly, she recalled the lone comment Cyril had passed in the paddy wagon on the way here: "We should never have had children."

Her greatest torment was separation from her husband, to whom she might at least have poured out her remorse. She worried about him, too. Kay herself was hardly enthusiastic about being persecuted, treated like an idiot child, and deprived more indefinitely of her liberty than the average murderer. (And for what? Criminally, they'd contemplated sparing both family and the NHS the price of their protracted decline.) But Cyril put even greater store in dignity than she did, and the man would be crazed. Righteous fury could get him into trouble. That enema was a warning: the slightest resistance would be met with crushing retribution. They made films about this stuff, and in retrospect it was ominous that Cyril had ardently watched *Cool Hand Luke* five times.

To her dismay the next morning, in what staff referred to smirkingly as the "restaurant," seating was assigned, and she and Cyril were separated at distant tables. She only managed to crane her neck and lock eyes with him once. Rather than glint with the steely, biding-his-time subterfuge she expected, his harrowed expression evoked a circuit board struck by lightning; why, she'd not have been surprised to see a wisp of acrid smoke rise from his head. He looked fried.

The glutinous porridge arrived so cold that, overturned, the oats would have stuck to the bowl. Her appetite wasn't improved by a stuporous lady opposite, who was smearing porridge into her mouth with three fingers as if plastering a crack in a wall. When Kay couldn't stomach even sampling the muck, a staff member gave his tablet a disapproving poke as he removed her bowl.

During the morning's desolate solitary, or "quiet time," looking forward to lunch proved a mistake. The undercooked boiled potato and overcooked grey meat were physically inedible, given that the "self-harm" regime allowed her only a blunt plastic spoon. The lime jelly was made with too much gelatine and almost as hard. How many meals could you refuse here before they stuck a tube down your throat like gavage?

Slipping her an indelible Sharpie, a kindly staffer warned as she left the "restaurant" that she'd better clearly label all her clothing or it would be swallowed forever in the bowels of the Close of Day laundry. Thus during the "rest period" after lunch—though from what exertions the residents might need to recover was opaque—Kay wrote "KW 114" on the tags of her tops, trousers, and frocks, as well as on the waistband of her knickers and the rim of each sock. The exercise was tedious; the Sharpie was running dry.

Perhaps she'd soon be grateful for a task of any sort. For Kay had made inquiries: there was no library and no gym. Residents were not allowed outdoors. The sole entertainment was the television in the communal day room, open only afternoons—where she prayed she might at least spend time with Cyril.

The large, dishevelled day room put Kay in mind of the ad hoc shelters organized earlier that year for British flood victims. Its few books were all for children: *We're Going on a Bear Hunt, The Smurf's Apprentice, Mr. Grumpy.* Broken-down sofas were lumpy with dog-smelling coverlets. As she scanned the room in vain for Cyril, the cacophony resembled the competing monologues of a modern-day train carriage, except that none of these people had mobile phones. "Her rose was a climber, right overgrown," one biddy narrated to no one in particular, "and well over the fence. I'd every right to lop it off. But the daft woman rung the council! Took on airs, that Stacy did . . ." Another resident's tuneless rendition of "Yellow Submarine" failed to overcome the TV's blaring rerun of *Come Dine with Me.* Kay finally spotted a staff member whose pocket sagged with the remote.

"Sorry," Kay said. "Might we watch something else? Say, BBC News 24?"

The gaunt young woman had the complexion of someone who actually ate this outfit's food. "Then we'd not find out if the chicken and Parma ham beat the Nigerian pepper soup, now would we, pop-pet?"

"I don't sense our friends here are terribly involved in the pro-gramme."

"Weekdays it's back-to-back *Come Dine with Me,*" the staffer de-clared flatly. "I'm more partial to *Ramsey's Kitchen Nightmares* at the weekend, but that's just me."

"Those are the only two programmes ever allowed on this television?"

"You're a quick study," the woman said deadpan. "This way, there's no fighting. Everybody love cooking shows."

"I don't," Kay said, but abandoned her petition on spotting Cyril, who'd a contusion on his forehead and his wrists zip-tied in front. His large male minders pushed him to a sofa and menaced from a step back.

"What happened?" she asked, kneeling. "How did you hit your head?"

"I lost control." His monotone implied less having regained control as having exhausted his lack of it. "I became violent. I had to be restrained."

"That's not like you."

"It turns out to be very much like me. We've never before been thrown in the Black Hole of Calcutta by our own children. In novel circumstances we find out new things about ourselves. Apparently, in the likes of *Close of Day Cottages*, I become resplendently violent. Why not? What can they do to me that's worse than this? Purgatory is liberating."

"If we've learnt anything in our practice of medicine," Kay whispered, "it's that there may be a limit to how healthy and happy a person can get, but there's *no* limit to suffering. So they can always make our lives worse. ECT?"

"I've already been threatened with solitary confinement." Cyril nodded at the codger still looping repeatedly through "Yellow Submarine." "Which might be a mercy."

"What'd I tell you?" the Keeper of the Remote exclaimed. "Chicken and Parma ham. No way them twee wallies in Somerset was going for Nigerian pepper soup."

"If you're put in solitary, we won't see each other at all, and I couldn't bear that," Kay said. "What are we going to do? It's only been a day. I'd rather be dead."

"You had your chance," Cyril said.

One of the beefeaters who'd dragged Cyril to the day room had been idly reading an *Evening Standard*, which he put down to check his phone. Cyril's bound hands snatched the newspaper to his lap, like a lizard eating a fly. As he struggled to conceal the paper under his gown, a hand clasped his shoulder from behind.

"How's our newbie doing, treasure? A little bird told me my pal Cyrus is having a wee bit of trouble adjusting to his new home." Dr Mimi grabbed the *Evening Standard*, which Cyril held onto until it tore. "Newspapers are contraband. All those terrifying stories about the coronavirus are just the sort of news our stakeholders find distressing."

"I promise not to share what's happening in Italy," Cyril said.

"I'm afraid I came over to break up the party. According to our records, you two may be a bad influence on each other. Goodness gracious me, your AMHP describes you as having formed a 'death cult.' Let's get up and circulate! It's best for our mental health that we make new friends."

Hence the spouses were kept apart again, and only filing out for dinner was Kay able to sidle beside her husband. "What sparkling fare might be on the menu tonight?" she muttered.

"Wild mushroom fajitas," Cyril supposed. "With a side salad of buffalo mozzarella, heirloom tomatoes, a sprig of fresh basil, and a balsamic glaze."

All too predictably, after breakfast the next day they were both handed paper cups of a dozen anonymous tablets. When Kay tried to slide the medication into a lower cheek, the nurse shouted, "Pocketing!" Another staffer held her mouth open as the nurse fished out the tablets and forced her to swallow the lot. The pills made her groggy and vague. It would be easy to fall into the habit of most residents: sleeping fifteen hours a day.

Despite the arduous Sharpie exercise, the first time Kay got her laundry back not a single item was recognizable. In trade for her becoming peach blouse with a cowl neck, the neat cream knit top trimmed with tiny black buttons, and form-fitting emerald trousers from Selfridges, she was bequeathed: a vast floral house dress, black polyester sweatpants with an exhausted waistband, and a loud men's shirt covered in golf clubs. Thereafter, she spotted a squat gentleman in his nineties wearing her cream knit top all twisted out of shape, with three of the tiny black buttons missing. Mindful of her appearance but no fashionista, Kay was surprised how personally obliterating it was to be deprived of your own clothes.

As Cyril had no better luck, before long they were both slobbing about in other people's clashing plaids and stained hoodies. Allowed to see the barber only once a fortnight, her husband could often have fit right in with the Romanian beggars sleeping rough around Marble Arch.

After that first load, Kay knew better than to abdicate to the voracious commercial laundry her birds of paradise kimono from Kyoto or the beloved dressing gown in black and crimson satin that Cyril had found on eBay—in which she would often swaddle herself luxuriously during long lonely evenings as a reminder of her husband. Well, so much for that. Both garments disappeared. She didn't have a key to her room, but plenty of the staff did. Any complaint about having spotted a certain portly nurse flouncing campily down the corridor in her satin dressing gown was bound to be unavailing.

Their first big group activity was an egg hunt on Easter Sunday.

As still more *Ramsey's Kitchen Nightmares* yammered overhead, residents were corralled in the day room for a stimulating exercise of intuition, problem solving, and spatial awareness. The objects of their "hunt," solidly coloured Styrofoam ovoids big as rugby balls, were hidden in plain view. They littered the carpet. They sat on the sofas. Curious, Kay lifted a cushion or two, but even concealing the odd giant egg under a pillow was considered too challenging. Nevertheless, the group was divided into teams, and their fellow inmates scurried round piling bright elliptical desiderata into plastic baskets with an impressive simulacrum of excitement.

"Now, princess," Dr Mimi chided, pointing to Kay's empty basket. "Let's see some team spirit!"

"Blimey," Kay said, staring at the red oval at her feet. "I'm stumped."

At last displaying a trace of subversive gumption, the residents started throwing the footballs at one another and bouncing them off the walls, until Dr Mimi exiled the delinquents to their quarters in disgust.

Weekly "exercise" sessions were equally demanding. Residents gathered in a semi-circle as a visiting gym instructor led them through a series of seated calisthenics: waving your hands urgently in the air, as if your car had broken down on one of those lethal new "smart motorways" with no hard shoulder. Stamping the floor, with its apt suggestion of a tantrum. Circling hands above the lap to execute what the instructor called "the muff." Jutting a leg out and rotating the foot, although this one was only for the "advanced." As a climax, the slow-mo Mr Motivator led them in a virtually stationary hokey cokey, though the turning-yourself-about bit for the wheelchair-bound tended to be fraught.

Cyril participated to the barest degree that would spare him punitive measures (cold showers, wheelchair confinement, sleep in restraints . . .). In the fitness sessions, he'd flap a hand two or three times like the final throes of a dying partridge. During group sing-alongs, he opened and closed his mouth in silence, with no one the wiser that he had once been the lead tenor in his men's choir. When in Arts and Crafts they fashioned landscapes out of corn kernels, kidney beans, red lentils, and mustard seeds, Cyril piled up a succotash that was mostly paste.

For her sanity, Kay took a different route. On May Day, she helped the more impaired to weave a May pole that was competent and attractive. On Father's Day, she assisted several residents with Alzheimer's in constructing cards with heartfelt messages, whilst keeping it to herself that the dads whom the tributes addressed were long dead. If Cyril opted for minimal compliance, Kay's strategy was overkill compliance. Her calisthenics were so wild and pacey that she got winded. She found she enjoyed singing—she'd always been self-conscious about the reediness of her voice in comparison to her husband's—and belted out "Baa-Baa Black Sheep," "If You're Happy and You Know it, Clap Your Hands," and "The Alphabet Song" with gusto. Kay's bean-and-seed landscape was meticulous, with more than a suggestion of Monet.

Socially, Cyril remained aloof, but Kay latched gratefully onto one inmate, Marcus Dimbleby, who was only seventy-seven and had his wits about him. The childless former estate agent had sold his home after being T-boned on the pavement by a mobility scooter, and his injuries made independent living difficult. But the posh care home called Journey's End he'd found outside of Aldeburgh was so expensive that it soon consumed his equity. Thrown on the mercy of the council, he'd been demoted here. She could listen for hours as Marcus detailed the fare at his Aldeburgh Club Med: freshly fried chips, steak and ale pie with button mushrooms, and proper green vegetables.

Kay took a still savvier approach to the underpaid staff, who hated their jobs. True, the worst of the carers took out their frustrations on the residents, but the employees weren't all bad apples, and befriending the young man who'd first slipped her that Sharpie proved a godsend. Leon risked sacking by loaning her his phone, if only for the thirty seconds it took to send Simon a cryptic SOS. The orderly also provided her with sachets of ketchup, mustard, mayonnaise, and vinegar that he pilfered from McDonald's, thus rendering their rations, if not palatable, at least disguised. Most crucially, Leon became her dealer for the cocaine of Close of Day Cottages: salt.

Yet even sodium chloride couldn't maintain their spirits. A single prospect kept the Wilkinsons alive in more than body. *Escape.*

When exactly the COVID care-home quarantine was finally lifted was unclear; the "shielding" regulations could have been relaxed for months by the time they were notified of their first visitor. Cyril was so incandescent over the children's betrayal that only his wife's beseeching persuaded him to meet their son. Even so, after Kay embraced their eldest in the day room, Cyril's mere handshake was stiff and withholding. Simon must have been mortified to see his once-stylish mother drowning in some stranger's shapeless paisley shift and his father's wide-boy shirt blazing with palm trees and parrots. Cyril hadn't had a shave in ten days. They both looked as if they belonged here.

"Can't someone shut up Gordon Ramsey?" Simon implored. Scanning the day room's petting zoo in a panic, he perched on the very edge of a folding chair. He might no longer have feared contamination by the virus, but he didn't want to catch the despair.

"So when are you springing us from this joint?" Cyril charged, skipping any prefatory niceties. "You kids have put your parents in hell—I'd say 'living hell,' but there's nothing living about it. What exactly did we do to you to deserve this? Give you life? Feed you, clothe you, care for you when you were sick, support you through university, and mind your children? Tell me, where did we go wrong?"

"I'm sorry if you're having a rough time," Simon said. "The online reviews of this place are pretty positive. Four and a half stars."

"But who would write those reviews?" Cyril pointed out. "We're not allowed access to the internet. The outside world, we're told, is too 'upsetting.' You're usually cannier than that, son. Because I'll tell you who writes those glowing reviews: the director. Who cuts so many corners that this building must look like a geodesic dome. Your parents are surviving on salad-cream sandwiches."

"Honey, we know this was more your sister's idea than yours," Kay said. For now, Simon was their only lifeline, and a barrage of hostility would not help their cause. "So never mind how we got here. The question is how we get out."

"The problem isn't Hayley," Simon said. "It's Roy. I thought at first it was a good sign that he wanted to take some responsibility for once, and I'm so busy . . . But now that he's legally your 'nearest relative,' it's a bastard to dislodge him from the position. And he's, um. Shifted into the house in Lambeth. I think he likes it there."

"Who gave that boy permission to live in our house?" Cyril asked in indignation.

"He doesn't need permission," Simon said miserably. "With power of attorney, he can do what he likes. He's managed to keep up to date on your mortgage by tapping your pension payments, and last I heard he was planning to refinance *again*. Meanwhile, he's been, ah, 'decluttering.' It seems to be fashionable."

"Decluttering what?" Kay asked. "I didn't decorate that house with any *clutter*!"

"I mean he's selling stuff off. Like those two end tables in the sitting room. He claims they didn't match."

"They're not supposed to match," Kay said, having trouble controlling her own temper, which was rare.

"The point is," Simon said, "there may be some protracted process by which Roy could be removed as your guardian, but I'd have to do some research, and probably hire a lawyer—which given present economic circumstances would be a stretch—and Roy would oppose it tooth and nail. There's no guarantee we'd prevail. So for now, you're going to have to sit tight. I can urge Hayley to visit, and maybe Uncle Percy, though I think I'll hold off on rallying my kids. If you don't mind. See . . . All this babbling and chaos . . . Geoff especially is fragile, and this place would mess with their heads."

Time was short, and during what remained of the hour they pressed their elder son for news of the larger world. One revelation of this Brigadoon was how integrally those big social stories that Kay had been so ambivalent about "returning to the library" on her eightieth interwove with their small personal ones. Having lived through the Second World War, the foundation of the British welfare state, all those assassinations in America, the miners' strikes, the fall of the Berlin Wall, the IRA bombing of Canary Wharf, the near collapse of the international financial system in 2008, their entire country being put under general anaesthesia during the hysteria over COVID-19 . . . Well, the totality of these events was part of who they were, and having observed, commented upon, and sometimes borne the brunt of this series of upheavals was for both spouses a vital aspect of being alive. So Dr Mimi having sealed them in a news vacuum like boil-in-a-bag vegetables induced a more clawing sense of starvation than salad-cream sandwiches ever did.

"I have to say," Simon said as they parted; the nurse who'd pilfered Kay's dressing gown was pointing sternly at her watch. "This place is way more depressing than I expected. I pictured you two, like, playing bingo—"

"Why would we have any interest in *bingo* merely because we're old?" Cyril said.

"No, I mean, maybe meeting with book groups and going to guest lectures and, I don't know, even going to wine tastings—"

Kay guffawed.

"But I won't lie to you. I can't promise I can get you out of here. I was surprised how easy it was to get you sectioned, and I only went along with it because I assumed it would be temporary. You'd get some therapy, come round to the view that you both still have plenty to live for, and then come home. I didn't realize it was only easy in one direction. Once the state sinks its claws into you—not to mention *Roy*—it's a bitch and a half to prise them out."

Simon's purported helplessness was disappointing, for it now looked as if no one would rescue them from the outside. But then, amongst Cyril's favourite films wasn't only the tragically messianic *Cool Hand Luke*, but *The Shawshank Redemption*.

Triumphing over distaste, Kay steadily ingratiated herself with Dr Mimi. Breaking the director down was tricky, because the woman was ensconced in multiple layers of phony sweetness, like a sugar-free jawbreaker. So Kay started with the obvious, admiring the garish designer suits and gaudy jewellery. She remarked in concern, "Are you eating all right? You look like you've lost weight." At Halloween, she feigned enthusiasm for the pumpkin carving contest, and never complained about having to sculpt her own entry with a plastic spoon. She commiserated over how wearing it must have been to lavish so much compassion on a population that rarely even said thank you. She bemoaned the fact that Dr Mimi was still so young and vibrant, and here she was exhausting her youth amongst the aged and infirm. She made collusive comments about a rebellious new admission who refused to participate in group activities but who would soon learn who was boss. After suggesting a print (something slashing and pretentious from Abstract Expressionism) and choice of rug (something shaggy with bits hanging off that feigned to be fabric art), Kay became her advisor on the redecoration of Dr Mimi's office.

The lubrication of obsequiousness soon loosened the administrator's tongue.

"It seems we're to be invaded Sunday week by a band of Smurfs, of all things!" Dr Mimi said, as Kay measured her window for blinds on the cusp of spring. "Some silly Belgian comic book has triggered a rage for fancy dress, and some of these groups have taken pledges for charity. I'm told all they'll do is leap about the corridors flinging sweets. I'd refuse permission, except they'll also make a substantial financial contribution to Close of Day Cottages. I don't mind telling you: I've often to reach into my *own* pocket to make ends meet, and a refund is more than overdue."

"That's frightfully generous of you to put up with such antics for our sake," Kay said. "In your place, heavens, my patience and good will would run clean out."

With the aid of *The Smurf's Apprentice* in the day room, Kay had her template. During Arts and Crafts, she pocketed pots of red and blue poster paint, as well as a packet of black pipe cleaners for the outsize glasses. She nicked cotton wool from a medical trolley; from housekeeping, she filched a yellow mop head. The foreign laundry circulating through their chambers netted two blue shirts, one pair of red men's trousers, and a pair of white leggings. For the hats with distinctive bloops at the tips, she swiped a couple of watch caps from the staff coat cupboard and bound a ball of socks in each crown. She drilled Cyril in advance that if they were caught, they were only *participating in group activities*, like good senior citizens.

The day the Smurfs descended, residents were allowed from their *private suites* to gawp along the corridors. As the costumed troupe exuberated down the hall singing, the youngsters tossed boiled sweets on either side, for which fitter residents happily scrambled. Face and hands painted blue, mouth smeared red, head draped with the yellow mop head and topped with the watch cap and its dangling sock bloop, Kay slipped into the visitors' manic parade wearing the white leggings and blue top. The hardest part at eighty with toe arthritis was to spring along the corridor in a convincing imitation of still being twenty-two. But the "la-la-la!" lyrics were easy enough to master, and she'd been practising her intonation in sing-alongs.

Once Kay threaded out with the rest of the troupe into the sunshine, the challenge was not to cry. But there wasn't time for exhilaration. When she spotted Cyril in his sagging white beard and ill-fitting red pants, it was obvious that their ad hoc getups wouldn't stand up to scrutiny in broad daylight. Besides, the young people piling garrulously into a coach all knew one another. And throwing themselves on the mercy of the revellers would be too risky. These innocents knew nothing of Close of Day Cottages; assuming the old dears had lost their wits, the Good Samaritans would turn them in. Shooting a bitter glance at the institution whose exterior she hadn't laid eyes on since they arrived, Kay grabbed her husband and pulled him behind a skip. The coach drove off.

They had no idea where they were. But by five p.m. they'd be missed at dinner, so time was short. Battling to the other side of a hedge, they struck across a patch of scrubland towards the drone of traffic. They scuttled up a hillock, to discover the very epitome of Western liberty: the motorway. But Kay's heart sank. With no services in sight, it was a smart motorway, whose hard shoulder, once a refuge, was an active lane. That made pulling over for hitchhikers the kiss of death, and that was assuming anyone would stop for an elderly couple painted blue.

"We have to get out of this vicinity double quick!" Cyril said, trying to catch his breath. Seated hokey cokey hadn't improved his stamina. "Or they'll send out the goons and haul us right back! After all, we hardly look inconspicuous."

"And how would you feel about being trapped there again?" Kay shouted over the rush of traffic, looking into his eyes.

"I think you know."

She kissed him deeply, the way they used to kiss for hours when they were courting, and withdrew from his lips at last with the same reluctance she remembered from those days as well, when they had to get back to their medical studies. That kiss sent a tingling shimmer through the entirety of their lives together, as if their marriage were a crash cymbal whose rim she'd just hit deftly with a felt mallet.

When they glanced behind at the scrubland, a posse of Close of Day Cottages staff was advancing fast.

Kay hollered as an articulated lorry boomed past, "Remember *Thelma and Louise*?"

It was awkward, what with Cyril's stenosis, but she kept Cyril from stumbling as she helped her husband over the barrier. Hand in hand, they rushed into the loving arms of the archetypal White Van Man.

8

Even More Fun with Dr Mimi

Shooting a bitter glance at the institution whose exterior she hadn't laid eyes on since they arrived, Kay grabbed her husband and pulled him behind a skip. The coach drove off.

They had no idea where they were. But by five p.m. they'd be missed at dinner, so time was short. As they battled through a thick hedge, Kay's mop-head wig snagged. Cyril's cotton-wool beard also snarled on the thorny bracken. By the time they extricated themselves, the door to the car park had opened. Spring hadn't quite sprung, and the budding hedge provided slight cover. They did escape beyond the property line of Close of Day Cottages, all right—about three feet.

Yet three feet was sufficient to establish that the Wilkinsons had not been impishly *participating in a group activity*. Thereafter, all Kay's sucking up to the director only heightened Dr Mimi's sense of betrayal—and she despised "Cyrus" already, if only because he insisted on calling her "Mrs Mewshaw." Her retribution would test Kay's theory that "there may be a limit to how healthy and happy a person can get, but there's *no* limit to suffering."

They were both consigned to lockdown, brought meals in their rooms. Out of some peculiar aesthetic sadism, the fare they were fed resembled the food one consumed in preparation for a colonoscopy: it was all white. Potatoes, rice, cream crackers, dry chicken breast, blancmange, all without adornment; even the fish fingers had the breading scraped off. They were given access to a shower only once a fortnight, and it was surely thanks to Dr Mimi that they were allowed to run out of loo roll for weeks on end. That summer, during a heat wave, the radiators in their quarters mysteriously warmed and clanked; that winter, the air conditioning kept coming on. If group activities were their own torture, banishment from group activities was even worse. Outside visitors were forbidden.

In protracted isolation, most people go insane. Kay held up longer than most. For months she kept up a routine of pacing, jogging in place, circling her arms, standing on one leg, and doing somewhat enfeebled star jumps. She recited Gerard Manley Hopkins. She sang what verses she could recall of Lonnie Donegan's "I Wanna Go Home," the Drifters' "Save the Last Dance for Me," Brian Hyland's "Itsy Bitsy Teeny Weeny Yellow Polka Dot Bikini," and Otis Redding's "(Sittin' on) The Dock of the Bay." She repeated the theme song of *Come Dine with Me*: "do-do do-do DOO! Do. Do." She even belted out "Baa-Baa Black Sheep," "If You're Happy and You Know it, Clap Your Hands," and "The Alphabet Song" with gusto.

But over time, she began to talk to herself, and the ceaseless monologue soon grew as disjointed and associative as the chronic mutterings in the day room. *Her rose was a climber, right overgrown,* she'd repeat word-for-word, *and well over the fence. I'd every right to lop it off. But the daft woman rang the council! Took on airs, that Stacy did . . .* Or she'd murmur urgently, *Mummy is jealous of Adelaide, so she has to be assured that there's nothing between Daddy and this poorly wisp of a girl, who's not long for this world anyway . . .* Her head swam with a grab bag of miscellany, like those big snarled bins in charity shops whose every item cost a quid. Suddenly that poofy green sofa in Rotherhithe would float across her consciousness like a cumulous cloud, and she would remember with a sly secretive grin what she and her husband had got up to on those pillows in the early days of their marriage. A funny little soap-dish box would loom in her mind pulsing with outsize powers, and the fact that for some reason the black box was always cold made it seem all the more excitingly sinister.

Without the aid of a computer or even his confiscated felt-tip and spiral notebook, Cyril was more successful in clinging to his own sanity by composing his memoirs, either *Fit for Purpose* or *Duty of Care* (he'd all too much time to decide on a title). He committed the text to heart as he wrote it, and ritually began each day by reciting his most recent chapter from the beginning. Reminiscent of *Fahrenheit 451*, in which memorists become walking banned books, the demanding exercise argued for concision. Thus to his own surprise he elided altogether the once-consuming debate over the EU—the better to skip to all the ways in which that bumbling, bovine Boorish Johnson had mishandled COVID-19.

Their solitary confinement was finally lifted three years later. The first time Cyril laid eyes on his wife again, she was slack and cadaverously thin, like a marionette slung on a hook. Her skin had turned the colour of their colonoscopy-prep diet, and she kept mumbling the plot of *Lawrence of Arabia*. When she said politely on their first afternoon in the day room, "You seem like a very nice gentleman," his heart fell.

At last allowed to visit, Simon explained that he, his siblings, Uncle Percy, and their grandchildren had been repeatedly turned away, because the care home's director always asserted sorrowfully but implacably that his parents were "unwell." Their eldest had, he claimed, made a stupendous effort to replace Roy as their nearest relative and so get the section lifted. But considering everything else that was going on in the UK, British functionaries couldn't be bothered about two modest burdens on the social-care system whose problems at least seemed sorted. The judge turned Simon's application down flat, and there was no mechanism for appeal.

Having learnt to trap his daily meds against the back of his throat, thereafter Cyril was able steadily to stockpile a reserve of tablets, which in quantity might grant him and his wife the merciful non-existence that appeared to be their only sure protection from Mimi Mewshaw. Once he'd probably accumulated a sufficiency but planned to store up one more handful just to be on the safe side, staffers did a room search and discovered his stash.

From there on in, rather than resist what was known as chemical cosh, both spouses gladly swallowed the tablets provided and slept most of the day. He and Kay had their chance to escape in March of 2020. The opportunity to call their own shots was not coming back.

9

You're Not Getting Older,
You're Getting Better

When the high-handed policeman demanded her details and got to the phone number, Kay drew an unprecedented blank. It was fairly commonplace not to recall your own mobile number, which one tended to communicate to others by texting or ringing up, and she'd misplaced her iPhone all morning (perturbing in itself). Of course she didn't know Cyril's; her phone knew Cyril's. Yet now she couldn't even retrieve the landline. When a selection of likely digits eventually danced in her head, she struggled to remember whether the last four numbers were 8406 or 8604. It is strangely difficult to locate your own phone number, and she excused herself upstairs to Cyril's study, rifling water bills and annual TV licences and finally scrounging a hard copy of a tax return from three years ago that included the land-line. Aside from changes to the London prefix, they'd had the same phone number since 1972. Rattled, she no longer gave a toss about the silly summons, and when she returned to the foyer the officer, who when she'd suffered her so-called senior moment had seemed to vacillate between pity and contempt, had clearly made up his mind. He went with contempt.

The sure sign that the peculiar lapse bothered her on a profound level was that she did not tell Cyril. Once the coronavirus upheaval finally settled down to some semblance of normalcy, she also did not tell Cyril that after a former colleague from St Thomas' reached out to her, she enrolled in a large double-blind drug trial being funded by the Gates Foundation and the Wellcome Trust. The researchers were specifically looking for subjects with no substantial comorbidities (happily, successfully treated hypertension did not count as substantial) who were over the age of seventy-five.

The likes of blanking out over their landline number did not recur. Not only could she rattle off those familiar digits—ending in 8406, by the way—but she could effortlessly produce her mobile number and, after giving her contacts list an idle glance, Cyril's as well. Why, she was able to rat-a-tat-tat through her every phone number since she was five. Furthermore, she'd no trouble reciting her favourite Gerard Manley Hopkins poem word-perfect. Cleaning the kitchen after dinner, she sometimes sang "(Sittin' on) The Dock of the Bay" or "Save the Last Dance for Me"—sotto voce, because she was always self-conscious about the reediness of her voice—and she correctly recollected the lyrics to the last stanza.

That strange cerebral seizure with the patronizing policeman had obviously been brought on by anxiety over being given a summons for the first time in her life, and perhaps as well by the larger emotional trauma of having come so close to calling it quits in perpetuity three days earlier; heavens, had she not experienced that sudden visitation of feminist agency in the loo (*Take back control!*), perhaps she'd have downed those tablets after all. Or maybe the explanation was more mundane: the temporary blockage of a neural pathway that happens to everybody. She really had to stop leaping to the conclusion that she was going bats just because her benighted parents had set such an unpropitious precedent.

Throughout her fifties and sixties, Kay had coloured her hair, covering the expanding streak of grey down the middle and returning her browning locks to the tawny gleam of her youth. But by her seventies, the discipline of monthly home treatments had grown tedious, and the lighter colour looked less natural. Thus for some years she'd let her hair go salt-and-pepper, a more seemly and not unattractive look for her age, and owing to the depressing follicular thinning of the menopause she always wore it snugly pinned in a French twist.

Yet removing the pins one night before bed, she noticed a surprising glint at her temples. Leaning towards the mirror, she flicked at a host of tiny sprouting hairs, very fine, altogether new, and strangely golden.

Over time, they grew longer and stronger. With no help from L'Oréal, her hair developed a brightening sheen, whilst it also grew softer and, though the transformation could credibly be all in her mind, thicker; regarding even delusional improvements to one's physical appearance at eighty-one, she would take what she could get. So one morning Kay impulsively refrained from binding the rope of her diminished tresses, but allowed the locks to flow free to her shoulders.

"You've not worn your hair down in donkey's years," Cyril commented. "It looks nice. Gentler. More feminine, if we're allowed to use that as a compliment any more. You should wear it down more often."

The new tufts were not only on her head. Those young women who fanatically lasered their nether regions had no appreciation for how bereft one becomes when most of those squiggly hairs down there disappear of their own accord. Kay herself hadn't realized that she rather cherished the coy disguising furze until bit by bit post-fifty it nearly all fell out. Now the undergrowth surged back: kinky, exuberant, and honey blonde.

Not only the hairs felt kinky. It had been a while, more than a while, and with this racy new frizz Kay couldn't resist taking it for a test run.

"You're frisky tonight," Cyril remarked in surprise, once she'd seized his joystick and shoved their bedtime reading up a gear. In the end, the experiment in nostalgia wasn't wholly a success, but no one was keeping score, and over the years they'd developed techniques for crossing the finish line by a variety of resourceful means. By custom, these improvisational encounters would mutually suffice for weeks thereafter. Consequently, on the following night, Cyril was begging to be allowed to sleep.

Although one always notices the arrival of the unpleasant, one often fails to notice the alleviation of the unpleasant. Hence Kay blithely thought about other things until finally realizing that she hadn't needed to tweeze out those ugly coarse dark hairs on her upper lip for months. If she picked up on the brightening at all, she dismissed the radiance of her teeth as a trick of the light, or attributed the sparkle to a reformulated toothpaste—as she also attributed the fading if not disappearance of the unsightly brown mottles on her hands to a rare beauty cream that actually worked. She'd certainly grumbled a fair bit to Cyril about how arduous it had become simply to arise from a seated position, but she went back to popping up effortlessly from her chair without remark. Kay had been consternated when she was diagnosed with hypertension, but when in taking her own blood pressure she discovered that it had dropped much too low, she simply stopped taking the medication, and once she regularly tested at below 120/80 she didn't give the matter a second thought. Months must have gone by before she did a double-take whilst brisking about the back garden: her toes didn't hurt. Her shoulder didn't hurt. After weeding, her knees didn't hurt when she stood. So she reinstated her original Sunday walkabout along the Thames, skipped the restorative coffee, covered the distance more quickly, then added an extra mile.

Whatever curious transformation was underway seemed not only to regard stamina and strength—she could now carry two bags of wood at a time to the log burner—whose increase she casually ascribed to being a bit more demanding of herself, and thus resisting the temptation in old age to reflexively rely on others. If you believed you could open the marmalade jar, it was amazing how by applying a tad extra determination the seal would break. She also evidenced a subtle shift in temperament, which was harder to explain away. A year previous when harvesting their fig tree, she'd never have risen on tiptoe on the ladder's penultimate step and leant so far over the party wall that the ladder began to topple, all for two pieces of ripe fruit— which if she wanted so badly they could always buy. That sort of lousy risk–benefit analysis was for kids, and Kay was old and wise.

She did seem to get more *done* lately. With fervid apologies for having abandoned the job halfway through, she returned to doing up Glenda's ground floor, going decisively with a hint of the Victorian that her best friend was sure to prefer to modern minimalism. Dispatching the makeover took half as much time as she'd expected. In preference to retiring altogether, she solicited still more design work; they needed the money. Finally accepting that she'd always hated the ungainly extra-terrestrial plant with blooms like eyeballs on sticks, she ripped out their deep-rooted fatsia in an afternoon. She reorganized the tool shed so that it no longer took half an hour to locate a screwdriver. Befuddled as to why the straightforward project had ever inspired such procrastination, she attacked her wardrobe and culled the clothes she never wore.

About to bundle the discards into a bin bag for Oxfam, she had a sudden change of heart. The frock atop the pile certainly didn't pass the standard test of having been worn at least once in the previous year. In a canary-yellow dotted Swiss, the dress was a peasant design, with puffed sleeves, a full skirt, a gathered neckline, and a black bodice that laced in a criss-cross pattern down the front. She'd looked quite fetching in the thing back in the day, like a cowherd in the

Alps, but had firmly slid the garment down the rail because there was nothing more embarrassing than women who didn't dress their age, and the styling was simply too girlish. But on a whim, she decided to wear it that evening.

"Bloody hell," Cyril said when she swanned downstairs to start dinner. "Gotta say, bab. It's not that you don't *always* look young for your age. But tonight . . . You look smashing."

She went to glance with satisfaction in the mirror of the downstairs loo. It was surely due to a fluke effect of the waning sun, but those harsh lines from her nostrils to the corners of her mouth did seem to have grown less pronounced; why, from this angle they appeared to have vanished. Likewise smoothed away were the pleats on either side of her philtrum that had made her lips look permanently pursed, previously imparting an unappealing schoolmarm disapproval. When she smiled, for once her face didn't look like a crumpled paper bag.

"I think eating more healthily has a perceptible knock-on effect on one's appearance," she said zestfully, whisking back into the kitchen and going at the courgettes, slicing three at a time. "During the hoarding of the coronavirus outbreak, you remember, we couldn't get green vegetables for love nor money."

"Yes . . ." he said, staring at his wife with unnerving intensity. "There's nothing like the tonic of vitamin C . . ."

"Also," she added, top-and-tailing the onions, "lately I seem to have embraced a more positive attitude. For a while there, I may have been a bit traumatized by our last-minute abortion of 'D-day.' At our age, being on the very cusp of disappearing from the universe, and then pulling back from the brink—well, it gives one psychic whiplash. From which it seems I've officially recovered."

They both seemed to notice it at once. Although Kay's swift, precise slicing of slender, uniform onion wedges was neither here nor there, it was extraordinary, not to mention dangerous, that she was

not wearing her glasses—without which she couldn't tell the difference between a root vegetable and her left hand. Casually, so as not
to be detected, she slid her gaze slyly to the open copy of *The Week* a
foot from the cutting board. She could not only make out the headline but the text, including the tiny italicized authorial identification
in the far bottom corner. It hit her at the same time that she couldn't
even remember the last time she'd worn her hearing aids, yet Cyril's
conversation was clear and crisp, as was the early evening birdsong on
the other side of the closed patio door. As a former registered nurse,
she was well aware that the stiffening of the corneas starting in mid-
life was a one-way process, and presbycusis did not improve.

"And, well, furthermore . . ." she said, faltering, and again unset-
tled by the piercing look in her husband's eyes. "It makes a big difference, to me anyway, not to be living under that sword of Damocles
all the time. In retrospect, I think it took a dreadful toll on me for
years, knowing that I'd committed to this . . . hard-and-fast . . . non-
negotiable . . . you know. So release from all that stress, and darkness,
and foreboding . . . It's made me feel better, and maybe even look
better."

She finally raised her eyes from the board and met her husband's
gaze.

"You could pass for thirty-five," he said accusingly. "I do not say
that to flatter you. I'm saying that as a fact. *What*. Is going on?"

That was when she broke down and told him about the drug trial.

The medication was fast-tracked and available on prescription three
years later. The National Institute for Health and Clinical Excellence
was sceptical at first, for so long as the drug was still under patent,
the price of approving it for NHS purchase was prohibitive. But once

the results across the ageing population were modelled, the regulatory body concluded that the cost of the prophylaxis would be overwhelmingly compensated by the money saved on treating the chronic conditions to which the elderly were prone. Besides, once the cat was out of the media bag, denying the British citizenry access to Retrogeritox would have led to widespread rioting.

According to rumour, which the subsequent longevity of a certain someone bore out, one of the first beneficiaries of the new restorative was the UK's official head of state, who, it was said, began discreetly popping the pills along with her nightly G&T whilst the drug trial, showing such early promise, was still underway. Consequently, the poor, inhumanly patient Charles, Prince of Wales, was unlikely ever to ascend to the throne after all; when the secret finally leaked, the Princess-Consort-in-waiting Camilla Parker-Bowles was livid. The country at large, however, was delighted. With the wildly popular Queen Elizabeth II installed in perpetuity, the monarchy was safe, a thriving British tourism industry guaranteed.

The wholesale transformation of the social landscape was gradual at first. A surprisingly considerable segment of Kay and Cyril's cohort was suspicious of fads, or resistant to taking experimental medication, or stuck irretrievably in their understanding of life, the world, and most of all themselves—they were old and their time was nigh—and it was fascinating how much some people were willing to sacrifice just to keep their version of reality from turning topsy-turvy. But the puristic hold-outs, well, obviously—in relatively short order, they died.

Little by little, the vista along the average high street included fewer and fewer pensioners—or at least pensioners who looked like pensioners. You didn't see many mobility scooters any more, until at length most of them were repurposed as go-carts for children. No one had to impatiently make their way round old ladies with walking frames when rushing for the bus. Meanwhile, care homes closed—including the appalling Close of Day Cottages, subject to a scathing exposé in the *Evening Standard*. Now notorious, the greedy, self-dealing director Mimi Mewshaw had deliberately withheld Retrogeritox from her wards, who had been imprisoned in an information vacuum and had never even heard of the revolutionary cure for ageing until they were freed.

Certain business sectors suffered. Demand for a variety of products and services shrank or evaporated: creams for the amelioration of spots, wrinkles, and eye bags; reading glasses and corrective lenses; hearing aids; in-home caretaking; walk-in bathtubs, shower-stall rails, transfer discs, and electric stair lifts; wheelchairs, canes, and walkers; a panoply of pharmaceuticals that treated the cancers, hypertension, heart disease, and strokes that soon grew exceedingly rare; artificial hips and knees; pacemakers and stents; pension fund management; the writing of wills and the settlement of estates. The confidence artist trade suffered a punishing contraction, with no more addled, credulous oldsters to prey upon. But the modest damage to the economy was more than made up for by the explosion of the working population, whose taxes now largely supported dependents who were under eighteen. Indeed, for the first time in its history, the fiscally insatiable NHS had its budget cut, and even the Labour Party didn't squawk.

Naturally, at first the ground-breaking therapy was largely available in richer countries, which gave horrifying new meaning to the "inequality" that had obsessed progressives for decades: now only the poor would get old. Talk about seriously unfair. But the UK soon devoted its entire aid budget to supplying the drug to Africa and other emerging markets; meanwhile, the patent expired, and the generic was dirt-cheap. Besides, after patients took the standard two-year course, the transformation of cell duplication turned out to be permanent, so the benevolence was a one-off. Best of all, parents who'd both drunk this contemporary Kool-Aid passed immunity to decay to their offspring. A whole new generation was born that would never see visibly elderly humans, save in archival photos and films—which terrified children, who perceived decrepit men and women with big hairy moles, bent backs, craggy faces, and crinkled, papery skin as monsters.

Inevitably, a demographic transformation on such a scale produced its share of doom-mongering naysayers—who in this instance had a point. Humanity continued to reproduce, but almost no one died. Of course, even sceptics were obliged to preface their cynical forecasts with assurances about how wonderful it was to have beaten death itself, now hailed as our species' crowning achievement. Nevertheless, were this situation to carry on, the population of the planet would go through the roof, thereby triggering a cascade of calamity: water and food shortages, horrific urban crowding, property prices unaffordable for all but the rich, and wars over territory and finite resources.

This argument was beginning to gain substantial traction when something happened. It was disagreeable. It was immediate—that is, not precisely overnight, but close enough, and far too rapid for any effectual social policy response or medical palliative to be formulated. In its mercilessness, it was almost kind (though no one said so at the time). The cataclysm's mathematical tidiness and uncanny uniformity of result across the globe suggested design. Like the stopped clock accurate twice a day, for once the conspiracy theorists were probably right.

The coronavirus panic of 2020 was, it transpired, a mere drill. Half the world's population died. Whatever it was that hit them, the half that remained were immune. Thereafter, an anonymous advert ran in all the major papers worldwide on the same day: **I HAVE BOUGHT YOU SOME TIME TO GET WITH THE PROGRAMME. YOU CAN HAVE ETERNAL LIFE, OR YOU CAN HAVE FAMILIES, BUT YOU CANNOT HAVE BOTH.** Together the American FBI and MI6 finally traced the advert to a cantankerous, misanthropic rogue demographer named Calvin Piper, who objected on his arrest that he had saved humanity from itself, "not that it especially deserved saving," and rather than be put on trial, he "should have a building on the Washington Mall named after him." Perversely, the villain who became far more notorious than Stalin or Hitler had refused to take Retrogeritox, for not only was he in his late nineties, but he looked in his late nineties—making history's most fiendish mass murderer appear uniquely and conveniently grotesque.

No one ever said so at dinner parties. Yet behind closed doors, more than one academic concurred that Calvin Piper's wicked pathogen—christened "Pachyderm," for it was derived from a virus that leapt the species barrier from elephants—achieved exactly what it was meant to. World population grew somewhat, until it gradually registered globally that procreation wasn't in the larger social interest if present generations weren't planning to leave the building any time soon, or possibly ever. In every country, pregnancy soon required a licence, only a handful of which were issued per year.

But back to Lambeth.

As the years had advanced since their wedding, Kay had unavoidably watched the dashing, energetic, idealistic young man she fell in love with metamorphose into what others would perceive as a grizzled crank. A once "slender" figure appeared closer to "scrawny." Stenosis crimped the ramrod posture. Soft chestnut locks turned the colour of lead. In their early days together, Cyril's absentmindedly allowing his hair to shag over his ears had been endearing; in later decades the same inattention to grooming made him look unkempt or even crazed. By about seventy, he developed a permanent scowl that, she teased in the twenty-teens, made him look like Jeremy Corbyn.

Scraggled in due course with single long, coarse hairs that didn't belong there, the smooth, firm chest on which she'd first laid her head as a bride inevitably began to droop. Meanwhile, her husband's keen features subtly lost definition, as if a Renaissance statue in Carrara marble had been eroded by acid rain. In accommodating these losses, Kay had been obliged to draw upon a mature sense of perspective, a more profound understanding of what a person is than she'd ever enjoyed when she married, a mournful resignation to the fleeting nature of beauty, a sense of humour, and a bottomless well of tenderness. (All frightfully character-building, though Kay had still been on borrowed time herself, and it had been difficult to see the use of continuing to build a character that would soon get thrown away.)

Witnessing the same transformation in reverse proved ever so much more palatable.

Oh, Cyril was still a fanatic. He was still inflexible. He was still an absolutist, and he still passed unequivocal judgements that could make him seem harsh. But all these curmudgeonly qualities were easier to take in a physically buoyant man whose occasional frowns instantly evanesced, whose posture was pillar-straight, whose pectorals once again resembled Italian marble, and whose lush chestnut hair had resprouted its disarming cowlick. Cyril looked twenty-five. Pretty much everyone looked twenty-five.

For a while, if only because they were still financially underwater after having spent down their assets in preparation for throwing in the mortal towel (what a dreadful mistake that would have been!), Cyril returned to the NHS as a GP. At that time, there were still pregnancies to look after, and people still injured themselves—though tending patients who healed so quickly was a joy. Cancers had always been depressing, and he was glad to see the back of malign cell production altogether. Colds and flus continued to come and go, but this newly resilient population bounced right back. In the old days, GPs were often overwhelmed, allowed only ten minutes per appointment, whilst many patients had complained that it was impossible even to get one. After the Retrogeritox revolution, Cyril went hours at a go with nothing to do.

By contrast, Kay had loads of interior design work, because everyone suddenly had so much energy, and in looking youthful they naturally assumed youth's impatience and appetite for novelty. The escalating demand for aesthetic variation displayed a trace of mania, which meant something, though in the first few years Kay wasn't sure what.

The fact that all the generations of their family now looked the same age had repercussions—neither good nor bad exactly, but interesting. Abstractly, in bygone times most children had made some effort to appreciate that their parents had once been young, but by and large this exercise of the imagination was half-hearted. Children didn't really want to picture their parents as contemporaries, and children didn't really want to think of their parents as regular people. Yet when a parent appeared a peer, no imagination was required. For Hayley in particular, the subjective experience of meeting her parents before she was born seemed uncomfortable, if not faintly obscene. She might have been irked that, of the two, by any objective standard her own mother was now by miles the more attractive. Although loath to compete with her daughter, Kay had merely to enter the same room for Hayley to glower in resentment. There was nothing for it. Kay wasn't about to live eternal life in a sack.

The sudden levelling of the generations exposed a chronic sense of superiority on both parties' parts. In the past, parents had always felt a trace of condescension towards their children, however warmly disguised. They'd already experienced what the kids were going through for the first time, and they knew better. But the condescension worked both ways: always more "modern," an upcoming generation also knew better. Even if they didn't yet enjoy position and wealth, the young had every other advantage: strength, looks, health, a future. It was their role, kindly or brutally, to discard and replace.

This subtle battle of mutual contempt was over. Simon, Roy, and Hayley could hardly write off their parents as yesterday's news when the children and grandchildren were no more "the future" than Kay and Cyril, whose life expectancy was now indefinite. As time went on, too, the family's power dynamic shifted dramatically, which was especially hard on Cyril. Once a father and son were both within a stone's throw of 150, seniority grew meaningless, and this rough parity translated into a dizzying loss of parental clout. The uniformity of the family's visual ages also made them feel more like friends than relatives—which sounds agreeable, save for the fact that kinship is ineluctable, friendship elective. Thus at get-togethers they all found themselves weighing up in the starkest of terms whether, love and the bonds of blood aside, they actually liked one another.

Roy was pissy because the very concept of inheritance had become an anachronism. (To be fair, in his disgruntlement on this point, their middle child was not alone. A host of entitled progeny who'd been waiting to come into trust funds would have to make their own way in life after all, and they weren't all eager to demonstrate their entrepreneurial pluck.) Of the three, Roy was the most inclined to regard everlasting life as a millstone, since living forever meant working forever. Hayley had also made the disheartening discovery that when all your cells replicate perfectly, your fat cells replicate, too. But at least she enjoyed a faster metabolism, and as for slimming? There was all the time in the world.

Therefore it turned out that the Wilkinsons needn't have been in such a rush to visit Australia, Japan, Key West, Las Vegas, and Malta. They sampled Russia, Tunisia, and the Philippines. They did mountain treks outside of Cape Town and took boat tours through the Amazon. They visited the obscure spice island of Pemba—where they were put up by an inhumanly generous expat New Yorker named Shepherd Knacker, whom not only his gorgeous wife Carol but the entire local population seemed to adore. In Thailand, they stayed with a fellow Brit called Barrington Saddler; once the booming bon vivant lurched off to bed, they whiled away the boozy wee smalls with his obliging sidekick Edgar Kellogg, musing together about how their overweight and self-satisfied host could be at once so damnably charming. They browsed for antiques in New England, where they made the acquaintance of a woman who seemed cold and standoffish at first, but Kay warmed to Serenata enormously over the weekend, even if the husband could grow tiresome if allowed to go on about LED streetlights. Kay and Cyril cycled alongside the Rhine and ploughed in a submarine along the Mariana Trench. Though they'd foresworn cruises as hedonistic and vulgar, they finally capitulated purely for the change of pace. Once such adventures became affordable, they spent a week in the International Space Station and went camping on the moon.

The NHS having downsized, Cyril was laid off as a GP, and resisted idleness by writing his memoirs. Unfortunately, infinite leisure to write a manuscript is not in any author's interest. He produced to excess. He revised to excess. He edited to excess, so that after whittling the record down to nearly nothing he was obliged to build the narrative back up all over again. He dithered over every adjective and rearranged every sentence. Sick of hearing about it, Kay insisted he commit to an inevitably imperfect version and submit the book as-is. But Cyril didn't find any takers. The whole subject of health care was of little interest to a population all biologically twenty-five, and with time stretching infinitely to the horizon everyone else was writing memoirs, too.

To her own surprise, Kay grew weary of interior design, and branched into landscaping. Then she qualified as an engineer, and for a while worked in bridge maintenance. As an escape from the responsibility, she tended a shop till, and then she tried acting in an historical television series on its 307th season, which comically entailed wearing elaborate make-up to look like the old woman she had once been in real life. A few years later she segued into municipal government, after which she experimented with what proved the purely theoretical satisfactions of manual labour and learnt to lay bricks. For everyone was swapping places. You could do whatever you'd always wanted to do, and then you could do whatever you'd never wanted to do. Yet it became ever trickier to determine what "wanting" was exactly.

Cyril had a harder time in the occupational realm, because he'd always been one of those people who'd known from an early age exactly what he wanted to dedicate his life to, and he'd never wavered from that purpose. But Britain no longer required many doctors. After the failed writing project, then, Kay encouraged him to expand his concept of healing and return to graduate school to get a degree in clinical psych. It was good advice. In the post-Retrogeritox world, the demand for counselling and treatment for mental disorders was soaring.

The drug didn't precisely eliminate death, as Calvin Piper's nefarious nostrum for his species' demographic ills had amply demonstrated. During what was thereafter referenced as "Calvin's Cull" back in 2042 (when world population had ballooned to an alarming 11.3 billion with no end in sight), the Wilkinson family would have been perceived as unusually lucky—though they didn't feel lucky. Oh, the loss of Simon and his son Geoff would have been devastating in any circumstance. But in a world in which both men could credibly have lived a thousand years, their demise was even harder to take. And now not only loveliness lasted forever. So did grief.

Still, as Calvin's Cull receded in memory and its survivors grew fanatically risk-averse, death became exceedingly rare. Consequently, death also became alien, and far more terrifying. Perhaps suddenly vanishing from the surface of the planet had always seemed strange, but now it seemed wrong, morally wrong; it was an abomination. Denounced as the ultimate violation, dying had lost any sense of inevitability, of nature taking its course. Whilst the bereaved of yore had often suffered depression, now even the loss of a not-especially-close friend could result in utter derangement.

After a long plateau of worldwide mortality, however, the death rate began to tick up—and not due to a freakish vogue for skydiving or rock climbing without ropes. Cyril's patient load increased, until once again his schedule was full to early evening. Universally, the psychic crisis was teleological. Having come within a hair of acting on the same impulse in 2020, Cyril was unusually qualified to offer succour and sympathy. For people came to Dr Wilkinson in droves because they couldn't stop contemplating suicide.

On the face of it, the pathology was baffling. The patients were healthy. They mightn't have all been devastatingly attractive, but the bloom of youth partially redeemed even the unprepossessing. None of them lived with the looming dreads that had haunted their ancestors: of physical dysfunction, aesthetic corruption, senility, irrelevance, loneliness, and the fearsome flop of the final curtain. If they didn't like their jobs, there was plenty of time to train to do something else. If they were unsatisfied with partners or spouses, so were loads of people, and there was plenty of time to find another soul mate as well. In a highly automated workplace, most employees didn't put in more than twenty hours per week, and the hobbies and holidays on offer were multitudinous. Why, Kay herself had learnt Portuguese, mastered caning chairs, and thrown mountains of ceramic flower vases they didn't need. Granted, it did transpire that she had no talent for ballet, was rubbish at tennis, and made an appalling jazz drummer, but there was always the tango, field hockey, and the pan flute. Whatever was these party poopers' problem?

"Well, that's it," Kay announced, colouring a dented rectangle with a magenta marker. "With Oman, it's a complete set."

She stepped back so they could both admire the artwork tacked to the wall: a variegated map of the world, every single country now coloured in. The Middle East had been low down their to-do list, since Kay retained a faint prejudice against places that had once compelled women to shuffle around in bin liners.

"Does that mean there's nowhere left to go?" Cyril asked, failing to disguise a hint of hopefulness.

"We could always start the exercise all over again and go to every country in the world twice."

"I'm afraid I may not enjoy travel quite as much as you do, bab."

"You have only said that three million times," Kay snapped. All right, that was a hyperbole. But given the longevity of their marriage, the notion of having heard the same sentiment word-for-word "millions" of times wasn't as great an exaggeration as all that.

"Roughly the number of times you've taken my head off for saying it," Cyril said. "What you dislike is not my repetitive conversation, but the truth of the sentiment. I've made a yeomanlike effort to overcome a general preference for staying home—"

"You have *infinite* opportunity to stay home!"

"I do not want to visit every country in the world twice," he said flatly. He might have looked twenty-five, but deep down inside that strapping youngster was a grumpy old man trying to get out.

"But since we've been there, all those places could have changed!"

"They most certainly will have changed," Cyril said with a know-it-all haughtiness that got on his wife's nerves more than ever. "They'll have grown more the same. With everyone trying on new countries like outfits, there's no difference between anywhere and anywhere else aside from the landscape. Everyone speaks English. Even here, forget regional dialects. There's no longer such a thing as a discernible British accent—much to the dismay of American tourists. So I don't see the point. We can find all manner of exotic foods, and all manner of people who at one time might have seemed exotic, in Lambeth."

Kay bombed to the sofa and glowered. Face it: she was irritable not because she disagreed with him, but because she felt the same way. Kay being the adventurous, curious one was a distinction between them to which she was attached. But the role had worn out. Oman had been boring, and she'd been glad to see the back of it. The trip had constituted the silly closing obligation of an arbitrary project, which had long before ceased to be an expression of genuine geographical appetite. Cyril was right about the creeping sameness, too, though the homogeneity was more overarching than a melding of global cultures, which had all blended into a giant mulligatawny soup. What was the difference between Kay and Cyril, or between Kay and anybody?

Which recalled the sage advice of her instructor in a metalsmithing class she took yonks ago. The woman said that in art your limitations are also your strengths. What you're not good at, what you can't think of, even the mistakes you make all contribute to your personal style. To have no such constraints is to be shapeless, she said, and to have no voice. This dictum helped explain Kay's growing identity crisis. She had been good at too many things: design, engineering, municipal government, all that. She had visited too many places and become "best friends" with too many people. As a result, the molecules of her disposition were spread so thin that her character was no longer solid matter but more like a formless gas.

Kay glanced dully around the sitting room. After about this interval she'd usually be getting ideas for another renovation. Although by all appearances this was still the same house, every joint, lintel, sill, door, and panel of plasterboard had been replaced multiple times. But now even her chronic dissatisfaction had exhausted itself.

As a perpetually peaceable coexistence would have been soporific, she and her husband tried to generate a few conflicts as a discipline, so maybe a trace of testiness this afternoon was all to the good. She wished she could return to the original exhilaration of watching her beloved age in reverse—but exhilaration by its nature is not an emotion one can sustain, and surety that her husband's face would always look that creaseless and his long legs would always remain that shapely made these attributes seem less dear.

They'd talked about getting divorced—and not in a state of raging hair-tear, but matter-of-factly, even frivolously. Like Oman, getting divorced was prospectively just one more thing to do. It was a matter of plain biological fact, much discussed because anything at all that there was to discuss had been much discussed: human beings were by nature serially monogamous at best. More marriages had gone the distance in the olden days because life was so savagely brief. Had Kay and Cyril married in 1841, when records began in England and Wales, actuarially Cyril would have died before forty, Kay by forty-two. (They'd looked it up. They'd looked everything up.) Thus their wedded bliss would have needed to last just sixteen years, and that was assuming Kay didn't die in childbirth. This was what, untampered with, the animal kingdom had in mind. But now? They didn't know a single other couple on a first marriage. It was not uncommon for people to have wed a hundred times—although "till death do us part" had been quietly dropped.

The Wilkinsons' secret, if you could call it that, wasn't being so supremely well suited or forging a love that was so fiery and true.

Rather, they'd both come to the same pragmatic conclusion. All around them people were romantically mixing and matching, as if running through a set of mathematical possibilities that might seem countless but that, with a finite population, a computer could calculate quite precisely. Theoretically, then, in this game of musical chairs, Kay and Cyril could both marry everyone else on the planet and eventually come back to each other, running out of options and having to repeat the sequence much the way they had just run out of map. Moreover, the freshly formed couples they encountered consistently seemed to recreate pretty much the same relationship as the last one, and the one before that. Why, look at Roy, who reliably found some woman, or man, or something in-between, depending on his mood, off of whom he could mooch and whose generosity he could abuse. So why bother with the change-up?

And it wasn't as if the Wilkinsons hadn't experimented. Oh, with newly nubile bodies, the sex had been ace at first, and neither wished to stray. But—surprise!—the sense of rediscovery didn't last. (That did seem to be the overall lesson: human beings now lasted forever, but nothing else did.) They agreed, tentatively at first, to explore an open marriage—which proved occasionally titillating, but most of the time gross. They tried three-ways, but someone always felt left out, and no one ever seemed to know what to stick where. With mutual permission, they both dabbled on the other side, though after Kay's awkward affair with Glenda the friends avoided each other for months.

They also went through a phase of changing sex, for transgenderism had become recreational. Kay quite liked having a penis, though Cyril admitted that he missed his, and he found breasts more exciting on someone else. Meantime, other people were getting tits *and* penises, or vaginas and phalluses side by side so you could poke one in the other and have intercourse with yourself; or they'd get three

breasts, or two penises, or an extra anus, but it all stopped being interesting (pornography was dead; rather than watch a lithe young Thai
ass-fucked by a donkey, most men preferred to do the crossword),
and, in the end, the Wilkinsons swapped back to their original equipment. For only one thing did not get tired: sleeping in each other's
arms. If there really was a secret to their marriage, that was it.

Kay roused herself from the sofa with the arduousness with which
she'd stood up at eighty, although the struggle was motivational. "So
what do you want for dinner?"

"I don't care," Cyril said.

"What have we agreed?" Kay said, swinging round and pointing
an accusatory forefinger. "*No apathy.*"

"Sorry," Cyril said, as he always did. "I could die for your wild
mushroom fajitas! And how about a side salad of buffalo mozzarella,
heirloom tomatoes, a sprig of fresh basil, and that fabulous balsamic
glaze?" The fervour was fake, but even theatrical enthusiasm beat all
too sincere ennui.

"Crikey," Kay said, filtering to the loo. "I do miss weeing standing up."

The one fad the Wilkinsons had resisted as pointless, possibly tasteless, and at length banal was switching race. After all the historical
agony over skin colour, perhaps it was passingly notable that virtually no one amongst what were once called "minorities" or "black
and brown people" or "people of colour" and finally "seeable people"
exhibited the slightest desire to become white. Repigmentation and
plastic surgery were all in the other direction, to the especial consternation of Jamaican Britons and black Americans, who could no
longer distinguish their "real" brothers and sisters from fraudulent

undercover crackers masquerading as hip and taking full advantage of their wholesale permission to use "the N-word" in all its six-letter glory. Black communities objected that they were being "infiltrated," "robbed," and "mocked." Yet bills to forbid the practice as the ultimate "cultural appropriation" were struck down by the courts, because lawyers defending the bans were unable to cite what legal principle the new conversion therapy was violating. Although the fashion eventually burnt itself out, the one positive result of no longer being able to distinguish between bona fide black people and the secretly naff incognito kind is that no one gave a toss any more what colour you were, until the very word "racism" came to refer innocently to an enthusiasm for driving cars around a track very fast—as in, "Yeah, Lloyd just bought another Ferrari, because he's really into racism." Besides, towards the end of the infatuation with skin treatments, the most popular hue was Smurf Blue.

War, too, was defunct. Sacrificing droves of citizens gifted with eternal life was unthinkable; famously, during the final attempted conflict, between Canada and Lapland, conscripts with too much to lose had refused en masse to fight. Criminal violence had also dried up. Murder seemed only more grievous when victims were robbed of godlike immortality, and "life imprisonment" might entail banishment to a small room for thousands of years.

Nevertheless, what with the odd accident, not to mention the perplexing raft of suicides whose rising incidence became the subject of numerous hand-wringing long-form essays, a smattering of replenishment human beings were still allowed to gestate. Kay and Cyril were fortunate in having already borne a family, but without lucking out in the Population Replacement Lottery, harder to win than the old kind with buckets of cash, their great-grandchildren were unlikely to become mothers and fathers. Being so scarce, children were universally spoilt, and immoderate doting didn't have an improving effect on the adults they became. Proud parents often kept their small people indoors, because word that a proper child had been spotted on such-and-such a street spread like wildfire, and in no time queues of rubberneckers would form, taking photographs and begging to pat the urchin's soft little head. Whereas in times past many parents had felt a touch of melancholy when offspring seemed to grow up too quickly, modern parents met the moment when their specimen of an endangered species turned twenty-five with full-tilt desolation: from then on physically ossified, their erstwhile status symbol looked abruptly like everyone else.

That said, young people who were authentically young—who not only looked twenty-five, but who'd truly been alive for only twenty-five years or so—were much sought after. Their artlessness, ignorance, transparent pretension to sophistication, unconvincing simulation of world-weariness, fierce certainty about what was wrong with society and how to rectify it, and genuine hunger for the experiences that their chronological betters had sampled up to the eyeballs? Well, the whole authentically fresh-faced package was intoxicating. They fell in love! Wretchedly and unrequitedly, and they thought they were going to die! They converted to Islam! They had crises of faith, and unconverted from Islam! But it took disappointingly few years for that faux world-weariness to morph into the real thing.

Every funeral was as costly, elaborate, and crowded as the ceremonies that once mourned a head of state. The public gloried in marking an event that was so rivetingly irrevocable. Indeed, the public had acquired an appetite for death, the sole remaining taboo; what replaced pornography was illicit videos of gory expiration by a raft of creative means.

Film, television, theatre, and fiction crafted before the Retrogeritox watershed—aka "pre-Retro retro"—were also unfailingly popular. For the narrative arts had gone flat. The quality of "edginess" was consigned to a bygone era. As stories cleansed of ageing and mortality didn't appear to function, all contemporary plotlines came across as inconsequential. Even grand star-crossed romance no longer scanned. What was the big deal? If a relationship doesn't work out, get over it and find someone else. Whenever modern directors attempted to recreate the epic tragedy, the most emotion that could be summoned from an audience was, "Well, that's too bad." Thus Kay never wearied of David Lean, and Cyril had now seen *Cool Hand Luke* several hundred times.

A birth here, a death there, but for the most part the human population of planet Earth was fixed. In the absence of an asteroid to take them all out of their misery, the people alive now would be the same people alive thousands of years hence. Perhaps that should have presented this uniquely privileged generation the opportunity to become wiser, better educated, more well-rounded, more compassionate, more insightful, more hilarious, and more spiritually advanced than their predecessors. Yet as for the cultivation of these many desirable qualities, most regular people soon approached a hard limit, whilst the truly distinguished members of this perma-cohort—the few artists who showed early promise of creating truly moving contemporary work against the odds, the scientific geniuses, the visionary philosophers, the great leaders—were the most likely to blow their brains out. The evidence was in. The betterment of only one human attribute was demonstrably boundless: the capacity to be dull as dog dirt.

"So, what do you think?" Kay proposed over still another wild mushroom fajita; it was tough to decide between eating the perfectly crisp, superbly gooey wafer and throwing it at the wall. "Should we kill ourselves?"

Naturally, they had conducted this conversation before, but their favourite topic was rationed. Technically today was Kay's birthday, though she'd lost track of which one. After so many, they didn't bother to celebrate birthdays any more, and licence for this parcelled exchange was the closest Kay would come to a present.

"Tell me," Cyril said, as he was meant to. "Why would we do that?"

"Well, what are we trying to achieve here? I'd hoped awfully that after hanging about all this time the nature of the project would become clearer. It hasn't done. I still can't get my head round what it means to be alive. I don't know what this place is, I don't know whether it's even real, much less whatever it is we're supposed to do here, and if I've wasted my time I still can't tell you what I should have done instead—though the whole idea of 'wasting time' seems to have gone by the wayside now that there's so bloody much of it. I've no more idea what matters than I did when I was five. I keep having this feeling that there's something I'm supposed to come to grips with, and there's not much chance of my grasping the nettle in the next hundred years if I failed to grasp it during the last hundred—which must have been full of nettles."

"Yes, you've said roughly the same thing more than once."

"*What* have we agreed?"

"No apathy."

"No, I mean what else?"

Cyril thought a moment. "That we won't give each other a hard time for saying the same thing over and over."

"Thank you. Go to the head of the class."

"Perhaps we should make another rule that even your birthday doesn't give you leave to be so snippy."

"Fair enough," she said sullenly. Kay was supposedly the one who knew how to enjoy life. Kay was the one who appreciated its many lulling rituals like cleaning the kitchen—AGAIN—in all their sumptuous mundanity.

"Why are you so impatient?"

"I don't know," she admitted. "There's no excuse, is there? We should both have nothing but patience. But: speaking of patients. Why do all these people you counsel claim to want to top themselves?"

"It varies a bit, but it's not as idiosyncratic as you'd expect. Their malaise is rarely triggered by a dire turn of events or a relationship gone rancid. My patients are lost. They can't enjoy anything. Sensory satisfaction doesn't work: sex, food, drink; even the effects of hallucinogens become predictable. They can't keep partners or spouses and they don't even care, though they still get lonely. They feel trapped— and at the same time they know they're experiencing more freedom than any human being in history, which just makes them feel worse."

"You know, this eternity we're stuck in almost replicates locked-in syndrome," Kay said. "The way you become inured to sensory input like taste, which is close to having no input. Remember when I stopped drinking red wine? I shocked myself, but I'd simply had enough red wine. And this passivity . . . I think unbridled freedom and passivity amount to the same thing. Being able to do anything is like being able to do nothing. We keep coming up with another career, or another hobby, or another friend who we convince ourselves is going to be different from all the other friends we tired of—but it's all a running in place. Nothing changes. As if the whole species is laid out on a hospital bed staring up at a stain on the ceiling the shape of Norway. Spiritually at least, we're paralysed. We're physically able to speak, but we can't say anything new, so what's the difference? Our only real activity is helpless mental churn. Because this whole ellipsis of ours feels like a dream. Some days, a bad dream. I'm one of the oldest people the world has ever seen, and I sometimes feel as if I'm not here at all, or as if I've never been here. It's getting . . . strangely horrible."

"I like that: locked-in syndrome. You've never said that before. Am I allowed to say that? That you've *never* said something?"

"Yes, my dear," she said, squeezing his hand. It was important to remember that they still loved each other, or more impressively still liked each other, even if frequently fractious exchanges could make it hard to tell. After all this time, they should more often commemorate the fact that they could bear to be in the same room together.

"These patients of yours, who are tormented by suicidal ideation," she added. "What do you tell them?"

"More improv! You've never asked me that."

"Haven't I? Why, that's appalling."

"I tell them that human beings have fought to locate a sense of purpose from the year dot—even back when most people dropped dead by forty. I say that, beyond mere physical survival, finding purpose is your job. And that job is never done, because you'll no sooner find an answer than you'll have to revisit that answer, which won't suffice on examination, and you'll have to find another one. The advice is a bit circular, but the hypnotic nature of anything that goes round and round has a calming effect. I'm really closer to a priest now than to a doctor."

"You didn't used to talk like this," Kay said. "It was all life expectancies and NHS budgets and bed-blocking."

"Well, that was one of *my* answers that didn't last."

So they'd made one more character swap. She used to be the reflective, musing, philosophical one, whereas Cyril was all brutal brass tacks. That impatience of hers, for example—a cut-to-the-chase what's-the-point—it used to belong to her husband. Apparently they weren't all just trading genders or careers, but trying on being completely different people.

"With some of my cleverer patients," Cyril added, "I suggest trying to get *beyond* purpose—because goal-directed behaviour is time-bound, and a consequence of mortality, as well as having been metaphorically borrowed from biology: the need to eat and sleep and mate to endure. But the universe simply is. It needn't justify itself, and by analogy we needn't justify our presence in it, either."

"Do you believe that?"

"I can't say I've mastered the art of purposelessness myself."

"You know, you've grown much more humble," Kay said.

"I feel more humble. It's surprisingly pleasant."

"But whatever happened to all your crying out for social justice?" she puzzled.

"After Calvin Piper's idea of a practical joke"—it had grown commonplace to elide the gravity of the tragedy by being flippant—"everyone may not be wealthy, but they are prosperous, and I'll not lose any sleep over whether they can all afford to dune buggy on Mars. Also, I came to worry that I championed social justice largely to think well of myself . . . Oh, right!" Cyril remembered. "The other thing I tell my patients is that, despite the impression they've been given that we're all immortal, it isn't so. At any moment, they could cross the street at an inopportune juncture and get flattened by an archetypal White Van Man. Believe it or not, that's the reminder that seems to cheer them up."

"You did have that one patient who died at her own hand. That was so hard on you."

"The inaptly named Jess Hope," Cyril recalled sadly. "Who jumped off Blackfriars Bridge chained to six kettle bells—not exactly a 'cry for help.' But most of these 'worried well' will never resort to anything so drastic. They'll just keep coming back to me, self-consciously complaining that they've nothing to complain about. Remember when you talked me out of taking the Seconal on your eightieth? You quite elegantly parsed the costs and benefits: much was potentially to be gained by living, and nothing to be gained by dying. You said the only good reason to commit suicide was to bring an end to suffering. But my patients aren't suffering—or not precisely."

"Maybe not suffering is a kind of suffering," Kay posited.

"You've never said that before either."

"This is almost like a real conversation!"

As she leant back to savour the rare spontaneity, Kay's gaze snagged on the framed photo on the bookshelf behind Cyril, from their golden wedding anniversary in that self-impressed restaurant. It was the one token image of themselves in real old age that they kept in open view, as it was a touchstone of sorts. Since she finished her last dose of Retrogeritox, Kay's face hadn't changed per se, but a chronically hard look in her eyes hadn't been there in 2013. The cold glare was the one expression her body could give to the tumultuous package of exasperation, fury, and despair that consumed her daily, but for which she had no earthly excuse.

"Do you ever look at that picture?" Kay asked, pointing.

"Often," Cyril said, not needing to turn around. "It presents something of a conundrum."

"I know what you mean. I look awful. I suppose you look awful as well, but not to me. My own face in that shot—I'm repelled by it, but it also makes me wistful. As if I've lost something, but what? What's valuable about looking like a dried fig?"

"I'm not only wistful," Cyril admitted. "I'm jealous."

"Isn't that odd."

"I'm jealous of our old *urgency*."

"Yes," Kay said gratefully. "That's it on the nose."

"So, thanks to my prescribing privileges, we still have a facsimile of Seconal in the fridge. I refreshed it recently. It's your birthday. What say you?"

"Oh, I don't know," she said, stretching and shooting a resigned glance at the dirty kitchen. "We could always do it next year."

10

Of Ignorance and Bliss

Typically for the posh establishments, residents of Journey's End progressed through three tiers. To begin with, if you could dress, wash, and feed yourself, and you were not incontinent or noticeably away with the fairies, you could live in a private flat, to which you were welcome to import your own furniture, wall hangings, and knick-knacks. As medical needs escalated, you shifted to a more hands-on situation with greater assistance, and then finally to full-time nursing care. Residents in the last tier were not, Kay noted, trotted out to meet prospective customers. Their tour guide merely opened a door and closed it again, eager to move rapidly on to the in-house cinema.

Talking up Journey's End as if it were a swanky country club, the more independent residents Kay and Cyril met tended to be highly educated professionals or successful entrepreneurs, so the social situation seemed promising. Though the fees were eye-watering, there was a waiting list—to which, were they to put down a substantial deposit, the Wilkinsons were free to add their names.

"I'm afraid I'm having second thoughts," Kay confessed at the kitchen table in Lambeth on return from the visit to Aldeburgh. "I mean, I've little doubt that Journey's End is the best we're likely to do. The facilities are fabulous, it's clean, and the staff seem personable. But I still found it depressing."

"Well, there's no getting round what it is," Cyril said.

"Exactly. I realize now that what bothered me about my mother's care home wasn't the cheap architecture and the bad food. However you disguise it, these establishments are warehouses for the pre-dead. With bars on the windows or chintz curtains, the residents are still battery hens being farmed for fees."

"I thought you were the one advocating that we be pragmatic, and face the future squarely, rather than lying to ourselves like everyone else."

"I still think there's merit to planning ahead and preparing for exigencies. We should probably keep that long-term care insurance just in case, even if the premiums are getting larcenous. But maybe there's such a thing as being too far-sighted, and skipping to the rubbish bit of our lives before we have to. We're not old yet, by most people's lights. Maybe we shouldn't push the programme."

"That administrator at Journey's End was very clear on the dangers of putting the move off for too long and deteriorating to the point that we won't be admitted," Cyril reminded her. "She said, 'Beware the five-minutes-to-twelve syndrome,' remember? It's the same mistake everyone seems to make, because they don't realize that five minutes to twelve is basically twelve."

"Maybe waiting so long that we miss out on a five-star funeral parlour is a risk worth taking. I'd rather have more good life, in which we control who our friends are and what we have for dinner, even if that means at the tail end we land in some geriatric madhouse doing the hokey cokey in wheelchairs."

"There is a whole movement that advocates 'ageing in place.'"

"I'm all for it," Kay said emphatically. "I like it here. I've put loads of work into this house. The conservatory is exquisite. I'm thrilled with the trailing orchid wallpaper in the sitting room. I want us to keep our garden. I want to pour myself a second glass of red wine without having some officious matron whisk it away because it isn't good for me."

"There's still the danger that *I* whisk it away," Cyril said.

"Just try."

In the end, they never put down that stonking deposit for Journey's End. Giving the ritzy safe haven a miss was a gamble, but, as Kay observed, every decision we make in this life is a gamble, isn't it?

That said, the couple did continue to organize their affairs with an eye to the future, keeping wills up to date, ensuring that the DNR directives in the event of mental vegetation were easy for the family to find, restricting their spending primarily to necessities, and investing their assets with caution. With no little sense of fiscal seasickness, they'd already survived the choppy waters of the dot-com crash and the market hysterics after 9/11. The Great Recession of 2008 proved especially worrying, because at sixty-eight Kay was just starting to draw down her private pension, which had nearly halved in value, whilst London property prices took a hit, making their six-bedroom backstop less of a consolation. But they'd no intention of selling their house and rode out the slump. The markets better than recovered, and even the financial apocalypse forecast by the Confederation of British Industries and the Bank of England in the event of a win for Leave in 2016 failed conspicuously to materialize.

Yet no investment strategy no matter how conservative could ever have countered the veritably worldwide economic shutdown during the coronavirus pandemic. Once the UK finally lifted the last of the restrictions on commerce and freedom of association, the much-hoped-for "V-shaped" recovery resembled a letter closer to the beginning of the alphabet: a backwards J. A host of businesses had been obliterated. The welfare rolls were groaning; unemployment was sky-high. It proved a great deal easier to shut down an economy than to rev it up again.

Like most other governments, Her Majesty's injected so much cash into benefits, interest-free loans, debt forgiveness, tax deferments, and infrastructure projects that early on in the give-away free-for-all the public lost track of the difference between "billion" and "trillion." All very well, save that the funds for these frenetic expenditures were borrowed. When in turn central banks across the world gobbled up sovereign debt and overloaded their balance sheets with government bonds through quantitative easing—QE7, QE8, etcetera, though governors stopped bothering to number the buying binges after QE12—the money was effectively conjured from thin air. Kay didn't understand this alchemy one bit, and often got angry with her husband for being such a bore about it. "Well, in a way all money is made up, is it not? I mean, money is an idea, a conceit. And I know you've explained it to me repeatedly, but I still haven't a clue what it means to 'monetize the debt.'"

"They don't want you to understand it," Cyril said miserably.

It was difficult to discern whether Cyril had grown habitually glum due to advancing age or to the gloom that had freighted the whole country ever since the likes of Trafalgar and Leicester Squares grew hushed and deserted as the moon—a gloom that had never entirely lifted, even throughout the cathartic exuberance over being allowed once and for all to *actually leave your own home.*

"You're not usually such a conspiracy theorist," Kay said.

"It's not a conspiracy," Cyril said, and he looked as if he could barely keep his head up. "It's worse than that. It's incompetence. Malfeasance on an incomprehensible scale, and all over the world at the same time."

"Please tell me you're not listening to that Shriver woman. She's a hysteric. And so annoyingly smug, as if she *wants* civilization to collapse, just so she can be proved right. I can't bear the sound of her voice." There was indeed an annoying American import—another one of those Yankee anglophiles who wouldn't go back where she came from—who kept claiming on Radio 4 that some book of hers had predicted the whole debacle now supposedly well underway. A handful of deluded groupies regarded the hyperventilating loon as a modern-day Nostradamus. But apparently the lady's stupid novel, *The Madrigal* or something, which Kay had zero interest in reading, made *no mention* of any pandemic, and the self-promotional author was obviously just trying to flog more copies with her irresponsible alarmism.

Throughout the 2020s, governments spent money like there was no tomorrow, but with all this pump-pump-pumping something didn't quite *work*. Collectively, these unrelenting rescue packages, tax holidays, universal-income experiments, and industry bailouts recalled the commonplace experience of inflating a bicycle tyre whose tube, unbeknownst to you, has a small hole in it. So you can depress the handle of the floor pump over and over, but the tyre never quite gets resiliently firm, and the moment you give the project a rest because surely that's sufficient, the tyre starts gradually to go soft again. Under pressure, too, small holes become larger holes, until eventually you frantically push and pull and push and pull, and the tyre sits flat on the pavement.

Kay didn't understand quantitative easing, but she did understand when the cost of Marmite—even more beloved as national metaphor than as spread on toast—doubled, then tripled. Although their NHS pensions were inflation-adjusted, official inflation rates from the Office of National Statistics grievously lagged reality on the street, and in due course the once-generous direct deposits barely covered the food bill. Then they didn't cover the food bill. Without abetting their income with private pensions, they'd be going hungry. But the markets, long anaemic, were sliding to worse than anaemic, and the Wilkinsons' pension pots were shrinking, too. To make matters worse, the elimination of cash had facilitated negative interest rates, meant to force "hoarders"—formerly known as "savers," who could no longer irately empty a bank account and flounce off with stacks of notes in a sack—to spend their selfish stash and so juice the economy. A hundred quid on the first of the month by the last became ninety-nine.

In the end, it was all a waste. The saving, the balancing of their portfolios, the penny-pinching and buying toothpaste on offer—all that painstaking preparation for an independent old age, the better to burden neither family nor the state. The couple had done everything right. They hadn't blown their assets prematurely on extravagant holidays or—as the tabloids had claimed the gaga elderly would all splash out on when foolishly allowed access to their own retirement funds—Lamborghinis. They'd bought their house at a provident time and paid off the mortgage. They'd both worked well past the point at which they might have comfortably retired. Besides their hard-earned pensions, neither had drawn on the public purse; to the contrary, they'd paid sizable tax bills without complaint. They'd put aside as much as possible for the rainy day presently gathering into a monsoon, yet increasingly their monthly income could barely purchase a tin of Baxters butternut squash soup and a packet of builder's tea. Even that long-term care insurance: the company went bust, so all those hefty premiums had bought them no more security than anyone else enjoyed—meaning none. Kay and Cyril Wilkinson discovered for themselves that there was only one thing worse than being very, very old: being very, very old and broke.

Frail but all there, both Kay and Cyril were proving remarkably long-lived. If, as news presenters compulsively observed, extended life expectancy was a stroke of great good fortune for everyone, enduring into their late nineties made the couple luckier than most. But were they lucky? As matters unfolded, this question was not as easy to answer as all that.

When Cyril turned one hundred years old on the twenty-second of January 2039, no one from the royal family sent a birthday card. That might have been because Buckingham Palace, along with all the other royal residences like Windsor Castle, was by then occupied by "asylum seekers" from a wide range of nationalities. For history, alas, does not instruct problems to politely wait their turn, even in a country with a reputation for revering the queue. Thus, on top of a Western-wide financial implosion that made the Great Depression seem like a pet death, the tide of tourists-for-life now rolling up from the global south made Europe's "migration crisis" of 2015 seem like a school field trip. Accurate numbers were impossible to come by, and anyone who claimed to know even roughly how many migrants had stormed the continent by foot, lorry, plane, and boat clearly had a political agenda. Leftists claimed that only a few million had breached the continent's borders, whilst much-demonized nativists were equally certain that the total well exceeded a billion souls. Just as they'd thrown up their hands when trying to keep track of "billions" versus "trillions" in government spending, most of the public settled on "a lot."

Many Britons who could afford to be charitable donated clothing, disposable nappies, bags of penne, and jars of pesto to support the incomers. The most considerable hostility to the influx was amongst first- and second-generation immigrants, sometimes from the very countries this more recent wave had fled. Having made it across the English Channel in time, Pakistanis, Afghans, Hindus, and Nigerians all demanded that the UK pull up the drawbridge. Yet the "drawbridge" in this instance was a useless figure of speech, and unless Britain was willing to come to the unacceptable conclusion that the unending flotilla of boats from France and Belgium was a military matter—in Turkey, troops had been ordered to shoot migrants on sight—policy decisions were nugatory. Besides, British bureaucracy was one of the last casualties of the onslaught, so that for the first few years every incomer was duly registered for a pittance of a weekly stipend, provided housing until there wasn't any, assigned a taxpayer-financed lawyer, strictly instructed not to work, and allowed to appeal denied asylum claims up to seven times. Any threat of deportation was empty bluster. Rather than remove the asylum seekers, it would have been cheaper and more logistically feasible to evacuate the English.

Meanwhile, the NHS, whose budget had so ballooned that the standing joke about Britain having become "a health service with a country attached" was no longer funny, was so inundated that doctors reminisced nostalgically about the coronavirus pandemic, when they'd naively had no idea what the word "overwhelmed" really meant.

"Being hospitable is the least we can do," Cyril maintained early in the surge, then predicted to soon subside. "Climate change is largely the West's fault. We're reaping what we sowed, so we'll simply have to move over and make room."

"Sorry," Kay said. "Europe, North America, and Australia have reduced fossil fuel emissions to practically nothing. Pounding one more nail in our economic coffin, we've bent over backwards to reach carbon neutrality by 2050—another one of those distant years that was never supposed to actually arrive, and now it's right round the corner. Meanwhile, China, India, and Southeast Asia have been churning out emissions to beat the band—"

"You can't blame poorer nations for wanting, and deserving, a Western lifestyle, bab."

"You've got to be joking!" Kay exploded. "We're living on mouldy toast. What 'Western lifestyle'?"

"If the UK weren't a massive improvement on their wretched

circumstances, these benighted refugees would never attempt the perilous journey across the Channel." Even in these early days, Cyril's soothing liberal platitudes had begun to assume the demented singsong of a nursery rhyme.

"I'm not convinced it is all climate change," Kay grumbled. "Or even primarily climate change. Africa and the Middle East are mostly desert, and they've always been desert. Those climates were abysmal even when I was a little girl. There've always been droughts there, and crop failures, locusts, and famines, because it's not a part of the world that's ever been equipped to sustain *billions* of people!"

"You sound as if you've been poisoned by the podcasts of that bitter lunatic Calvin Piper. I don't say this about many people, but that demographer is evil."

"I concede the codger is unsavoury, but he may have a point. As for this knee-jerk mea culpa of yours, which means we're supposed to just sit here whilst our country is overrun—"

"Watch your language!" Cyril said.

"What am I supposed to say? 'Whilst our country attracts an unusual number of visitors'?"

"All right. That's better."

"What is our fault is curing all the diseases that once kept population growth in those parts under control."

"Enough! You're a *nurse*. What's got into you?"

"I'll tell you what's got into me. Hyde Park and Kensington Gardens are encampments and no-go areas. You can't walk along the South Bank for all the families huddled in blankets with cups out. And it's not only here. In Paris, they're all along the Seine, on the bridges, around the Eiffel Tower and clumped around the pyramid of the Louvre—whose panes they've all smashed. In Italy, they've set up tents in the Roman ruins and turned the Coliseum into a homeless shelter. There's hardly a solvent government in Europe aside from

Sweden, and Sweden only barely, because they have more *visitors* per capita than anybody. Even you and I can barely afford one miserable sausage between us. What's this country supposed to do with them all?"

"You don't talk about 'them' as if they're real people," Cyril admonished.

"They're real as sin! But just because they're 'people' doesn't mean I'm required to like having them here!"

"I'm ashamed of you. I've never known you to be so selfish." Cyril had always been one of those types—why was it always men?—who was big-hearted in relation to strangers, but often pitiless with people he knew.

"Biologically, we have to be selfish to survive," Kay said. "Blindly altruistic cultures would die out. And what's the purpose of a country if not to protect its people? To put the interest of citizens *above* the interest of outsiders? Otherwise citizenship is meaningless. If the rights of inhabitants are put on a par with the rights of everyone else in the world, there is no country."

"The purpose of a country," Cyril said, eyes narrowed, "especially this country, is to preserve a set of values. To which the beggar-thy-neighbour policies you're advocating are anathema."

"So to save Britain—which according to you means rescuing our sucker *values*—we have to destroy it."

"I would rather die with integrity than thrive as a savage."

Kay arose from the table so quickly that her chair fell backwards. "You are barking! That's the kind of empty armchair aphorism which . . . which . . . which is fatuous, and amounts to a kind of preening. What's going on right now all over Europe is real, not a page torn from a book of lofty political philosophy, and your response is to flatter yourself. Because we're both over a hundred bleeding years old, and it's getting dangerous out there!"

"Understandably. Many of these asylum seekers are desperate, and they'll do anything to feed their children."

"Uh-huh. And what if they thumped *me* over the head? To *feed their children*?"

"I would be sorry," Cyril said with elaborate condescension, "but I would still be able to contextualize your misfortune."

"I ask you: is there any limit? In your mind, is there any limit to the number of *visitors* this country should let in—five million, ten million, fifty million? Or is it all the-more-the-merrier to you?"

"The numbers have been grossly exaggerated," Cyril said coldly. "I cannot emphasize my concern strongly enough. I fear you've been contaminated by ugly, bigoted propaganda, and *that's* what's dangerous."

Cyril was quite right about the rise of prejudice. To the horror of most Britons, who in truth had always cared more for fairness and decency than for disciplined supermarket lines, vigilante groups multiplied. From fishing vessels, these ruffians took pot-shots at overloaded dinghies in the Channel. They beat up the undefended with cricket bats and set fire to tented encampments. When not explaining why the sudden deluge of migration was all the audience's fault, the BBC spent the abundance of its coverage of "The Great Flood" bewailing these hideous far-right attacks in ghastly detail. What few minutes remained to *Newsnight* thereafter were lavished on poignant stories of individual suffering and persecution amongst the new arrivals. They were gay, from countries where homosexuality was illegal. They were transgender and denied transition surgery. They were fleeing mandatory conscription, or they'd dared voice opposition to totalitarian regimes and had narrowly survived attempts on their lives. They had escaped from endless, vicious territorial wars. Most commonly, of course, they had trekked from villages that had no water and no food, having often lost family members to starvation and poor health care. The portraits were unfailingly sympathetic, and every single one of the supplicants the corporation interviewed seemed deserving of what any human being should rightly expect: safety, sustenance, and shelter. Obviously, anyone who argued that these lovely people should be turned away was a monster.

Unencumbered by this high regard for civility amongst the British mainstream, in the end the newcomers had the advantage over the violent outliers on the home team, first due to the ruthlessness of their determination to find "a better life," and soon due to their sheer numbers—whatever those were, as the Home Office had long ago stopped even pretending to keep track, and the Home Secretary had abandoned her cabinet post and absconded, it was rumoured, to the Hebrides. For despite repeated reports that the surge had peaked, massive caravans of pedestrians, bicycles, burrows, camels, jalopies, and overloaded coaches continued to form to Europe's south, stretching for miles into the distance in drone footage.

Further contributing to the festivities, the anti-climate-change Extinction Rebellion, once so popular amongst affluent young white Britons, had merged with the antinomian No Lives Matter movement to become "Extinction!" full stop. Gathering a fearsome strength, the faction urged a pagan embrace of the very apocalypse that the original eco-activists had aimed to prevent. Regarding themselves as sharing common cause with the asylum seekers, these young people weren't pummelling immigrants or torching encampments. They were smashing anything that smacked of a hoary old civilization that had had its day, and the targets of their arson were larger than tents— like the Houses of Parliament. According to Simon and Hayley, the Wilkinsons' now-teenage great-grandchildren had joined the anarchists and were out marauding across London all night long. The UK having bred the disaffected punk scene, it made sense that the country would also give birth to an antisocial movement far less decorative and middle-class (for Britain no longer had a middle class), which quickly spread to the continent. Once the restoration of Notre Dame was finally completed for a second time, within a fortnight a rabble of young white Frenchmen in *Extinction!* T-shirts burnt the cathedral to cinders.

"We've no need for six bedrooms. In a way it's fair." Cyril's stock social justice had grown lacklustre, and he pitched the platitudes in a mocking minor key.

"I'm sick of you telling me I have to learn to share, like some toddler," Kay whispered hoarsely. "I hate having these people in our house."

They were holed up in the loft, to which the homeowners had been banished by a good thirty *visitors* who had co-opted the rooms below.

"At least Simon *tried* to evict them," Kay added.

"Bab, it's hard for us to get our heads round it, but Simon is seventy-five. The display of loyalty was terribly touching, but banging on the door and making empty threats about ringing the police—what police?—simply put him at risk. Even most of the adults downstairs are less than half his age. He's lucky they merely laughed at him. It could have been much worse."

"It's Roy who could organize our rescue if he wanted to," Kay said.

Of their family members, Roy alone had flourished in the chaos, having got in on the ground floor of people-smuggling for the refugees who were better off. It was a lucrative trade. At seventy-two, he'd finally found his calling.

"True," Cyril agreed heavily. "He has the underworld connections to mobilize a mob on command. But let's be honest. Roy's only interest in this property would be as a safe house for his customers."

"Maybe we're lucky that he hasn't personally chucked us in the street, then," Kay said. "At least Hayley seems to have learnt her lesson after that abortive performance art. She claims to have nostalgically returned to the 'social distancing' of the coronavirus outbreak, a fancy way of saying that she never leaves the house."

Hayley had chosen the worst possible historical juncture to revive her arty ambitions from university. The piece she staged for the tent city in Regent's Park was bound to end in tears. To illustrate "inequality," she sat on a plush stool wolfing profiteroles as actors pretending to be refugees looked mournfully on. The actors were robbed, the profiteroles seized: far edgier theatre.

"Hey," Kay said. "Did you see they took apart those lovely end tables and fed them to the log burner? And the kids used the charcoal afterwards to draw pictures on the sitting room wallpaper."

"It was getting a bit faded," Cyril said with a sigh. "Sod the wallpaper. The real problem is the plumbing. London's sewage system is fragile enough, after all those wet-wipe and PPE fatbergs. But they don't seem to realize what you can and can't flush. I barely got the upstairs toilet working this afternoon, but when I sneaked down the ladder just now it was backed up with shite and overflowing again. Sorry, bab. Back to the bucket."

"Got to feed the oldies, ya?" came from below. Having joined a contingent of local anarchists, the guests of their impromptu Airbnb hailed from multiple countries, so at least communicated with each other in English.

The retractable ladder rattled down, and their personal chef rose only the few steps required to fling the evening meal on the dusty floorboards. The lone main course was, as ever, a small mound of cornmeal mush, which might just have passed for polenta except it contained no butter, no parmesan cheese, and more fatally no salt. The plate was a piece of their wedding china: chipped and cracked but still attractive, with its cream centre, emerald border, and glint of silver on the rim.

"Don't know why we bother with them," came a female voice as the ladder was slammed closed again. "Food bitching to find. Waste of good ugali. Means time, Sarina get too thin."

Once their overstaying houseguests had tromped away, Cyril whispered, "I'd enough time to get a partial charge on my phone today, because the others were mostly out—foraging, I suppose. But the electricity is bound to be cut off eventually. Our pensions no longer cover the British Gas bill, and the direct debit won't have gone through for the last two months. They won't be lenient forever."

"Hurry up and check the BBC website, then!" Kay urged. "What's the news?"

Cyril inhaled, scrolled, and sighed.

"What? How much worse can it be than yesterday?"

"They've rappelled up the Bank of England and bashed in the windows. It's suspected they murdered the governor. In any case, it's now another squat."

The headline was of a piece. August university campuses from Cambridge to Bologna were occupied by needy arrivals, and what few courses were still offered were conducted patchily online; Hayley's husband had long before been made redundant at UCL, as the last thing anyone had time for was linguistics. The British Library was covered with plywood, whilst the Booker was long gone, and even Sweden had dropped awarding Nobels for the last three years. The looted V&A was empty of artefacts, if full to the brim with exhibits of human desperation and ingenuity. Would that the paintings in the National Gallery had been stolen, but instead the canvases were hanging in shreds from attacks with penknives. Gaudi's architecture in

Barcelona had been vandalized into gaudy loose chippings. The stark blocks of the Holocaust Memorial in Berlin had been systematically pulverized by sledgehammers, which the Germans tried to blame on neo-Nazis, but the rioting nihilists weren't driven by any so constructive a purpose as the resurrection of the Third Reich.

"Goodness," Kay said. "That building is a fortress. Was it Extinction!? Or the migrants?"

"Both. They're operating in league now. And getting better organized. Funny, that: even anarchists gravitate towards order."

"Maybe the Bank doesn't even matter," Kay said hopelessly. "Sterling is worthless anyway. You know"—she nodded at their supper—"this is grim enough without our kindly caretakers refusing to give us our own cutlery."

"It's cultural," Cyril said, but his heart wasn't in it. "I think by custom most of our downstairs neighbours eat with their left hands."

They tried to maintain a semblance of civilization by sitting formally on either side of the plate, the sharp bones of their buttocks padded by quilts passed down from Kay's grandmother. After dipping her hand in a bucket of their only once-clean water, she politely divided the mound into two portions with a forefinger, trying to give Cyril the greater amount; he was a man, and however nominally now the larger. The fare was hardly appetizing, but they were starving, and it took discipline not to fall upon the muck all at once. Instead, they always tried to draw out their mealtimes with reflective conversation, just as in the old days. Cyril lit their last candle stub, which created a cosy atmosphere, whilst helping to dim the heaps of bric-a-brac stashed under the eaves that might have "someday come in useful."

"Back when we decided not to end it all on your eightieth," Cyril began, "you told me that you 'wanted to know what happened.' You felt as if you were in the middle of all these stories, like climate change and the coronavirus and, heavens, I think at the time you even mentioned

Brexit, of all things, and Donald Trump. You said that calling it quits in March of 2020 would be like returning a pile of unfinished novels to the library."

"And *you* said," she remembered, "that whenever we died, we'd always be in the middle of some unresolved historical plotline, so leaving loose ends dangling was part and parcel of mortality."

"But I wanted to ask you something. The collapse of the pound, the soaring crime, the loss of all our savings. The flooding of New York City. The cricket-bat-wielding rampages through the British Museum. The descent of most of Europe into autocracy. Our own house occupied by strangers. Are you glad to have lived long enough to see all this? Or would you rather have opted out earlier and spared yourself? Looking back, how strong is your 'narrative curiosity' when the end of the book is this depressing?"

"Hmm," Kay grunted. "I surprise myself a bit, because I'd have imagined that 'narrative curiosity' of mine was properly keen. But I'm not that curious. If I had it all to do over again, I think I'd accept the grand bargain you first proposed in 1991. Looking back, I think it must have been right around my eightieth birthday that everything started to go wrong. Maybe I'd rather have died in a state of innocence, or even delusion. Because I wish I'd never seen news photos of a Caravaggio sliced to ribbons and hanging from its frame. I wish I'd never seen the Houses of Parliament burnt to the ground. I wish I'd never seen the flowers in Kew Gardens trammelled and covered in human faeces. I'd love to turn back the clock to the twenty-ninth of March in 2020, toast our wonderful marriage with a glass of good cabernet, and knock back a handful of tablets to induce—well, whatever you call amnesia that allows you to forget the future. I'd have happily dozed off in our house, when it was still *our* house, nicely done up, where we'd conducted so many lovely evenings with dinners better than cornmeal caulking. I'd love to have left this world with no idea what awaits on the horizon, which, as I close my eyes for the last time, still looks bright."

Cyril frowned, staring into the middle distance, which meant looking no further than the closest cobwebbed roof beam. "I may not feel the same way, and that surprises me as well. The last twenty years have been painful, but they've been interesting. If this descent into bedlam was going to happen anyway, then I'd prefer to have been around to see it. I don't fancy delusion. I've always tried to look life square in the face."

"Oh, you have not," she said with a smile, leaning over to kiss his cheek.

"Of course, take the long view," he said more cheerfully, "and we may be witnessing creative destruction. Something different and sometimes better always arises from the ashes, does it not? Look at the Renaissance."

"True. But the Middle Ages lasted a thousand years."

"Look at it this way, then. Mostly, we've led wonderful lives. We only got old enough to truly understand the Second World War once it was over, when we knew that the white hats had won. We lived through the Marshall Plan and the triumphant rise of a cradle-to-grave welfare state. We had long, useful careers. We raised three healthy children, at least one of whom turned out to be an agreeable human being. We availed ourselves of affordable labour-saving appliances. We got in on computers, and owned more than one, and then we were blessed with the internet, which however broadly misused is still a miracle. For four-fifths of our lives, technology, the alleviation of poverty, the powers of medical science—everything did nothing but improve. We've watched great films, read great books, and gone to great exhibitions. Before the last few years, we've walked the streets without fear. We've lived largely in a state of social order, which has made all our higher pleasures possible.

"But none of the angry young people ransacking the last of the West End theatres can say any of these things. They've experienced nothing but hardship and decline. They have no future, and they know it. The fundamentals of the Western world entered a fatal disequilibrium well before the rabble-rousing of Extinction! tearaways. Maybe those hooligans are just trying to get the inevitable demolition over with as fast as possible—"

"*Sh-sh*," Kay said.

"Where you go?" came a female voice from the floor below.

"Got to get the plate from the oldies," said the man who'd brought the mush. "We running low, 'cause they keep breaking. And got to empty they fucking bucket. *Whoo-ee!* Nothing that smell like oldie poo-poo."

"*Why* you keep bothering with them shrively white folks?" the woman demanded. "We need the mealy-meal for the children. They stink, and they never stop running they mouths. *Mumba-mumba-mumba* come from the ceiling all day long."

"Kokie, me soft lad, the queen's spot on," said a booming male voice in a strong Scouse accent. "Don't make no sense, know what I'm saying? Scran's proper tight, like. Might as well feed a boss tea to a pair of mangy dogs."

"But they elders!" the minder protested. "They due respect!"

"Leave that guff back in the old country, mate," the big male voice said. "Practical times call for practical measures."

The catch on the hatch moved, and the loft ladder unfolded with a violent clatter. Kay clutched Cyril's arm and their eyes met.

"What you gonna do, Dicky?" their minder pleaded from below. "What you gonna do?"

The man who emerged from the hatch was a massive, heavily muscled white fellow of about twenty-five they'd never seen before. He was carrying a machete. Had she downed that Seconal in 2020, it was one more image Kay would have spared herself. But at least the vision of her husband's decapitated body didn't burn on her retinas for more than a second or two.

11

Love Doesn't Freeze

"There is a whole movement that advocates 'ageing in place,'" Cyril noted.

"I'm all for it," Kay said emphatically. "I like it here. I've put in loads of work on this house. The conservatory is exquisite. I'm thrilled with the trailing orchid wallpaper in the sitting room. I want us to keep our garden. I want to pour myself a second glass of red wine without having some officious matron whisk it away because it isn't good for me."

"There's still the danger that *I* whisk it away," Cyril said.

"Just try."

In the end, they never put down that stonking deposit for Journey's End. Giving the ritzy safe haven a miss was a gamble, but, as Kay observed, every decision we make in this life is a gamble, isn't it?

Yet in the exuberant years of celebration, rejuvenation, and rebirth that followed the conclusion of the coronavirus crisis, Kay and Cyril felt abruptly at odds with the buoyant social mood. The inevitable economic slump in the immediate aftermath was later classified as creative destruction. Soon new restaurants opened and new businesses blossomed. The FTSE traced not a mere V-shape, but a J—soaring stratospherically and fattening everyone's pension plans. The Wilkinsons felt as if they'd not been invited to the party. Oh, their own private pensions were bursting, but what good was money that they wouldn't live to spend? First Cyril was diagnosed with pancreatic cancer, and on top of the disease's universally poor prognosis the NHS diagnosed it on the late side. On the heels of this crushing news, Kay learnt that the persistent pain and weakness in her shoulder, along with muscle cramps, increasing difficulty walking, and a sudden inability to open her own marmalade jars, had been an early sign of amyotrophic lateral sclerosis—or ALS.

"I'm rusty after having left St Thomas' so many years ago," Kay said limply at the kitchen table. "So I had to look it up. I might live another four years, but I'll progress quickly towards paralysis. My favourite symptom: 'inappropriate laughing or crying.' In time, I'll not be able to eat, or talk, or breathe without a ventilator. Maybe it's time to source that Seconal again."

"I have another idea," Cyril said. Though scheduled for chemo, he hadn't yet committed to a gruelling treatment that for a man of his advanced age would undoubtedly fail. "They've made massive leaps in cryogenics the last few years. None of this sticking-you-in-preservative-fluid-like-a-pickle business, but proper suspended animation. You remember that package we saw on Channel Four. They kept a hamster perfectly inert for eighteen months and then woke it up again, to run happily round its cage. What've we got to lose? If it turns out that at some later date we can't be revived after all, we're goners anyway—and set to die in the most dreadful manners imaginable. There'd still be a sliver of a chance that it works, and by the time we're revived, pancreatic cancer and ALS are curable."

"Sure, why not?" Kay said carelessly. So far, a death sentence had inclined her to be flip, even giddy—perhaps as a forerunner of all that *inappropriate laughing or crying* to come. She leant to seal their agreement with a peck. "My very own Rip Van Wilkinson."

The fact that the outer office of Sleeping Beauties Ltd was decorated with Disney paraphernalia didn't encourage confidence. Rather, cartoons of bunny rabbits and dwarves increased the sense that this dubious endeavour was having a laugh at the clients' expense. Most of the exhaustive paperwork was to absolve the company of any legal liability. At least the extortionate fees didn't make either spouse blink. Facing oblivion, these lifetime tightwads had finally registered that money had no value in and of itself, but was only a means to an end, and was therefore only valuable when you spent it. Barring the success of this kooky experiment, both a fiver and £5 million would soon be equally worthless.

"So what's your prob?" the receptionist asked with the distinct air of not giving a monkey's. The skinny young woman wore athletic gear to work, and she was chewing gum.

Disinclined to confide their heartache to a bored pencil pusher, Cyril said tersely, "ALS and pancreatic—"

"Yeah, we had a few of those. Pain in the arse, innit?" she said, not moving her gaze from the computer screen. "Any time limit?"

"No, the period is indefinite," Cyril said. "As we've specified, we're not to be revived until both conditions can be alleviated by medical breakthroughs. The fees are indemnified by a trust. We sent in all the documentation."

"Does it hurt?" Kay asked with sudden urgency. She'd been too embarrassed to ask before.

"How should I know?" the receptionist said, *smack-smack*.

"At least at Dignitas we'd get better service," Cyril grumbled to Kay under his breath.

"Do we need to disrobe?" Kay asked anxiously as the girl led them to the inner sanctum.

"Puh-lease," the receptionist said. "This is a cryogenics lab, not a naturist camp. And no offence, but I could skip looking at your wrinkly ass."

"Oh, no offence taken," Kay said sourly.

"Sarky, for a past-sell-by." She seemed to mean it as a compliment.

Two capsules were open and lit from within. There was no getting round their resemblance to caskets.

"Are we supposed to simply—lie there?" Kay asked.

"What else would you do in that thing, Morris dancing?"

"You could be a bit more respectful," Cyril said. They were both getting rattled by the disconcerting lack of ceremony.

"Look here, you lot getting cold feet?" the receptionist asked. "'Cause you're gonna get cold feet, even if you go through with it." She tee-heed. She'd made the joke before.

"Could you give us a moment alone, please?" Cyril requested firmly.

"A minute or two," she said. "But if what you're really up to is waffling on and bottling it, I got to warn you that the penalty for pulling out at this point is, like, I don't know, a gazillion quid."

In their brief window of privacy, Cyril kissed his wife deeply, the way they used to kiss for hours when they were courting, and they withdrew from one another's lips at last with the same reluctance they both remembered from those days as well, when they had to get back to their medical studies. That kiss sent a tingling shimmer through the entirety of their lives together, as if their marriage were a crash cymbal whose rim he'd just hit deftly with a felt mallet.

"See you later," Kay said.

"See you later," Cyril said.

The last thing they heard was the sound of that woman's gum.

A few seconds after that—or what seemed a few seconds—Cyril opened his eyes to find a dusky-skinned woman of indeterminate race staring down at him with an expression of clinical curiosity. "Hearm ca? Seem ca?"

His eyes were dry and painful. The sound of the woman's voice hurt. But the pain seemed deeper than his response to sensation. Being here hurt. Being at all.

"Turn lighden," the woman said, standing upright. She was at least eight feet tall.

The illumination dimmed, which helped the agony of seeing, but only somewhat. Cyril tried to form a word, but making his mouth move was hard work; even harder work was thinking of what to say. Either his neurological system was suffering from a mechanical creakiness, or his brain and facial nerves were functioning perfectly well—in which case what was keeping him from speaking was his mind's stark instruction that anything that he might say was not worth the effort because it was stupid.

"Waa," Cyril croaked weakly.

The woman in peculiar clothes—her form-fitting gear was covered in sleek black feathers, as if she were a superhero crossed with a crow—squirted an aerosol into Cyril's mouth. "Secure!" she said over her shoulder. "Sum viol." Then a large man with the same indeterminate complexion and gear of blue feathers came to stand watchfully beside the supine specimen.

Whatever had happened to the outside world in that blink of an eye between the closing of the capsule and the raising of its lid again, something had happened to Cyril. He felt like a copy of himself—a poor copy, like the decayed kind you got when you didn't photocopy from the original, but copied the copy, then copied that copy, and he seemed to be the result of at least ten reproductions on. When he struggled to retrieve his recent memories, the recollections were in fragments: dwarves, bunnies, and a woman's Lycra workout shirt floated by. Again his mind directed that he needn't fit the scraps together because they were stupid.

Cyril managed to lick his lips. "Could you please tell me where am I?"

The several people in the room all burst out laughing.

"Pardon me, did I say something humorous?" he puzzled.

They cackled again.

"Sar," the woman in black feathers said. "Sounya ha!"

"I hate to cause any trouble, but it would be awfully helpful if you could find someone for me who speaks English." Of course, the request was absurd if no one spoke English. "*English?*"

As the team crowding round the capsule continued to find him hilarious, Black Birdwoman asked, "Angle?"

"Google Translate?" Cyril proposed with little optimism. These people did not look right, dress right, or talk right. Wherever and whenever he was, the chances of a rather imperfect smartphone application still being extant half a million updates later were nil. Not that it mattered. Not that anything mattered.

His minders conferred, poking at whatever mechanisms a human race over eight feet tall poked at, until at length a hologram of an older man in a suit of fine golden feathers appeared beside the capsule. Experimentally, Cyril struggled to a sitting position. Everything ached. Not just the bones. Every cell.

"Allowest I introduce I-self," he said grandly. "I expertise on loster dialection. Service at your. Trans."

Some expert. Cyril said, "Maybe you could start by explaining what language these people are speaking."

The "expertise on loster dialection" looked shaken, but when Cyril repeated the request much more slowly he seemed to get it. The holographic projection appeared to be the current equivalent of Hayley's husband: a linguistics professor. "Angle," the prof said. "Ang*lish*."

"*English*. Seriously." Cyril felt an unfocused dread, because if these people were speaking whatever hash his mother tongue had become, then they would require an amount of effort that his belligerent mind was informing him point-blank it would refuse to make. "And could you be so kind as to tell me where I am exactly?"

The audience was hooting again, and the hologram shot them a chastening look. "Lun," he said.

"London?" Cyril inferred. "London, England, in the United Kingdom."

The interlocutor was having trouble again. "Lon-*don*," he seemed to remember. "Ing, Unite King?" he said. "Go more no."

Well, they predicted the breakup of the United Kingdom after the UK left the EU, and though Cyril was once a passionate unionist—the factual information was available to him; it just needed dusting off—now he didn't care. The Scots were always troublemakers, and the Barnett formula for the distribution of revenue had never been fair to English taxpayers.

"So the *Unite King go more no*," Cyril recapitulated caustically. "Could you also—"

"Sar!" the hologram said. "How say you 'Unite King go more no'?"

"The United Kingdom is no more." Back in the world ten minutes and he was already teaching his captors, or whatever they were—who with their poncy future what-all might instead have been teaching him a thing or two, and Cyril was already tired.

The hologram punched excitedly at a device. "Treasury grove of lingualistic histrionics!"

"Treasure trove of linguistic history," Cyril decoded, bored. "And sorry to be so basic, but I seem to have been down for the count rather a while. What year is this?"

The answer was incomprehensible. After more agonized back and forth, Cyril at least established that they no longer dated years from the birth of Christ, and it was pretty much impossible to establish what, you know, Star-date Whathaveyou it was in relation to the 2020s. Luckily, the year was a matter of supreme indifference, really.

Yet amidst the extensive back and forth about base ten, which was apparently like asking these people about cave drawings, it dawned on Cyril that he should have asked a pressing question at the very first. Having still not asked it was disturbing, insofar as Cyril could be disturbed at all—although he sensed that his previous incarnation would have been quite disturbed indeed. How could he have taken so long to inquire: where was his wife?

Cyril was assured he could soon reunite with the other ancient hominid in the second capsule of the pair, but beforehand they were both required to undergo a thorough health check.

When his species' amiable descendants helped him out of the capsule, Cyril was relieved that his legs bore his weight; suspended animation didn't appear to entail the muscle wastage of lolling in bed. But as a young man, he'd been tall for his generation, a generous six foot one. Now he stood a good two and a half feet shorter than these strapping new-age specimens, beside whom he looked like a dwarf. The literal loss of stature smarted. By inference, then, however peculiar he felt, some inner kernel remained unchanged: a sort of underseer that had always been there waiting and watching from within. The man he had been before taking the cryogenic plunge would have disguised this quintessence from himself as something loftier or more ineffable, but his newly brutal iteration had no problem identifying the kernel for what it was: ego.

The childlike humiliation of staring straight at his caretakers' diaphragms was intensified by self-consciousness about his clothing. Amidst this sleekly aviary kit, a navy woollen cardigan with wooden buttons and a roll collar, a once-crisply-ironed ivory button-down that had badly creased, and comfortably roomy belted slacks with a break in the leg could as well have been the ruffs, pantaloons, tights, and pointy buckled shoes of a comedic BBC period drama.

As the team led their historical curiosity gingerly towards some sort of medical facility, they treated him with the exaggerated care with which palaeontologists might handle a rare, newly unearthed fossil. Given the task ahead, Cyril was obliged to dredge up one memory that remained sombrely intact, and that alone seemed capable of making him feel something—in this case, tainted, corrupted, and doomed.

Awkwardly, the words "cancer" and even "cell" left his holographic translator baffled. Thus Cyril was obliged to elaborate about many proliferating bad creatures attacking and overwhelming the good creatures and then rushing to other points in the body to do more bad things . . . He sounded like an idiot. In the end he simply located his pancreas as best he could and pointed.

He was led into another unadorned room. A woman shone an orange light in both eyes, and a moment later he was lying on a gurney naked under a blanket, so he must have been sedated.

"All fix," the hologram said, a little smugly.

It was more than the British Cancer Society could ever have dreamt of.

Once again Cyril had the nagging sense that he probably should have asked another question earlier, and once again having failed to ask it didn't especially distress him, but before he awakened as a photocopy of himself this apparent absence of concern would have distressed him greatly. Could they also cure ALS?

During the two days the time traveller would be kept under medical observation before he could be reunited with his spouse, the golden interlocutor suggested that Cyril do both himself and his keepers a favour by sitting down to converse at length. Their dialogue would be fed into a self-learning computer, the result of which would be, effectively, Google Translate.

Over the course of their discussions, the hologram explained in his groping way that homo sapiens sapiens of today regarded itself as a single organism (what he actually said was "singular orgasm")—which as a socialist Cyril should have found appealing, and didn't. (The teeming hive concept did help explain why so far his caretakers had neither asked his name nor introduced themselves by name.) Because this collective entity required few components to function efficiently, the number of humans on the planet had been greatly reduced. Old Cyril would have been anxious about how this diminution was accomplished. New Cyril was merely relieved that maybe this meant he wouldn't have to meet all that many eight-foot-six strangers after all. When he asked why everyone seemed to be the same agreeable walnut colour, the translator was stymied by a concept of "race" that didn't mean "human race." Well, thank God for that. Interbreeding? However the homogeneity of hue had been achieved, Cyril was glad to see the back of the cosmetics contest.

All this stuff was vaguely interesting to the extent that anything was, but by their last morning Cyril was distracted. About to reunite with his wife that afternoon after however many zillion years, he felt not eager anticipation but anxiety.

After a revoltingly bitter lunch—something dreadful had happened either to human taste buds or to the ability of the species to cook—Cyril's new best mate led him into a simple room with a small table, two cups of liquid, and two simple chairs. A moment later from an opposite door a very short figure, almost a midget, entered with a female escort. The tiny person looked incredibly old and rather shell-shocked. Beside her minder's streamlined plumage, the pocketed below-the-knee dress looked sack-like and frumpy. Surely this gradual, arduous process of "recognizing" his wife was not the form. In the past he would simply have seen her.

When the hologram moved towards the door, Cyril panicked. "You're not going to go?"

"You speaken same losted linguilism, yes?" the hologram puzzled. "So no requiration of trans."

"Oh, right, of course," Cyril said. He wasn't about to say aloud that he didn't want to be left alone with her.

When Kay's escort departed, he could swear that she also shot her minder a mournful glance. Cyril walked more slowly and stiffly to his seat than recent awakening from suspended animation justified, for his body having been put on pause had made moving around again no harder than pressing *play*. The only activity he found fiendishly difficult was existing at all.

Perhaps if there'd been time to script this reunion in advance, they'd have blocked the scene with an embrace. As it was, not only did they not touch, but neither party acted as if it occurred to them to do so. They took their time sitting. When Kay finally looked up, her eyes were cardboard. "Hello," she said.

"Hello," Cyril said.

Time passed.

"How was it for you?" Cyril asked. A trite inquiry after sexual congress, but neither took up the joke.

Her face flickered with annoyance. "There is nothing to remember. So what kind of a question is that?"

They sat.

"Did they cure the ALS?" Cyril remembered to ask.

"Yes," she said stonily.

Of course, he might have noticed when she walked in that she no longer displayed those classic symptoms of stumbling and poor balance. But picking up on these improvements would have displayed the kind of attentiveness that came naturally in relation to someone whose pains were in some sense your pains too, whose death sentence was your death sentence too, and this woman could have been anybody.

Cyril took a sip of the liquid and made a face. He hadn't even wanted any, since the flavour was as punishing as he'd anticipated. But it was something to do.

"The food here is terrible," he said.

"I think they think it's very sophisticated," she said, though her delivery was aimless. "I think we're being fed what to them is haute cuisine. They think they're feeding us like royalty." The thought seemed to exhaust her, and her gaze kept sliding off her husband's face as if it were covered in cold cream and she couldn't get visual traction.

"The English they speak now," he said, realizing with embarrassment that he was "making conversation" in a manner he couldn't recall ever having done in previously effortless exchanges with his wife. "There are no more adverbs. There are no declensions—no *I* versus *me*, *she* versus *her*. In the written form, after everyone got hopelessly confused about how to use commas and semicolons, they reduced all punctuation to the forward slash. All letters are lower case, and all spelling is phonetic. Those fashionable truncations from our day—*prob* for problem, *cab* for cabernet, *uni*, *bro*; the way Hayley started saying *obs*, which got on your nerves—now they've done it to everything, chopped all the long words into snack size. Their vocabulary is miniscule, because it's 'more efficient.' If we want to learn to communicate, mastering the dialect is probably doable, even at our age."

"Uh-huh," she said dully. "I can't say that I care."

Factual memory informed him that this woman was once vigorously, even frenetically interested in everything—often to no purpose. Perhaps her current apathy was "more efficient."

"Do you feel . . ." He wasn't sure of the adjective. "Lost?"

Kay had the look on her face of a classic stroke victim with "slow processing speed." "That's too specific," she said at last. "I'm not sure what feeling is."

The whole texture of this encounter recalled his ungainly efforts at courting at *uni*, before he met Kay. It was the texture of a bad date.

"Well, it worked," Cyril said, unable to repress a note of sourness.

"What worked." Again, the irritation.

"Our grand plan," Cyril said, with corresponding irritation. "We went into cold storage. When we woke up, both our terminal conditions were curable."

"Oh, that," she said. "So?"

He had no idea what he'd ever seen in this woman.

When they were finally rescued from each other what seemed like hours later but was really more like ten minutes, the hologram told Cyril that he would now need to see a different kind of doctor.

"You and your spouse are the oldest cryogenically preserved specimens we have ever revived," the Different Kind of Doctor said clearly and grammatically. Wearing a flashy feather suit whose crimson was reminiscent of the male cardinal, he had a diode or something attached to his head. Google Translate was a success. "I cannot believe how long it takes to say anything," he added under his breath.

"Cryogenics was still in its infancy," Cyril said. "But if we didn't give it a try, we were going to die."

"Why did you not want to die?"

"That seems like a stupid question."

"If our research on much fresher specimens is any guide, you now think everything is stupid."

Cyril felt caught out, and also resentful, as if the therapist had been spying. "In this future—"

"It is not the future. It is the present. That is one of the many things you are going to have trouble with."

"In this present, then. You don't fear dying or try to avoid it? Or do you not die?"

"We die," the human cardinal said blithely. "But all that matters is the continuation of . . . I am not happy with this expression of yours, 'the hive.' I detect it refers to insects. This is too reductive."

Cyril proposed, with a nod to the counsellor's garb, "How about, 'Birds of a feather flock together'?"

The therapist's expression remained flinty. Perhaps such a psychic high priest was above a sense of humour. "The whole to which I refer is something you have no understanding of, and no capacity to understand."

"Sorry, but I'd call that rather insulting."

"We aren't troubled by offending your vanities. There was a time, when the unity of our greater organism was more fragile, that we'd have regarded your primitive individualism as a grave threat. Had you been reanimated in an earlier era, you might have been stoned to death. But now our solidarity is unassailable, and we're more likely to regard you as quaint, or more probably as pathetic."

"With all due respect"—the standard introductory flourish with which Members of Parliament had always begun an abusive harangue—"you don't know me at all. I've never advocated 'primitive individualism.' All my life, I've been an ardent socialist . . ." Cyril's huffing and puffing collapsed. One of the most dreadful side effects of suspended animation was a horrifying inability to lie to himself. He had been neither a socialist nor an egalitarian. He had espoused socialism in the interest of his own glorification, and he had always felt superior to everyone else.

"That's a prime example of what we find pathetic," the doctor said. "This idea that there's such a thing as 'getting to know you.' As if others will be mesmerized by your unplumbable depths, and we're sure to be fascinated by your amusing eccentricities, ironic inconsistencies, and arresting complexities. There's nothing special about you, as there's nothing special about any of us. Your only personal distinction is hubris and ignorance. We know we're all the same, and being interchangeable doesn't bother us in the slightest. That's why death leaves modern humans unfazed. Whereas for you the notion of being just one more fungible worker bee, to use your disagreeable analogy, is intolerably demeaning, and you cling to the farcical fancy that your subtraction from humanity would leave a gaping hole."

"Maybe I used to think that," Cyril said glumly. "Not any more."

"We have digressed. If I may resume: from what we've patched together, there were a number of ghastly instances in which cryogenics went wrong. More than one subject was buried alive. Or bodies were put into perfect stasis but the minds remained alert—much like what you call 'locked-in syndrome'—so that by the time the subjects were reanimated, they were irretrievably insane, and a danger to themselves or to others. Sometimes consciousness was revived in decomposing corpses. As a result, for a long period whilst you and your wife were in a state of hiatus, the practice was banned. So you're quite a rarity. The records from your era are nearly all destroyed. You might usefully fill in some gaps for us. But I'm here to warn you that you are in imminent danger of wilful self-destruction—colloquially, 'topping yourself.' That would entail our so-called *hive* losing a valuable asset. To prevent that loss, I need to prepare you for what to expect. At the moment, you are thinking that the immediate shock of emergence into a new world is the hard part. You assume that later you will get acclimatized, and learn the language, make friends even, and fit in. It's therefore important for you to understand at the outset that your experience of a time in such contrast to your own will only get more difficult. You will never get acclimatized or make friends as you understand them. You will never fit in."

"That's not very welcoming," Cyril objected.

"I want you to imagine you are a dinosaur in a natural history museum that has been miraculously brought to life. So you can pound down the street. Are you going to fit in?"

"You got that from my conversation with that professor chap. It was a metaphor."

"The dinosaur is a good metaphor. You stand out in the landscape. People will stare at you. You are clumsy and can't communicate. The only thing wrong with the metaphor is that you are freakishly stunted."

Once more, Cyril was stung. "I used to be considered on the tall side."

"Get over it," the clinician said brutally. "We are in the early stages of developing full clairvoyance, which is one reason language is being minimized; it will soon die off, like the vestigial tail or the appendix. You will feel left out. I assure you that being in a room with people nodding and laughing whilst not even needing to say anything is a great deal more isolating than being at a party where all the cool people give you the cold shoulder."

"You can read my mind?"

"Crudely. If I care to. Though to be honest, your head is not a place where I particularly wish to go."

Cyril was about to say defensively, "Being me isn't that bad!" but stopped himself. It was that bad. It was terrible, and he did not know why.

"You see, when you opted to 'go to sleep,' as you're prone to misconceive suspension," the therapist continued, "you didn't take seriously the possibility that when you 'awoke' all your acquaintances, your colleagues, your friends, your family, including your own children and their children, would have long before vanished. We've had cryogenic revivals make absurd efforts to locate blood descendants. Even when successful, they discover they've no connection to their progeny either emotionally or, to the eye, biologically. These great-great-great-etcetera children who never asked to be tracked down tend to regard their resurrected ancestors as pestersome and in no little part repulsive. That pasty skin you've got. It's disturbing, like the colour of a naked mole rat."

"My, you certainly don't beat about the bush."

"At best you will be seen here as circus acts," the therapist continued, as if being called pestersome and repulsive wasn't cruel enough. "Your sense of yourself is constructed more than you realize from the other people you've known and cared for. Even the nemeses you've despised have helped form your defining context. Now all you have for context is your wife."

Cyril looked to his lap. He felt inklings of something like shame. "Kay," he said heavily, though he wondered if citing anyone's name in this communitarian blob was an act of sedition. "Something has happened to her."

"Something has happened to you both," the therapist corrected. "Previous interviews would suggest that you'll find what has happened to you even harder to accept than the changes in your spouse."

"I don't understand it," Cyril said. "When we signed the papers at Sleeping Beauties Ltd—a ridiculous name for a scientific enterprise— I didn't have any real confidence that we'd survive. But to my astonishment, although I may still be in my eighties, I can walk, eat, and sleep; as far as I can tell, my body is working as well as before, and now if I can believe your medic I don't even have pancreatic cancer any more. So why is everything so . . . stark, and . . . plain, and . . . dead?"

"Recall a packet of mince that's been in the freezer for a long time," the therapist returned. "When you thaw the meat, it's still made of protein, and it will still nourish you in a purely nutritional sense. But all its delicate flavours have been lost. On the edges, the colour has gone grey and the texture is dry; the water has separated from the fibres, which have become unpleasantly tough and chewy. As we don't eat 'mince' today, I took that image from your memory, so I'm certain you know what I'm talking about. And I have to say, I picked up that memory and fled, because I don't know how you can stand it in there. Your mind is a cold cave, and I'm still choking on its dry dust."

Cyril was strangely certain which memory the therapist had pilfered. With great fanfare, he had presented his wife with a cubic chest freezer for their first anniversary, making them brave early adopters of what was not yet a standard-issue middle-class white good. As if to please the Gods of preservation, they offered up to the appliance a ritualistic pound of mince—for in those days, freezing was an entertainment. Perhaps in time the totemic packet was simply forgotten and obscured by fresher fare. While the lump knocked about for years, its butcher's paper tore and its twine loosened. She finally thawed the once-ceremonial mound when they were preparing to move to the house in Lambeth. The meat was awful. The family stoically suffered through their patties anyway.

"Not only your body was metaphorically put on ice," the counsellor carried on, "but also, well, your essence, your finer feelings; if you will, your soul. We've seen it before. In fact, we've seen it every time. For lack of a better term, you have freezer burn."

The Wilkinsons were provided shared quarters, which like all the structures in this future—this *present*—were simple and serviceable. Had she ever pursued that absurd whim of hers to become an interior designer, Kay would have scavenged few clients here. Like the language, the décor was pared down to essentials.

They stood that evening gawkily, unsure whether to stand or sit or sit where, as if they'd not spent over sixty years going about their business and intersecting by chance and then convening to a purpose in the same house.

"I talked to some sort of therapist," Cyril said. It didn't seem right to say absolutely nothing.

"Yes," Kay said. She still had that dazed look, as if she were in a cartoon, a bear in a bow tie had just hit her over the head with a skillet, and the animator had drawn asterisks for eyes. "I talked to one as well."

"I didn't find him comforting."

"I don't think the intention was comfort."

This woman who was his wife had a peculiar smell: musty with a disturbing overlay of sweetness, like an unpeeled onion. Indeed, the odour was worse than peculiar; it was repellent. Yet his mind informed him that this was the same way she had always smelt. He'd no comprehension of how he had ever been able to stand it.

". . . Do you suppose they can fly?" Cyril proposed lifelessly.

She looked at him as if he were daft. "What."

"The suits, covered in those fine feathers."

She couldn't rouse herself to a reply. The conversation was going nowhere.

"Shall we go to bed?" Cyril suggested in desperation.

"All right."

As he undressed, he didn't feel shy or embarrassed—in the glare of that pernicious plainness, the unveiling of a naked body didn't appear to expose anything other than what-was—nor did he feel ashamed of a figure whose droops and mottles also simply were. He did shoot a glance at the shrivel between his legs in idle wonderment that a woman would ever have found it captivating, and that made him realize that he'd never asked if these neo-humans still had sex. But of course he hadn't asked. His curiosity was desiccated.

Kay also undressed with plainness. They looked at each other unclothed and it was the same as looking at the wall or a chair. Nothing stirred.

Cyril had always slept on the left-hand side of the bed, territory he reclaimed reflexively. It was already difficult to remember that, however many eons had elapsed in real time, subjectively only a handful of nights had passed since they last shared a mattress. Yet this evening he nestled awkwardly against a foreign body. Throughout the night as well, Kay was constantly flopping an arm across his pillow or kicking him in the shin, and he found it hard to quell his irritation even though he knew she wasn't assaulting him on purpose. She mumbled in her sleep, and he was confounded how he could ever have found these habitual vocalizations of dialogue in her dreams the faintest bit endearing; only a proper English upbringing prevented him from exclaiming, "Shut *up*!" Whenever she flung off the bedclothes he got cold; whenever she pulled them up he got hot. An instep shoved against his calf would shock him awake with its Arctic, scaly skin, whilst a hand splatted against his neck made him feel the same panic to get it off him that he might have felt had a bat dropped from the ceiling. It wasn't a large enough bed to establish a separate fiefdom, and no matter how he lay beside, wrapped around, or intertwined with this woman who was still his wife, he could not get comfortable. Nothing fit.

When Kay first opened up the pound of thawed mince after a long day of packing their possessions for the removal men, he'd noticed her poking at the meat with a sigh of disappointment before breaking it in half to begin forming patties. In the very middle of the mound, perhaps no more than an ounce had still looked like beef. The remnant remained a vibrant red, and one might postulate that if this central titbit had been rescued from the rest, it would still have retained its original flavour. Something at the heart of Cyril's psyche had been preserved in just this manner, and in the early hours before dawn it was this morsel that wept and wept and wept.

12

Once Upon a Time in Lambeth

"Hold on. Let's be clear." Kay swung her feet back to the floor and sat up straight. "You're proposing that we get to eighty and then commit suicide. You didn't use the word. Anyone who concocts a plan like that shouldn't rely on euphemism and evasion."

"Quite right." Cyril recited, "*I am proposing that we get to eighty and then commit suicide.*"

"Oh, for pity's sake, Cyril Wilkinson, don't be ridiculous. Honestly, sometimes!"

Cyril looked wounded. "I was serious."

"I know," Kay said, standing up. "That's what makes it ridiculous."

"How do *you* propose we avoid your father's fate, then?"

"I don't. Our destiny isn't wholly in our hands. I realize you don't like that about the world, but there's an upside: our destiny isn't wholly our responsibility, either. Or, if we end badly, our fault."

"I don't appreciate you simply dismissing an idea that I've given a great deal of thought." He was sulking.

"You have any number of brilliant ideas, my dear," she said, kissing the top of his head. "This simply isn't one of them. By contrast, your proposal that we add a second skylight to the conservatory is spot on."

"What's wrong with planning for a clean break?" he asked petulantly.

Blimey, he simply wouldn't let it go. "Some silly, numerically arbitrary suicide pact is psychologically unrealistic, and besides. I don't want to kill myself. Is that good enough for you? Occasionally people conduct an old age that is fulfilling, active, and rich. If believing in such a possibility is like believing in fairies, then fine. I believe in fairies."

Kay put both attractive sherry glasses in the dishwasher. What on earth had she been thinking, drinking at such an early hour? It would have been one thing had she been driven to drown her sorrows over her father, but she was not sorry he was dead. She was merely sorry that she wasn't sorry.

It was only four years later that Kay opted for retirement from the NHS at fifty-five. Before she announced the decision to Cyril, she was anxious that he'd regard leaving the service at the earliest opportunity as a betrayal. Worse, she worried that the second career she hoped to cultivate thereafter would elicit his derision. The occupation she aimed to train for wasn't morally freighted; it had no moral qualities whatsoever. The arrangement of surfaces, shapes, and colours had nothing to do with doing good, though properly pursued it could entail doing well.

Yet when she laid out her tentative plans—nervously, in a spirit that implied she might forget all about the whimsical notion in the face of the slightest discouragement—her husband was astonishingly supportive. He commended the redecoration she'd done in their own home and saw no reason why her innovative design instincts couldn't be scaled up. He assured his wife that she'd more than put in her time at St Thomas'. He even confessed to a cheerful envy of a trade that could provide her such broad opportunities for creativity. That night, she'd never felt more certain that she'd married the right man. He wasn't nearly as rigid as the children seemed to imagine. Though he could get wrapped up in his own ambitions and his own way of seeing things, he had a warm nature. He cared passionately about her happiness. He might have been raised in an era when women were expected to assume a muted, subordinate position, but he was not stuck in the 1950s and he was capable of change.

After she graduated from Kingston, the jobs for friends and friends-of-friends eventually gave her a long-shot crack at doing over the lobby of a flash, relatively new hotel called One Aldwych in Covent Garden. Not only did she snag the commission, but her bold yet cosy revamp won a major national design award. Having made the leap to commercial properties, she was soon commanding considerable fees and able to pick and choose which spaces she found inspiring. She acquired a coveted reputation as a designer who never sacrificed functionality for high concept, and who believed that interiors could convey modernity and style without being cold and inhuman. She might have been concerned that Cyril would feel overshadowed or even a trace resentful, but instead her husband was bursting with pride, constantly dragging their friends into restaurants whose dining room décor his wife had devised even when the food was rubbish.

Meanwhile, Cyril finally gave himself credit for having paid his own dues to the NHS. When he retired at sixty-two, the fervent send-off at his Bermondsey clinic moved him to tears, and he forbade any of the nurses, physicians, and receptionists from leaving the do until they'd helped him finish off their farewell gift of a twenty-five-year-old single malt. Back home, he wasn't long footloose before he started in earnest on his memoirs. He was apologetic about the project at first, claiming that the manuscript was really for his own satisfaction. Although he harboured small private hopes that perhaps the children might be interested in an account of their father's life, he nursed no serious expectation that the memoir would ever see print. The process of reviewing his life proved enjoyable for its own sake. When he shyly allowed Kay to read the final draft, Cyril was as abashed by her effusive response as he had been by the unstinting admiration of his former colleagues in Bermondsey. "You needn't exaggerate!" he begged her. "Darling, it's enough that you didn't find the thing unbearably tedious." Only at her insistence did he email the file to a fellow member of his men's choir whose wife was an editor at Orion.

Given how riveting she'd found his account, Kay claimed that matters proceeded precisely as she'd expected, but Cyril himself was gobsmacked. Orion made an offer on the memoir within the week, and the size of the advance on the table made him blush. On publication, *Fit for Purpose* became an instant *Sunday Times* bestseller. At the urging of his editor, Cyril embarked on a companion volume, and eventually authored a whole series of medically oriented books for laymen, with a wildly popular mix of health tips, folk wisdom, philosophizing about mortality, and anecdotes about anonymized patients. Cyril varied his more humdrum workdays at the computer with signings, festival appearances, and formal lectures at medical schools. He was open-handed with the press in granting interviews.

Indeed, their home in Lambeth became a Mecca for junior doctors suffering from a crisis of commitment, unsure they could take the long hours, the sacrifice of family life, and the devastation of losing patients. Meanwhile, aspirant designers rocked up to see Kay and pick her brain on challenging aspects of their fledgling projects. The mentors were generous with tea and wine, and their house often teemed with young people clamouring for advice, shyly soliciting compliments that would probably mean too much to them, and sharing stories from that poignant phase of life that combined crippling under-confidence with wildly unjustified arrogance within the same five minutes. The young blood around the kitchen table was a tonic.

When the acolytes made profuse professions of veneration, the couple were embarrassed at first. Yet they soon learnt to take the tributes in stride, never letting it go to their heads when told repeatedly, "You're way more fun than friends my own age," or, "You two understand me loads better than my parents," or, "Come on—you could both pass for thirty-five!"

Leery of getting separately caught up in the stratospheric successes of second careers, the spouses made time every year to travel to all the destinations that Kay had pined to visit in the days they'd never have afforded such extravagance. Cyril held back at first, acceding to these forays largely as a favour to his more adventurous wife, but after a trip or two he caught the bug as well, launching into excursions to Australia, Malta, Key West, Las Vegas, and Japan with enthusiasm. What a perilous pitfall, he noted: falling into a rut in one's latter years and getting overly attached to routine.

Once they bought a palatial holiday home in the Algarve region of Portugal, they also reserved time to spend a rambunctious fortnight every August with the whole extended clan. Like most families, theirs had suffered from frictions. Having nursed artistic ambitions when she was young, Hayley was frustrated in middle-aged motherhood. The other two were jealous of Simon's income as a trader in the City, whilst in turn Simon worked until so late at night that he rarely got to spend it, much less see his children. Long ago, Roy had nobly volunteered for the role of black sheep, the way other sons joined the army.

Yet their parents' late-life flowering inspired all three kids to locate the same optimism and resourcefulness in themselves. Following her mother's lead, Hayley opted for further education, devoting her creative flair thereafter to teaching special needs children from deprived areas of London. Beavering about town to help others less fortunate than herself, she dropped a few pounds and ceased to resent her wiry mother; the two grew close and were often mistaken for sisters.

Packing it in at his brokerage firm, Simon moved to Devon to establish a wind farm. Responding to a population with the same outcast status he'd been lumbered with his whole life, Roy started working with asylum seekers, securing them English classes, coaching them on the Life in the UK citizenship test, and helping them navigate the arcane bureaucracy of the Home Office. He finally settled down, too, marrying a gorgeous woman from Senegal; their four mixed-race children were exquisite, the colour of walnuts. Although on the old side to become parents, Kay's brother Percy and his husband had fraternal twins with a surrogate from Laos. As the older grandchildren came of age to date a Taiwanese law student, a Colombian osteopath, a Jewish coder from South Africa, and a footballer from Samoa, their once narrowly Anglo-Saxon tribe soon duplicated the multicultural crowd shots in insurance adverts—making family get-togethers so much richer than the stiff, civil convocations of boring old English people.

Now so much more personally contented, the Wilkinsons' three children grew more appreciative of parents whom they'd previously taken for granted or deployed as unifying targets of shared sibling mockery. Hayley went out of her way to express gratitude to her mother for being such an exemplary role model, with both long unstinting public service and a brave, no-guarantees departure into a more imaginative field. Simon bought stacks of his father's books to distribute to his wind-farm employees at Christmas. And perhaps Roy's turnaround was the most moving. Though he made a pittance as the deputy head of Hospitality House, he had clearly been saving for years to be able to announce that he was taking his parents on an all-expenses-paid expedition to meet his in-laws in Senegal, and he refused to accept a penny to help finance the trip. The shindig was a huge success. Though Roy's in-laws spoke no English, everyone communicated by sign language with often hilarious misunderstandings, and they all agreed to a reunion as soon as feasible.

Well before they hit seventy, Kay and Cyril had realized the supreme importance of taking care of themselves, and together they
embarked on a project of strenuous but entirely pleasant exercise. No
longer merely strolling beside the Thames, Kay took advanced spinning classes and became a passionate fan of bone-chilling wild swim-
ming throughout the winter. Cyril took up mountain climbing and
unfailingly fascinating free weights. In total agreement, as they seemed
to be about everything these days, they resolved henceforth to make
their holidays more vigorous, canoeing the Amazon, cycling between
Michelin-starred restaurants in France, and hiking the Appalachian
Trail in America—overtaking many a younger party on steeply rising
switchbacks.

In kind, although Cyril lent a considerable hand in the kitchen
now, Kay took it upon herself to improve their diet. Leaving behind
the stodgier fare of shepherd's pie and bangers and mash, she introduced more nuts, seeds, olive oil, and leafy greens. Cyril didn't especially fancy kale to begin with, but the more Kay served it the more it
grew on him, until on those occasional evenings she steamed pointed
cabbage instead he could grow petulant. Where was the kale? Once
she weaned them off nutritional traif, they both lost any taste for red
meat, sugar, butter, and cream, and their favourite pudding was a
refreshing branch of celery.

Thus throughout their seventies, both spouses were lean, tan, and
sinewy. If anything, the two were more attracted to each other than
they'd been as newlyweds. So electrifying and various had their sex
life become that they would sometimes catch each other's eyes across
a table in a crowded restaurant with a distinctive knowing smile—a
smile that remembered the night before and promised for the night to
come. Carved with wry humour and hard-earned wisdom, their faces
as they aged grew in many ways more beautiful than the smooth,
bland countenances of their callow youth. It was not unusual for the

couple to glide gracefully down the pavement hand-in-hand and turn the heads of Londoners in their twenties.

The referendum on the UK's membership of the European Union might have been an occasion for the rest of the country to cleave into hostile, irreconcilable camps, but for the Wilkinsons the run-up to 23 June 2016 was a welcome opportunity to have long, in-depth discussions in which they shared what began as divergent positions. These conversations were thoughtful, productive, and open-minded. Both spouses had so much respect for their better half's fine analytic mind that each couldn't help but entertain the validity of the other's view. So as their compatriots tore into each other at dinner parties, the gentle antagonists in Lambeth came only to a deeper appreciation for the opposite side—so much so that when the day of the ballot came round, Cyril had grown convinced that on balance Britain was better off on its own and voted Leave, whereas Kay, having gained a far better understanding of the many regards in which their country benefited from the political solidarity and market access provided by the EU, voted Remain.

Although the initial months-long coronavirus lockdown appeared to be trying for everyone else, the couple found it terribly touching how loyally all three children rang every day to make sure that their parents were well. The Wilkinsons weren't sure what so many other older Britons were whingeing about, because they had no problem securing weekly delivery slots from Waitrose. Moreover, given that Cyril had been repeatedly jetting off to literary festivals in Zagreb or Mumbai, whilst Kay had often been up to her neck in choosing sofas for some Saudi prince's mansion on Kensington Palace Gardens, the period of enforced stay-at-home orders proved one of the most tranquil and luxuriously intimate few months of their marriage. Cyril apologized profoundly for having been "unforgivably" patriarchal in the early years of their relationship, and Kay forgave him anyway.

"I'm curious if you remember a certain early evening," Kay recalled during the gradual lifting of restrictions that summer, about which they were both mournful. They'd come to love their captivity. Like so many of their fellow Britons, they'd lost any desire to return to a frenetic life in which one dealt with troublesome other people and onerously earned one's own keep. "It would have been 1991, right after my father's funeral. You proposed we kill ourselves at eighty."

"Of course I remember," Cyril said, faintly affronted. "I remember everything." The assertion was no exaggeration. As they'd been doing Sudoku puzzles and the *Times* crossword, their memories were eidetic.

"If I'd gone along with your scheme, we'd be dead as of three months ago," she noted.

"I wonder if I wasn't going through some undiagnosed depression," Cyril puzzled. "That proposition was abnormally defeatist. Why, I've more energy, I feel healthier, and I take more enjoyment in life at eighty-one than I did at twenty-five. I feel more fully connected to the rest of humanity than ever. I love being eighty-one. I don't think I'd want to be any other age."

"So how will you feel about turning eighty-two, then?" she teased.

"Why—I imagine I'll love being eighty-two even better."

And so it transpired. Being eighty-two was delightful, an experience topped only by being eighty-three, so there was no reason to do anything other than look forward to turning eighty-four. Oh, they both felt an occasional twinge in a joint or minor ache in the lower back when rising from a chair, but these tiny reminders of ageing were always passing, and merely served to make them more grateful for their wonderful lives, their wonderful occupations, and their wonderful marriage. Because they ate so many vegetables, naturally neither came down with any illness more serious than a bout of sniffles, whilst daily squats, lunges, planks, and press-ups (Cyril still did 200 every morning, albeit, he was quick to modestly point out, in two sets) kept their muscles firm, their limbs flexible, their skin radiant, and their bones strong.

Meanwhile, events in the larger world seemed to mirror the unremitting improvement of life in Lambeth. After the scare of what, in historical retrospect, proved a relatively brief economic downturn following the global lockdowns to suppress COVID-19, an obliging monetary theory was demonstrated to be faultless. Lo, it was more than possible for the government to print an infinite amount of money and then give the money to its citizenry to buy things. If the citizenry ever wanted to buy more things, then the government could print still more money so that the citizenry could buy more things. Everyone marvelled at why retrograde economists had ever installed the unnecessarily convoluted business of employment and taxation. The technique caught on all over Europe, effectively establishing an indefinite lockdown, except in this one you could leave the house.

Earlier concerns about the potential for uncontrolled migration from "overpopulating" countries in Africa and the Middle East proved altogether unfounded, and a certain demographic grump named Calvin Piper, with his alarmist, racist predictions that Europe was sure to be "swamped" with refugees, became a byword for there being no fool like an old fool. As long forecast by more upbeat observers of the continent, Africa became the global nexus of technological innovation and eventually overtook China as the world's economic powerhouse. Far from forcing their starving or disaffected inhabitants to flee abroad to seek a "better life," African leaders implored their countries' diaspora to please come back home and take high-paying jobs that were going begging. (Roy's Hospitality House started running so short of asylum seekers that the charity was obliged to reorient towards tutoring underachieving working-class white kids.) Women having been granted full political and social equality in the Middle East helped to make the likes of Iran, Afghanistan, and Iraq peaceful, affluent societies that no one would dream of leaving, and the region's only serious problem was so many infatuated American tourists overstaying their visas. Meanwhile, Muslims having joined Christians in a new worldwide religion ("Jeslam") meant the end of terrorism.

After reducing carbon emissions to absolute zero in perfect unison (because who didn't care about their children's future?), all the nations of the planet kept atmospheric warming to a level low enough to be widely hailed as beneficial. If nothing else, the minimal rise in average global temperature had a salutary effect on the quality of British sparkling wine, which overtook champagne as the go-to bubbly even in France.

Thereafter, it was discovered that energy could be extracted from carbon dioxide (after all, if trees could do it . . .), so fossil fuels and even the likes of Simon's wind farm became anachronisms. Energy was free, just like all those products in Europe. Also free, and effortless, was the new process of desalination, so that the fresh water shortages that had seemed so ominous a few years before turned out to be one more product of a neurotic scientific establishment reliant on an infinite supply of insoluble problems to justify its existence. Likewise, antibiotic-resistant bacteria naturally evolved to be resistant to themselves.

Alas, however harmonious, prosperous, and environmentally sustainable, it was still a world in which people died. Yet for the Wilkinsons, a final leave-taking was merely one more occasion to pull off with panache.

Once Kay and Cyril turned 110 and 111 respectively, they had perhaps slowed an increment—Cyril's morning press-ups had dropped to 180—yet they were otherwise fit, healthy, and so stunningly attractive that artists would stop them in the street and plead to be allowed to paint their portraits. The pair were more curious than ever, jollier than ever, and more involved with the lives of others than ever, as a consequence of which they were also ever more beloved. Cyril had just received the proof of the thirty-second book in his medical series, concentrating on the breakthrough cures for pancreatic cancer and ALS, whilst Kay was debating whether to accept the commission to redecorate Windsor Castle. Sure, they took a tincture of quinine to ward off muscle cramps and popped the odd low-dose aspirin to reduce the risk of untoward vascular events. Otherwise, it was full steam ahead.

Nevertheless, there came a day in late May when Kay turned to her husband at dinner and said, "My dear? I don't know how to explain it, but I feel a bit odd."

"Yes, now that you mention it," Cyril said, "I feel a measure peculiar myself."

"It's not that I feel unwell," she assured him.

"Certainly not, bab," Cyril said. "We never feel unwell."

"It's more like a tingling. An inkling. An intimation."

"Foreknowledge," he said gravely. "Does it make you—sorrowful?"

"No," Kay said in wonderment. "Not at all. It makes me feel complete."

"That's a good way of putting it. I would miss your insights, your ways of putting things, if I were going to be around to miss anything."

"Looking back, I don't believe we've missed anything whatsoever. But I do sense we've time to make preparations."

Kay and Cyril literally put their house in order. They went through their drawers and threw out all the instruction booklets for printers, toasters, electric griddles, and microwaves that had broken years ago. Kay reserved a small selection of exotic apparel from their travels for Hayley, then carefully folded the rest of her wardrobe for the charity shops. They disposed of all their old bills, tax returns, and bank statements, whilst Cyril compiled a scrapbook of his own rave reviews, Kay's design awards, and appreciative correspondence that might mean something to their descendants when they were gone. Kay went through the larder and chucked open bags of grains, seeds, and flours that might attract vermin if the house were left idle for a protracted period. In general, they agreed that the last task they wanted to bequeath to their progeny was clawing through drawers full of crenulated knickers and orphaned socks.

"I think we owe it to all those great- and great-great grandchildren to gather the troops," Kay suggested.

"Yes," Cyril said. "I keep picturing a bed. Us in our bed upstairs with lots of pillows, holding court."

"That's the cliché," Kay said. "But I don't want to loll about having my cheek kissed, smelling of camphor and having to listen over and over to what a bloody marvellous example I've set. It sounds terribly staid and like something out of Tolstoy."

"That may be why I keep picturing the scene in sepia tones."

"I think we should hold our own wake. None of this lazing-abed business. A proper knees-up, in the Irish tradition, when everyone gets stewed."

Naturally, none of their family, friends, and disciples took the nature of the invitation seriously. It was assumed that the Wilkinsons were being droll—as if such roundly revered luminaries needed an excuse for a party. This wink-wink "wake" was widely regarded as the highlight of London's social calendar for 2050, and regrets were not merely few; they were non-existent.

By late afternoon, the house in Lambeth was overflowing. Having failed to register the sincerity of the purported occasion, most guests arrived with presents, which toppled in mountains by the door. It was midsummer, and the weather was warm and fair—as Kay had somehow intuited it would be. Murmuring tenderly to all she met, the hostess sipped champagne that never went to her head. She'd reluctantly acceded to having the do professionally catered, after Cyril called her attention to the length of the guest list; she shouldn't spend this of all days filling trays in the kitchen. Mischievously, they'd agreed to serve all the creamy, carnivorous fare they'd spurned for decades, and when Kay sampled a passing almond tart the shock of sugar was subversively thrilling. They'd also compiled a playlist, so the property-wide sound system cycled through favourites from the era in which they wed: Shirley Bassey, the Everly Brothers, Tommy Bruce and the Bruisers.

Kay wore a long flowing dress in white rayon that she hadn't donned in eons, whereas Cyril, who wanted more than anything simply to feel comfortable, wore his usual ivory button-down and roomy trousers with a break in the leg, keeping his navy cardigan with wooden buttons and a roll collar at the ready for later in the evening when it was bound to get cool. In context, he was conspicuously underdressed, for their guests had gone all out. Kay was especially touched that Hayley (now seventy-eight, but also benefiting from her parents' enchanted genes) must have spent hours swirling her hair up with chopsticks, the better to match the gifted birds of paradise kimono.

There were testimonials, and in truth they grew a tad trying; it was funny how weary you could grow of listening to what a wonderful person you were. After one of the great-great granddaughters finished reciting a Gerard Manley Hopkins poem, the couple gently urged their admirers to wrap it up.

It was light until well after ten. As the sun faded reluctantly from the long-shadowed garden, Kay and Cyril slipped out back with re-charged glasses (in this white dress, she might have declined to switch to red wine, but given the reason for this party a drop or two on the rayon would hardly matter). The garden, too, was full of revellers. Yet as the fairy lights came on, the hosts located a deserted copse with two weathered teak chairs and a table for their drinks. On this private patch of lawn, Kay and Cyril slow-danced to a Van Morrison rendition of "I Wanna Go Home" and the Drifters' "Save the Last Dance for Me." But it was only once "(Sittin' on) The Dock of the Bay" came on that Cyril announced, "They're playing our song."

They sat. Kay sampled the cabernet (which she never called a "cab"). Her table manners faultless to the last, the white dress remained immaculate.

"So you feel it, too?" she asked.

"Of course I do. I feel as if we've been in the process of convergence since 1963, and finally we're in perfect sync. I wouldn't say we've become the same person. It's more as if we *make up* the same person." He inquired in sudden concern, "Not in any pain, are you, bab?"

"No, no, not at all," she assured him. "It's only that feeling of *resolution* again, but much more intense."

To emphasize the heady sensation, she inhaled a lungful of the cabernet's concentrated fruit. There had always been a touch of the immoderate about Kay's passion for red wine, and now no purpose would be served in its restraint. Yet despite the implicit permission of the moment, she wanted to face this mysterious frontier in a state of clarity. Her single blissful sip was chaste.

"I must say, we chose the red splendidly, my dear," she added, dabbing her mouth with a napkin. "Robust, and balanced. Just like you and me."

They held hands and kissed deeply, the way they used to kiss for hours when they were courting, and withdrew from each other's lips at last with the same reluctance they remembered from those days as well, when they had to get back to their medical studies. That kiss sent a tingling shimmer through the entirety of their lives together, as if their marriage were a crash cymbal whose rim they'd just hit deftly with a felt mallet.

Kay's head dropped onto Cyril's shoulder. Cyril's cheek rested against her crown. None of the other tipsy partygoers raising glad voices and breaking into spontaneous waltzes on the main lawn noticed—just as the couple preferred. Whilst the moon rose behind Kay's resplendent white hair and created a silvered corona, Cyril murmured his wife's final benediction: "Robust, and balanced."

Fortunately, it turned out that there was life after death after all.

13

The Last Last Supper

All day, Kay had been lifted by this peculiar floating sensation, as if she were drifting two or three inches above the floor, the way a hovercraft glides across the waves without touching water. Her pervasive giddiness, detachment, and lack of seriousness were awfully inappropriate considering, as if the guiding principle for all their major decisions for decades were merely a fanciful leg-pull. As she sipped the last of her champagne, this feeling of fizzy levitation intermingled with the refreshing spritz of bubbles on her nose, but the buzz wasn't from the wine. She felt as if she *were* the champagne, rising into the air, *pip, pip, pip*. The whole evening, she should have been consumed with dread and anxiety, and instead she couldn't remember a night in recent memory when she and her husband had had a better time.

She considered going on a riff about the many news stories they were stuck into whose resolution they would now never learn, but at the moment all those erstwhile nail-biters seemed to bob by like passing flotsam. The pro-democracy protests in Hong Kong, the pandemic, and the perilous health of Britain's prime minister might have been those ocean-clogging plastic carrier bags that David Attenborough was always on about. Shutting the book on these ongoing dramas was far from a frustration; au contraire, the disengagement came as a great relief. The floating sensation persisted, except that now she was soaring even higher, until she was suspended hundreds of feet overhead and looking down at all the little people scurrying and clashing and fomenting as they always did. Her gaze wasn't precisely pitying, but it was close.

"What do you suppose we'll miss?" Kay posed more generally instead, rising to open a pricey bottle of cabernet that she was damned if she'd leave for Roy.

"Each other," Cyril said.

"Yes, of course," she said with a smile, pouring the wine with a heavy hand. "But whatever is going to happen to this place?" It was already "this place," at a remove. Perhaps she had finally mastered the government's mandatory *social distancing*.

"Good things. Terrible things. The usual," Cyril said. "I'm tired of worrying about it—as if worrying does any good. Look at the economic disaster we're in the midst of—"

"It's so quiet," Kay observed wistfully. "You'd think disaster would make more noise."

"Yes, it's eerie, isn't it? I'm reminded of that novel, *On the Beach*. Remember? They're in Australia, where everything is calm and the weather is warm and the skies are clear, but they're awaiting the inexorable arrival of nuclear fallout. If the Tories keep their lockdown lunacy in place for months, we'll be fortunate to escape this hysteria's fallout, which could be just as dire as the radioactive kind. In fact, the catastrophes we're sure to give a miss are countless. Who knows—an invasion by aliens, like in H. G. Wells. Or even a return to the plain old want and scarcity that you and I grew up with. I'd hate to try to survive in a world in which my wife can't get her mitts on a bottle of red wine."

"Very funny." After taking a defiant slug, Kay excused herself with theatrical umbrage to the loo.

"But it's also possible," she said zestfully on return, "that medical science comes up with a cure for ageing. What fools we'd seem then!"

"Or cryogenics could take a great leap forward," Cyril posited, "and it could become possible to awaken in a world hundreds of years hence. So if you're going to be that way, we're turning our backs on time travel as well."

"Or maybe we'd find out that Alzheimer's is only wretched for the people around you—but actually *being* demented is jolly good fun, like watching a reel of your lifetime's highlights. Maybe we'd find out that a care home is just like a Butlin's holiday camp, and we'd make fast friends playing bowls."

"Or for all we know, I'd drop dead within the year anyway, and you'd have a whole second marriage to a younger man who voted for Brexit, just like you."

"A second marriage? That sounds exhausting."

"I'm the one who's been exhausting," Cyril said.

"Better you said that than I."

Finishing off the cabernet allowed for generous musing over the fate of their children—Kay was convinced that because Simon's long office hours were courting divorce, the lockdown might at least save his marriage, whilst Cyril maintained that suddenly being trapped with one's family all day could as readily end in mass murder—after which they left the dirty dishes on the dining table and didn't clean up the kitchen. The neglect was so liberating that before departing for the sitting room Kay gave in to an earlier impulse: she picked up her china dinner plate and dropped it on the floor.

Cyril merely raised an eyebrow. "I'd have thought you'd want to keep the set complete for Hayley."

"Hayley will never use our wedding china. It's a generational thing. She'll try to sell it, find out there's no market, and break half of it on the way to Oxfam."

"Port and crumble?" Cyril proposed.

"The crumble, my dear, came out rubbish, and I'm damned if I'm leaving this earth with the taste of failure on my tongue. And sod some twee thimbleful of port. I'm opening another cabernet."

"Why do I get the feeling this is your real, intemperate self coming to the fore—the secret sot who's lurked in there for years and has finally got out?"

"Perhaps you're right." Kay pulled the cork with a resonant pop. "That's one sound I'm truly sorry to hear for the last time."

"Now," he chided. "Who says you can't open a third bottle?"

"You know, when you're on the cusp of oblivion, Mr Wilkinson, I rather like your style."

For himself, Cyril took out the single malt that his colleagues had given him at his retirement.

"I can't believe you're still hoarding that," Kay said, extending on the sofa with her crystal globe filled nearly to the brim. "Selfish git. You should really have shared it with all the well-wishers at your farewell party."

"I decided to save it for a special occasion. And what could be more special than this one?"

"Special or not, it's the only occasion we've got left. Now, I'm curious. Given tonight's spirit of fuck-everything—"

"I'm not sure I've ever heard you say that word."

"I know. I thought I'd try it out. Everyone else seems to use it with such abandon now. FUCK FUCK FUCK FUCK FUCK! Interesting. The sky doesn't fall."

"That was loud enough for the Samsons to hear."

"I couldn't care less. But I was asking: are you planning to be a stickler and insist on the stroke of midnight? Down to the wire, remaining the same letter-of-the-law fellow I've lived with for fifty-seven years?"

"Have I really been such a tyrant?"

Kay considered. "Yes!"

They laughed. Cyril slid beside his wife on the sofa. They were a nice fit, even sitting.

"I feel this question is an obligation," Kay said. "Any regrets?"

Cyril said without missing a beat, "I could have skipped every single one of those foreign holidays."

"What?" Kay exclaimed, sitting up straighter.

"You thought I was going to say, no, not a regret in the world, didn't you?"

"A little white lie would have been nicer. And what you might have properly regretted is being such a tit when I wanted to study interior design, especially since I made a grand go of it after all."

"At the time, I was giving you my honest opinion."

"Which happened to be wrong."

"Which happened to differ from yours, which is not the same as 'wrong.' And you? Regrets?"

"I should have said *fuck* more often."

"Kay, seriously," Cyril said, draining his whiskey; he seldom used her Christian name. "Is this a daft idea? Would you like to forget it?"

"Then we'd have to do the washing up."

"I wasn't joking."

"Nor was I. I really don't fancy doing the washing up."

"We could leave the dishes for tomorrow. Be rash."

"But we're skint. We spent everything. We can't afford to not go through with it."

"We have our pensions. We could always sell up and rent a flat."

"I'm positively looking forward to Roy finding out there's no inheritance. I wish I got to watch his face."

"You changed the subject. You've been noticeably ambivalent about this pact of ours from early on, bab, and I'm not going to push you to do something so irrevocable if you don't want to."

Kay put down her glass with a sigh. "That's true. I have been . . . what? Uneasy, conflicted. But you didn't marry such a timorous doormat that we've got all the way to the very brink of my eightieth birthday—the last two hours of my eightieth birthday—before I can finally bring myself to propose like Fred Astaire, 'Let's call the whole thing off.' I've been anxious about this scheme of yours, and I've hoped awfully that some archetypal White Van Man might cut us to the quick on a zebra crossing and spare us carrying it out. But we've looked both ways before crossing the street, and here we are.

"Honestly, I've gone back and forth. Especially during this last year, when it's looked as if we'll be put to the test after all, I've considered bowing out ahead of time more than once. But I didn't sign up to the idea in the first place only because I'm a pliant pushover. It's not been in the forefront of my mind without cease, but the cautionary memory of what happened to my father, and to a lesser extent my mother, is still quite keen. You didn't browbeat me into going along with this business, and a great deal of your hectoring about 'bed-blocking' and the costs of the 'old-old' to the NHS has been gratuitous, because in the main I already agreed with you. You're the one who sounds as if you're losing your nerve, which is frankly gobsmacking. Since when do you of all people lack the strength of your convictions?"

"It's worth looking at the matter for a last time, isn't it? If looking at the matter for a last time is the last thing we'll ever do? And my convictions, well. They've always seemed a bit beside me." Cyril lifted his wife's memorial service printout. "As if I could pick them up and put them down."

"I wonder if I believe in this project more fervently than you do, then. Because what's at stake doesn't feel abstract or at arm's length to me, or not any more," Kay countered. "It's true that we're not in as bad a shape as we might have feared. But we're nothing like what we were, my dear. I look at old photographs of us and my heart melts—the way one's heart melts looking at photos of people who've died. We've made all manner of compromises, but in that gradual way, in our own peripheral vision, so we almost haven't noticed. I suspect that's the form. You gave up the men's choir. I do less gardening, and now we hire Dan to do the strimming. I never formally quit design work, but I might as well have. You have that stenosis, and although sometimes you seem to be playing up the pain, other times I think you play it down, and that's when it truly hurts. You could get surgery, but the prognosis at your age would be poor. I never told you, but I've been diagnosed with hypertension—"

"Since when?" Under the circumstances, it was insensible for him to be worried about heart disease, but Cyril wasn't beyond being injured by her concealment.

"We may be married, but there's still such a thing as my business," Kay said. "Apparently my blood pressure is all over the map, which makes it much harder to treat. Obviously, that increases the risk of stroke, which—I need hardly tell a GP—can effectively end one's life without warning over the course of a few minutes, and some of the worst outcomes are those in which one survives. I also have a persistent pain in my right shoulder, which I haven't mentioned either. It sends pain down the arm and sometimes feels numb; the problem is clearly neurological and could be a symptom of something grave. Aside from joint replacement, there's no cure for arthritis, and mine is getting worse. I could probably manage no longer being able to walk, but I don't *want* to manage not walking.

"Because it's not as if we can't live with these ailments. The trouble is that we can live with them, as we can also live with all the other ailments that are coming soon to a theatre near you. We're already well into the process of whittling away what we've always done, who we've always been—making sacrifices by degrees, like frogs in a heating pot. So it's already out of the question that we'll live some sort of fantasy old age in which we're wise, spry lives of the party until we're a hundred and ten."

"That would never have been possible," Cyril said. "I was no life of the party when I was twenty-five."

"You were the life of my party," Kay said. "And tonight's party has been splendid."

"It will still have been a wonderful evening even if we get cold feet about the pièce de résistance."

"But if we go ahead and simply do the washing up, it's actuarially likely that you predecease me. I don't know about that second marriage to a strapping Brexiteer—I'm not sure I'd have the energy, and I worry that he'd never shut up about fishing rights—but I could probably function on my own. I dare say that I could get to the shops, and warm up a tin of beans—"

"You'd do better alone than I would. You're more sociable."

"Possibly, but the question is whether I'd have an appetite for that life. Whether I *want* to shamble to the shops for beans."

"Come, come," Cyril said. "It's 2020. You could at least make it penne and pesto."

"I'm being serious. I want to let all this go when it still *hurts* to let it go. When we can still feel a sense of loss. When what we're losing is still whole, and not corrupted, and diminished, and made dreadfully sad. When other people will still be sorry to see us go. I'm not sure about Roy, but I'm certain that Simon will be sorry. To be fair, Hayley will be sorrier than she expects to be. She's such a drama queen that it's hard for her when she has to feel real emotions. She apes so much. It's a form of avoidance, really, all her histrionics. Funny how pretending to feel things is really a way of not feeling them."

"That's what I find hardest to abandon," Cyril said. "Your asides. They've made the course of my days infinitely more stimulating."

"But what I'm saying is no aside, and it should be music to your ears. There's only one thing you love better than a good steak and ale pie, and that's *being right*. So, back in 1991? You were *right*. I know I'm always castigating you for being such an obdurate ideologue. But every time I've struggled against your unnatural proposition, I've ended up boomeranging back to your way of seeing things. Eighty years, whether it feels that way to us right now? It's a long time. We've had a good run. And we—not you and I, but the Big We—we're getting into the habit of destroying everything good about ourselves before taking our belated leave. Remember those horror films we grew up watching? About zombies, and mummies, and Frankenstein's monster, staggering around with gaping mouths and vacant eyes? Those creatures played on a primal fear: of living death. And despite the fact that it's one of our mythic terrors, that's what we're trying to arrange for everyone now: a living death. It's a defilement! A desecration—!"

"You always get louder when you drink," Cyril said.

"Oh, everyone gets louder when they drink," Kay said, irritable at the interruption.

"It's just, the Samsons—"

"FUCK FUCK FUCK!" Kay shouted at the window. "Is this the last night of our lives, or isn't it?"

"I thought that's what's under discussion. And on every other night of our lives, we've tried to be considerate of our neighbours, so we should also be considerate on the last one."

"I was trying to say," Kay said, at an elaborate if condescendingly reduced volume. "Our lives are our artworks. Sure, we can do a deal with the devil. We can accept decrepitude in trade for remaining technically alive—as a travesty of what we used to be, a walking—or not walking—self-humiliation. But that's like vandalizing our own creations. It's like destroying what we love in order to keep it. You and

I, we can still talk, and make sense. We can still enjoy each other's company. Other people can still enjoy our company. You were a fine tenor. Let's go out on a high note."

"You're absolutely certain?"

"I keep getting the impression that I'm more certain than *you* are."

"But there was something suspiciously . . . lofty about that speech of yours, being our own 'artworks.' Suspiciously high-flown. As if you were talking yourself into something."

"I'll keep it simple, then. How much better are our lives going to get than they are right now? What are the chances that everything gets worse from here on out? Not only a bit worse. Loads worse?"

"One hundred percent," Cyril said.

It was Kay who fetched the water, the tumblers, and the funny black soap-dish box, Kay who first raised her glass with a palmful of tablets and waited for her husband to do the same before giving a quick sharp nod, like the start of a pork-pie-eating contest or party game, and Kay who pulled Cyril to her good shoulder and placed a warm, consoling arm around his back. But it wouldn't do to sink into the cushions of the sofa whilst letting so much of that good cabernet go to waste, so before closing her eyes and kissing the silky hairs on her husband's forehead she downed the rest of the glass.

About the Author

Lionel Shriver's fiction includes *The Motion of the Body Through Space*; *The Mandibles*; *Property*; the National Book Award finalist *So Much for That*; the *New York Times* bestsellers *The Post-Birthday World* and *We Need to Talk About Kevin*, the international bestseller adapted for a 2010 film starring Tilda Swinton. Her journalism has appeared in the *Guardian*, the *New York Times*, the *Wall Street Journal*, *Harper's Magazine*, and many other publications. She's a regular columnist for the *Spectator* in Britain. She lives in London and Brooklyn, New York.